Skios

Michael Frayn was born in London in 1933 and began his career as a journalist on the *Guardian* and the *Observer*. His novels include *Towards the End of the Morning*, *The Trick of It* and *A Landing on the Sun*. *Headlong* (1999) was shortlisted for the Booker Prize, while *Spies* (2002) won the Whitbread Novel Award. His fifteen plays range from *Noises Off* to *Copenhagen* and, most recently, *Afterlife*.

Praise for *Skios*:

'Hugely entertaining.' *Daily Telegraph*

'The pieces of this intricate farce click into place with all the assurance you'd expect from the author of *Noises Off*.' *Daily Mail*

'Frayn at his comic best . . . A transfixingly witty novel about riding one's luck and being undone by it.' *Financial Times*

'A wonderfully diverting entertainment, something Wode-house might have written if Blandings Castle had been perched on the edge of the Aegean.' *Evening Standard*

'Truly does make you laugh out loud.' *Observer*

'A masterful comedy of errors.' *Sunday Express*

'Effortlessly funny.' *Herald*

'A rattlingly paced and amusing farce.' *Independent on Sunday*

'A perfect summer read . . . he's a literary genius.' *Tatler*

'Expertly written, genuine fun . . . Frayn builds his puzzle so painstakingly and tells his story so engagingly, you want to jump in his lap and build a nest.'
New York Times Book Review

'Are you, perhaps even now, searching for the perfect comic novel for the beach, the hammock or some lazy summer weekend? . . . By page 2, readers will know without any doubt that they are in for a wonderful time.'
Washington Post

'Blissfully funny.' *Country Life*

'Frayn's own technical skill, when it comes to farce, is of the highest order, and this is a very funny book.' Book of the Week, *Tablet*

'A light-hearted comedy of mistaken identities and sexual subterfuge . . . *Skios* will undoubtedly amuse you.'
Sunday Business Post

by the same author

FICTION

The Tin Men
The Russian Interpreter
Towards the End of the Morning
A Very Private Life
Sweet Dreams
The Trick of It
A Landing on the Sun
Now You Know
Headlong
Spies

PLAYS

The Two of Us
Alphabetical Order
Donkeys' Years
Clouds
Balmoral
Make and Break
Noises Off
Benefactors
Look Look
Here
Now You Know
Copenhagen
Alarms & Excursions
Democracy
Afterlife

TRANSLATIONS

The Seagull (Chekhov)
Uncle Vanya (Chekhov)
Three Sisters (Chekhov)
The Cherry Orchard (Chekhov)
The Sneeze (Chekhov)
Wild Honey (Chekhov)
The Fruits of Enlightenment
    (Tolstoy)
Exchange (Trifonov)
Number One (Anouilh)

FILM AND TELEVISION

Clockwise
First and Last
Remember Me?

NON-FICTION

Constructions
Celia's Secret: an investigation
    (with David Burke)
The Human Touch
Collected Columns
Stage Directions
My Father's Fortune

MICHAEL FRAYN

SKIOS

A Novel

faber and faber

First published in 2012
by Faber and Faber Ltd
Bloomsbury House
74–77 Great Russell Street
London WC1B 3DA

This paperback edition first published in 2013

Typeset by Faber and Faber Ltd
Printed and bound by CPI Group (UK) Ltd, Croydon, CR0 4YY

A CIP record for this book
is available from the British Library

ISBN 978-0-571-28145-9

FSC
www.fsc.org
MIX
Paper from
responsible sources
FSC® C101712

2 4 6 8 10 9 7 5 3 1

Skios

'I just want to say a big thank-you to our distinguished guest,' said Nikki Hook, 'for making this evening such a fascinating and wonderful occasion, and one that I'm sure none of us here will ever forget . . .'

She stopped and read the sentence aloud again to herself, then deleted 'fascinating and wonderful' and inserted 'unique and special', which sounded a little bit more, well, unique and special. A little bit more Mrs Fred Toppler, in fact, which was what counted, because it was after all Mrs Fred Toppler, not Nikki, who was going to be so grateful, and find it all so extraordinary. Nikki was merely Mrs Fred Toppler's PA. She provided the thoughts for Mrs Toppler to think, but in the end it was Mrs Toppler who had to think them.

Outside the windows of Nikki's office the tumbling gardens and hillsides of the Fred Toppler Foundation were vivid in the blaze of the Mediterranean afternoon. Cascades of well-watered bougainvillaea and plumbago challenged the saturated blue of the sky. The fishermen's cottages along the waterfront and the caiques rocking at anchor on the dazzle of the sea were as blinding white and as heavenly blue as the Greek flag stirring lethargically on the flagpole.

Nikki, though, looking out at it all as she composed Mrs Toppler's thoughts for her, was as discreetly cool as the air conditioning. Her discreetly blonded hair was unruffled, her white shirt and blue skirt a discreet echo of the Greek whites

[3]

and blues outside, her expression pleasantly but discreetly open to the world. She was discreetly British, because Mrs Toppler, who was American, like the late Mr Fred, appreciated it. Europeans in general embodied for her the civilised values that the Fred Toppler Foundation existed to promote, and the British were Europeans who had the tact and good sense to speak English. Anyway, everyone liked Nikki, not just Mrs Toppler. She was so nice! She had been a really nice girl already when she was three. She had still been one when she was seventeen, at an age when niceness was a much rarer achievement, and she remained one nearly twenty years later. Discreetly tanned, discreetly blonde, discreetly effective, and discreetly nice.

As Nikki watched, people began to emerge from the fishermen's cottages and drift towards the tables scattered in the shade of the great plane tree on the central square. They were not fishermen; they were not even Greek. They were not tourists or holidaymakers. They were the English-speaking guests of the foundation's annual Great European House Party. They had spent the day in seminars studying Minoan cooking and Early Christian meditation techniques, in classes watching demonstrations of traditional Macedonian dancing and Late Mediaeval flower-arrangement. They had interspersed their labours with swims and siestas, with civilised conversation over breakfast and mid-morning coffee, over pre-lunch drinks, lunch, and post-lunch coffee, over afternoon tea and snacks. Now they were moving towards further intellectual refreshment over dinner and various pre- and post-dinner drinks.

Tomorrow evening all this civilisation would reach its climax in a champagne reception and formal dinner, at the end of which the guests would be spiritually prepared for the most important event of the House Party, the Fred Toppler Lecture. The lecture was one the highlights of the Greek cultural calendar. The residents would be joined by important visitors from Athens, ferried out to the island by air and sea. There would be articles in the papers attacking the choice of subject and speaker, and lamenting the sad decline in its quality.

Please God it wasn't going to be too awful this year, prayed Nikki. All lectures, however unique and special, were of course awful, but some were more awful than others. There had to *be* a lecture. Why? Because there always had been one. There had been a Fred Toppler Lecture every year since the foundation had existed. They had had lectures on the Crisis in this and the Challenge of that. They had had an Enigma of, a Whither? and a Why?, three Prospects for and two Reconsiderations of. As the director of the foundation had become more eccentric and reclusive, so had his choices of lecturer become more idiosyncratic. The Post-syncretistic Approach to whatever it was the previous year had caused even Mrs Toppler, who was prepared to thank almost anybody for almost anything, to choke on the task, which was perhaps the unconscious reason she had left the 'not' out of this being an occasion they would not forget in a hurry. Nikki had seized the chance of the director's absence on a retreat in Nepal to choose this year's lecturer herself.

'Dr Norman Wilfred needs no introduction,' Mrs Fred Toppler would be saying tomorrow when she introduced him. Nikki looked at the unneeded introduction that followed, paraphrased from the CV that Dr Wilfred's personal assistant had sent her. His list of publications and appointments, of fellowships and awards, was mind-numbing. Lucinda Knowles, Nikki's counterpart at the J. G. Fledge Institute, had assured her that Dr Wilfred was both a serious expert in the management of science and a genuine celebrity. Her friend Jane Gee, at the Cartagena Festival, said he was the lecturer everybody currently wanted.

So this year – *Innovation and Governance: the Promise of Scientometrics*. There was something about the word *promise* that made Nikki's heart suddenly sink. Her choice was going to be just as awful as all the others. Even now he was five miles up in the sky, on his way from London, above Switzerland or northern Italy. She had a clear and discouraging picture of him as he sat there in business class sipping his complimentary champagne. All those committees and international lectures would have taken their toll. His jowls would be heavy with importance, his waistline thick and his hair thin with it. He would have dragged *Innovation and Governance* around the world, from Toronto to Tokyo, from Oslo to Oswego, until the typescript was yellow from the Alpine sun, tear-stained from the tropical rains, and exhausted from repetition.

She printed up the unnecessary introduction and the big thank-you, the solid bookends that bracketed whatever was to come. Too late now to alter what that was going to be. It was coming towards them all at 500 mph.

She looked at her watch. She had just the right amount of time in hand to deliver the texts to Mrs Toppler and then double-check a few things on her list before she left for the airport. She stepped out of the door of her office into the great brick wall of late-afternoon heat.

Why does one do it? thought Dr Norman Wilfred as he sipped his complimentary business-class champagne and gazed absently down upon the world five miles below. Why *does* one do it?

Round and round the same treadmill one went. Another view like all the others over some unidentifiable part of the earth's surface five miles beyond one's grasp. Then another airport and another waiting car. Another eager assurance that everyone was so excited at the prospect of one's visit. Another guest room with two towels and a bar of soap laid out on the bed. The Fred Toppler Foundation, it was true, had a reputation in academic circles for treating its visiting lecturers well. He foresaw drinkable wine and comfortable chairs set out in soft sunshine or warm shade. All the same, when he thought of the performance he would have to go through to earn these small compensations, he felt a familiar weariness in the marrow of his bones.

'Dr Norman Wilfred?' people would say when introductions were made, and he could already see the way the expressions on their faces would change. He could feel the way he would smile and incline his head slightly in return. Once again he would bring out the topics he kept ready for the obligatory mingling with his fellow-guests. Once again he would lay out his little stock of unusual knowledge, original thoughts, and interesting opinions. He would offer the scraps of gossip he had brought. He would tell the tried and tested stories.

And then the lecture itself. The faces raised expectantly towards him. The fulsome introduction with the record of his career paraphrased from the CV that Vicki had sent them and edited down to manageable length by omitting, always, the most important publications and appointments. His head modestly lowered as he listened to it all once again, revealing the way the years were beginning to extend his high forehead up over the top of his head.

The applause as he goes to the lectern and opens the text of his lecture . . .

His lecture! Had he got it? He felt in his flight bag once again, just to be sure. Yes, there it reassuringly was. He always kept the text of his lecture with him on his travels. He and his luggage had become separated too often over the years for him to take any risks. Toothbrushes and pyjamas could be replaced; the lecture was part of himself, flesh of his flesh and bone of his bone. He took it out of the bag, just to be doubly sure. The same scuffed old brown binder that had travelled so many thousands of weary air miles with him, personalised by the red wine-stain it had acquired in Melbourne, the smeared remains of some small tropical insect in Singapore. He would add a few introductory remarks, as he usually did, to make clear the special relevance of the lecture to this particular time and place, but the body of the text was the material that had slowly taken its present form, like his scalp, over many years. A whole lifetime of thought and study was concentrated in these pages, its expression gradually refined and adapted, like all human knowledge, to current circumstances. The carefully crafted phrases were as familiar and reassuring as the wine-stain and the dead insect. 'Perhaps foremost among the challenges facing us today . . . The hopes and fears of mankind . . . Within an overall framework of social responsibility . . .'

He saw the words as they would look up at him from the warm pool of light on the lectern, like well-behaved children at their fond father. 'These problems must be squarely faced . . . And here a note of caution must be sounded . . .' He heard the accomplished but still apparently spontaneous delivery. The little extempore variants and asides. The laughter. The reasonably prolonged applause at the end. The words of appreciation from his host – 'thought-provoking, insightful, fascinating' – not all of them perhaps entirely insincere . . .

Why did one go on doing it, though? When one could be sitting in one's office at the institute and doing real scholarly work. Struggling to understand the latest research by younger rivals who had invented some incomprehensible new vocabulary of their own, or to master the institute's draft accounts before the next meeting of the committee of management, or to sort out the muddle into which the manuscript of one's new book seemed to have descended.

And instead, here one was again, five miles up, glass of champagne in hand. Why, why, why?

It was true that there was also some satisfaction to be derived from being Dr Norman Wilfred. Purely as a consequence of his being who he was, seriously worded documents drafted by the labour of others were placed in front of him to be signed. His advice and his skills as a chairman did not go unappreciated. As soon as people heard the name they knew exactly what they were going to get. They were never disappointed. Dr Norman Wilfred was what they expected, and Dr Norman Wilfred was what they got.

And if there were benefits in being Dr Norman Wilfred, he thought, as the cabin attendant refilled his glass, then God knows he had earned them. He had arrived at being who he was only slowly and with sustained application, thought by thought, opinion by opinion, appointment by appointment. There had been many let-downs along the way; many failures, rebuffs, and slights; many mornings when he had looked in the shaving mirror and seen someone he didn't much like the look of gazing back at him. He had his problems even now. His blood pressure had to be kept under control. He had developed a serious allergy to onions. He suffered perhaps from a slight tendency to take himself too seriously.

Also from this apparently incurable propensity to find himself on planes with a glass of champagne in his hand, and the prospect of yet more debilitating comfort and flattery in front of him.

3

Nikki walked slowly through the green territory of the foundation, up and down the winding hilly paths, looking out at the bay and the piled summer clouds. The light was softening as the afternoon slipped into evening. There was a suggestion of gold in the air.

She loved this place. Everything was so at ease with itself, so delicately balanced, like the works of a good watch, or nature itself. The web of pipes and sprinklers that kept everything green was discreetly concealed. So was the flow of money that kept the sprinklers sprinkling. It was a complete world, a miniature model of the European civilisation that it existed to promote, and she could almost feel it sitting in the palm of her hand, its clockwork quietly humming. The only piece of the machinery that stuck a little, that threw the whole clock slightly out of true, was the bit that was concealed behind the closed shutters of Empedocles, the villa high above all the others, where the emaciated and failing director was hidden away. Though perhaps for not much longer ...

From the fishermanless fishermen's cottages along the waterfront, and from suites in villas hidden among the trees all over the headland that the foundation occupied, from Leucippus and Anaximander, from Xenocles, Theodectes, Menander, Aristophanes, and Antiphanes, more and more of the House Party guests were emerging, looking for food and drink. Two hours or more had gone by since they had last been fed and watered.

She imagined that she was seeing it all for the first time, as Dr Wilfred would shortly be seeing it. How would he feel it compared with all the other foundations and institutes that he had spoken at around the world? She imagined him at her side, looking and listening appreciatively as she explained it all to him. He might be a more sympathetic person than she had supposed as she transcribed his CV. He *was*, she could feel it. He was someone you could talk to.

'Most of our guests are from the States,' she found she was telling him, her words as inaudible to anyone else as he was invisible. 'All horribly rich, of course, or they wouldn't be here. But awfully nice people, or they wouldn't be interested in the kind of things we do.'

She waved to an elderly couple with apple-cheeked smiles. 'Hi, there!' she called. 'Oh, Nikki, honey,' called the woman, 'we're having the best time! All thanks to you, of course! And we know you've got a treat in store for us tomorrow!'

'Mr and Mrs Chuck Friendly,' murmured Nikki to the disembodied treat walking beside her. 'I understand they're the second-richest couple in the state of Rhode Island. They've been coming to Skios every year since the House Party started. Sweet! Most of the guests are couples, others are hoping to be, so watch out!'

Two men were strolling thoughtfully together in the shade cast by the Temple of Athena. One of them took the pipe out of his mouth and raised it to her like a glass of wine, the other salaamed.

'Alf Persson,' she explained to Dr Wilfred, 'the Swedish theologian. Quite well known, I believe, in the theological world. And V. J. D. Chaudhury, the great authority on comparative underdevelopment. Two of our embedded intellectuals! You're not the only distinguished visitor, you see!'

They crossed the ancient agora, where men were unloading caterer's tables, gilt chairs, carpets, and bales of linen from electric trucks. 'That stone floor is three thousand years old,' she reminded the foreman. 'You will make sure the carpets are down before anything metal touches it?'

To Dr Wilfred she added modestly, 'My Greek is still a bit rudimentary, even after five years here . . . Oh, and this is another of our embedded intellectuals.' She waved to a young man who was gazing gloomily out of the window of Epictetus. 'A Brit, this one, like me. Chris Binns, writer in residence . . . Chris, will you do me a favour? Tomorrow, when we get to questions at the end, and no one wants to be the first, we don't want one of those terrible silences, like last year. So will you have a question ready?'

'A question?' said Chris Binns. It seemed to be a word he hadn't come across before.

'Anything,' said Nikki. 'About his work. Prospects for international control. Whatever. You'll dream something up. You're a writer. Just to get the ball rolling . . . At the lecture. You *are* coming to the lecture tomorrow?'

'Sure,' said Chris. 'Of course. Absolutely.'

'He's so wrapped up in his work!' whispered Nikki to Dr Wilfred, as they continued on their way. 'He didn't know there *was* a lecture tomorrow!'

'Perhaps it's the sight of *you* that makes everything go out of his head,' she imagined Dr Wilfred saying. She laughed. 'Now, now!' she said. He really was more charming than she had supposed. And had got a good deal younger and slimmer.

'Jesus, Nikki,' said an elderly lady, dabbing a little eau-de-cologne-soaked lace handkerchief to her brow as they passed her near the Aphrodite fountain, 'you always look like something out of a deodorant ad. I don't know how you do it.'

'I think cool thoughts, Mrs Comax,' said Nikki.

Her cool thoughts were that she herself was as discreetly necessary to the workings of the foundation as the water in the buried pipes and the mysterious flow of funds through the balance sheet. She didn't like to say this to Dr Wilfred, but probably he could see it for himself. Particularly when she took him on a slight diversion backstage. Screened by dense shrubs was a world not of traditional stone cottages or villas with the names of philosophers and poets, but of prefabricated sheds with no designation at all.

'This is where the staff live,' she explained. 'Will you wait here for a moment? I've just got to put my head into the kitchens.'

'*Now* what?' shouted Yannis Voskopoulos, the *chef de cuisine*, over the clatter of stainless steel on stainless steel and the roar of the air-extractors, and the endlessly Levantine pop wailing of the woman on the radio. 'I don't know what you gonna tell me but you told me already! Twice! And we done it! Twice over!'

Some of the white-robed ghosts looked up from ovens and worktops and waved amiable ladles and cleavers at her. Some looked up and didn't recognise her.

'But these new guys, Yannis,' she said, not in Greek but in American English, because Yannis had worked in America and liked to keep the language up. 'The agency guys. You've got your eye on them?'

'Got my eye on everyone, Nikki. Everyone and everything. The same like you.'

'Last year you forgot kosher.'

'Nikki, you wanna see kosher? Look – kosher. Halal. Diabetic. Vegetarian. Gluten-free, nut-free, salt-free. Vegetarian kosher. Diabetic halal. Gluten-free diabetic. Salt-free nut-free vegetarian. Get outta here, Nikki!'

'And onion-free?'

'*Onion*-free?'

'Salt-free onion-free! For the guest speaker! I told you!'

Yannis looked at the ceiling, then wiped his face on the oven-cloth he was carrying. He sighed.

'When I was a kid in Piraeus,' he said, 'was only two sorts of food. Was food, and was no food.'

'You see why I check everything?' said Nikki.

She rejoined the imaginary Dr Wilfred and walked on with him towards Parmenides, the quietly luxurious guest quarters where he would be staying. He was already impressed, she could see, as they climbed the hillside towards it. When they got inside and she opened the shutters to let in the great sweep of bay below, the piled cumulus above the horizon, and the rocking caiques along the waterfront, she thought she could hear him catch his breath. Just as well he was seeing it now – it would probably be dark by the time he actually arrived.

She checked the air conditioning, topped up the water in the vases of yellow lilies and white roses, and put a recirculating disc on the CD player. A quiet murmur of plainsong softened the air.

'The monks of the local monastery,' she explained.

She took the whisky out of the sideboard and put it by

the tumblers on top. 'A rather rare straight malt,' she said. 'Is that all right?'

She went into the bedroom, turned down the cover, and laid out the white bathrobe and slippers, as richly fluffy as the hide of a sub-tropical polar bear. Moved on to the study: stationery on the desk, yes, directory of services, history of the foundation. The kitchen: champagne in the refrigerator, together with two flutes, a good local white wine, and two litres of chilled water.

'From the foundation's own spring,' she told him. 'It's famously pure.'

She took the grapes out of the refrigerator and a bowl from the sideboard to arrange them in. 'Thrown in the foundation's pottery room,' she explained. 'It shows that bit in Homer when Odysseus landed on Skios disguised as an itinerant knifegrinder.'

She took a last look round before she left . . . The lilies . . . Oh my God! Better double-check that, too . . .

She touched 'Vicki' on her phone. She'd had the number stored for the last six months.

'Vicki . . . ? It's me yet again, I'm afraid – Nikki. So sorry . . . PA to PA – the well-worn back channel once more! He's on the plane . . . ? Yes, well, I think we're all ready for him, only I had a last-minute panic . . . Lilies! I've put lilies in his room! And I've just thought, wait a minute, if he's allergic to onions . . . ! Onions – bulbs . . . Bulbs – lilies . . . ! No? Oh, wonderful . . . Bless you . . . So sorry to bother you. We're all so excited!'

Far too excited in her case, she thought as she put the phone back in her bag. Dr Wilfred had suddenly slipped back to being the overweight, self-important figure she had originally expected. Though you never knew. He was only sixteen years older than she was, after all, according to his CV. She remembered a discreet but lyrical episode three years before with *The Challenge of Post-Modernist Topology*. The laughter in the warm darkness – his lips coming close to hers – the softly invading hands . . . So there were surprises in life. She also remembered driving him back to the airport the following morning to return to his wife . . .

There was nothing in Dr Wilfred's CV, so far as she could remember, about being married. Not that she herself had any ambitions in that direction. She loved it here, she loved her work. All the same . . .

All the same, it was time to go to the airport.

4

The ping of the seat-belt sign coming on and the feel of the empty champagne glass being taken out of his hand woke Dr Wilfred from the doze he didn't realise that he'd fallen into. He looked out of the window. There was a scattering of small rocky islands in the sea below, and then the coastline of another, with buildings, streets, and the first lights coming on here and there as the day faded. Skios.

For no identifiable reason his spirits rose. This time it would be different. New dishes, new wines, new weather. Views over the sea not quite like the views he had seen before, fellow-guests not quite like any other fellow-guests. A woman would come up to him after his lecture. Lightly tanned, slim, smiling. An American, from a rather well-known university. With tenure already. No, without tenure yet – someone who would be prepared, if she met the right companion, to reshape her life, to change universities and continents. It was seven years now since he had last been in that kind of relationship.

'Dr Wilfred,' she would say. He would smile and incline his head. 'I found your lecture fascinating. It raises so many issues that I'd love to pursue with you. I don't know whether you have a moment . . . ?'

It might happen even sooner. The woman who would be looking after him, and who would be meeting him just the other side of Customs and Immigration. 'Dr Wilfred? We're all so excited!' Vicki had exchanged many e-mails and phone calls with her already. And she was professionally and personally committed to seeing that he had a good time. She would be lightly tanned. Discreetly blonde, perhaps. In her thirties . . .

He checked the right-hand inside pocket of his linen jacket. Passport, credit cards. He checked the left-hand pocket. Phone, three condoms.

You never knew. All you knew was that it was either stored in the long causal chain of the universe or it wasn't. If it was going to happen, it was going to happen.

*

Nikki tapped on the sliding glass window of the lodge. Elli waved at her. She was busy smiling her wonderful dark Greek smile into her headset, which seemed far too skimpy to accommodate it. Nikki knew what she was saying, in English smoothed and streamlined by so many repetitions over the years: 'Fred Toppler Foundation. How my dreck your call?' She was the voice with which the foundation spoke to the outside world, the finger that pressed the buzzer to open and close the barrier keeping the confusion and shabbiness of that world at bay, the hand that sorted the incoming mail. She also looked after all the keys. Which was why Nikki was waiting.

Now Elli was frowning her wonderful dark Greek frown. The unseen caller's answer to her perfectly formed English question was evidently also in English, which she couldn't always understand.

Nikki waited. She had time in hand. Of course – she always had, in spite of having so much to do. She thought another of her cool thoughts. This particular cool thought was a recurring one: that quite shortly now the director would be out of Empedocles and on a plane back to his native Wuppertal. She knew it from the way Mrs Toppler pronounced his name these days.

So the post of director would be vacant. The appointment would have to go before the Board of Trustees, of course, but what could the Board of Trustees do except what the money told them to? The money was Mrs Fred Toppler. And, of course, her friend Mr Vassilis Papadopoulou, who had been such a patron and benefactor of the foundation. In Athens Mr Papadopoulou made ministers and broke them. No one in Greece who had any hopes of remaining alive and well would want to put obstacles in the way of a candidate supported by Papadopoulou. And there was a candidate to hand whom he might just possibly favour. Someone who over the past five years had gradually made herself indispensable to both Mrs Toppler and Mr Papadopoulou. 'Oh, that Nikki!' as Mrs Toppler so often had cause to say. 'Whatever should we do without her?'

And now this year she had organised the entire House Party. She had chosen the Fred Toppler lecturer. Mr Papadopoulou would be present at the lecture himself, and he had invited a number of his business associates. Last year Mr Papadopoulou and several of his guests had fallen asleep in the lecture. If this year they managed to remain awake . . .

Well, you never knew in life. You never knew.

Elli slid back the glass and held out a car key.

'Nikki, you should be late! The plane comes in half an hour!'

'It's ten minutes behind time. I checked.'

'Oh, yes, you check,' said Elli. 'Of course.'

'Everything,' said Nikki, smiling her nice open smile. 'Always.'

She walked unhurriedly towards the brilliant wall of bougainvillaea that concealed the car park, still thinking her cool thought.

Elli watched her go, thinking a cool thought of her own: if Nikki becomes director, Mrs Fred Toppler will be looking for a new PA . . .

5

Dr Wilfred had established himself in the prime position by the carousel, identified through long experience and granted by right of being in business class and so among the first off the plane: hard up against the track, close to the point where the tide of tumbled black wheelie bags would at any moment burst through the doors, but just far enough away to get a good sight of them approaching before they reached him. His own was easy to spot, because its red leather address tag made it stand out from the sea of black all around; the fruit of experience once again. Which reminded him of his flight bag, and the lecture inside it. He checked. Yes, wedged safely between his feet, where he could feel it while he turned his phone on and found out what tedious demands upon him had accumulated while he was airborne.

Five e-mails and seven texts. Would he consider . . . ? No, he would not. Would he address a conference . . . – no . . . ! – in Hawaii? Oh God, Hawaii again. Well, possibly. Would he write, join, read, judge . . . ? No . . . yes . . . maybe . . . Nothing that Vicki couldn't deal with. Except one e-mail from Vicki herself. Did he wish to respond to the attached? It turned out to be a review of his life's work from some publication he had never heard of in Manitoba, and it was entirely ridiculous. The author was disabled by stupidity and ignorance, motivated by spite, and didn't understand what 'disinterested' meant. It was not something he would dream of responding to.

He was about to put the phone back in his pocket when one particular phrase in the article suddenly came back into his mind. 'Dr Wilfred's entirely mystical faith in reason.' He switched the phone on again. His thumbs began to move, almost of their own accord. 'I should not normally accord uninformed abuse of this nature the dignity of a reply,' he typed, 'but . . .' His thumbs flew back and forth over the keyboard like eager pigeons snapping up seed. His response was effortlessly authoritative, pleasantly amused, and totally devastating.

Even in the crowded baggage hall of a strange airport he was a master of his craft.

*

Nikki Hook felt the back of her shirt, to make sure that it was still tucked into her skirt, then touched her hair to check that it had not been blown out of place by the air conditioning in the car. She could see the passengers through the glass screen as they emerged from passport control and crowded around the carousel like impatient pigs round an empty trough. There were twenty or so other people on either side of her, holding clipboards and lists, also waiting. Chauffeurs, drivers of taxis and limousines, representatives of tour operators. Some of the women from the tour companies were tanned and blonde, but none of them was as lightly tanned or as discreetly blonde as Nikki, and even the ones in their thirties, like her, were not as tastefully ensconced in them as she was. All these people, young and old, had their own opinions and memories, their own secret weaknesses and choice of underwear. In their own eyes, in the eyes of boyfriends, wives, children and grandchildren, of employers and fellow-employees, they were all no doubt whoever they were. But only Nikki Hook, she couldn't help being aware at the back of her mind, was Nikki Hook.

This was always a slightly tense moment, though. She imagined an actress standing in the wings waiting for her entrance on a first night. Not the star of the show, perhaps, but that long moment of waiting for her cue, of checking yet again that she remembered her first line, was just as long for her as it was for the star. And it wasn't possible to run through all the rest of her part. She couldn't know how the volatile combination of her and her fellow-actors, of text and set, of audience and circumstance, was going to turn out.

No doubt each of the visiting lecturers she had met year by year felt something similar. But then it wasn't their responsibility to charm and flatter *her* – it was hers to charm and flatter *them*. Some of them could absorb amazing amounts of charm and flattery and still not show the benefit.

On the other side of the glass a klaxon sounded. The carousel began to turn. A series of irregular black shapes shouldered their way through the flaps from the outside world, like swaggering cowboys through the doors of a saloon. The passengers pressed impatiently forward to greet them.

All around Nikki the waiting drivers and tour operators lifted up little placards. 'Merryweather,' said the signs expectantly, some handwritten, some printed. 'Horizon Holidays . . . Johanssen . . . Βαςςιλικι . . . Sand and Sun . . . Purefoy . . . Silver Beach Hotel . . .'

Nikki lifted hers. 'DR NORMAN WILFRED', it said in neat, clear capitals. She softened the set of her mouth, relaxed the skin around her pleasantly open eyes, and became a couple of years younger.

6

Why, though? Oliver Fox asked himself. Why do I do this kind of thing?

His tumbled dish-mop of hair was as blond as blanched almonds, his soft eyes as brown and shining as dates. His thoughts, though, were as black as the tumbled black wheelie bags coming towards him along the carousel. Why? he thought as his eyes jumped from one to the next. Why, why, why? It had seemed so natural to start with. So inevitable, even. But now, with the black bags filing past him like mourners in a funeral procession, he could see that it was going to turn out as badly as all the other adventures he had launched upon so lightly.

Georgie, this one was called. And he scarcely knew her! He'd only ever met her once! And now here he was, on his way to spend a week with her in a villa he'd borrowed from some people he knew even less. Why *did* he do it?

He'd watched her across the bar for some time, it's true, over the shoulder of a man he was having a drink with, before he'd introduced himself. He'd also subsequently spent many hours on rather complex detective work to find out who she was and where she lived, on flurries of increasingly frequent messages and phone calls, and many changes of plan – because *her* plans depended upon the plans of someone called Patrick, and Patrick's plans on the plans of the three colleagues from the trading floor he was going yachting with. Now here Oliver was, watching the bags plodding round the carousel, and there Georgie was, waiting for him on the other side of Customs, if the plane had arrived on time from wherever it was where she had been, seeing Patrick safely out of the way on his yacht. They were going to have to talk to each other for some of the time, and there wouldn't be anything to talk about. They were going to have to share a bathroom and a lavatory. She was going to find out that he wasn't as charming as he had seemed for that brief moment in the bar.

So why had he done it? Because he couldn't help it! It was just another sudden bit of being Oliver Fox. And being Oliver Fox was destroying his life.

As soon as he had seen that the man she was with (Patrick, of course, as he later discovered) was outside on the street, smoking and talking on his phone, and that she was on her own for the length of a cigarette, he had known what he had to do – what he had been born to do – what he was obliged by the laws of God and man to do – what he was *going* to do. It was stretching out before him as frightening and irresistible as the tightrope before the tightrope walker. Suddenly, once again, the world had darkened, and there was only the narrow spotlit wire above the abyss, the unstable narrow line that had to be walked. And already there he was, just as he had known all his life he would be, sliding his first foot over the dark depths of failure and humiliation, not looking down, his shining eyes fixed on some dim goal he could scarcely see. Already he was slipping into the empty chair beside her . . .

She was almost as irresistible close up as she had been across the bar, though rather older than he had supposed. But this wasn't really the point. The point was that the chair beside her was empty, and he had probably only three or four minutes at most before her companion came back to claim it.

What had he said to her? He couldn't remember. All he could remember was how she had responded. She hadn't laughed, or ignored him, or told him to get lost. 'You're Oliver Fox,' she'd said.

He had been unable in all honesty to deny it. This was the trouble. He was Oliver Fox. In the kind of circles he moved in, everyone had heard of him even before they met him. Friends of friends – even complete strangers, sometimes – started laughing as soon as they were introduced, waiting for him to be Oliver Fox in front of them. He had tousled blond hair, and soft smiling eyes that fixed on yours, and no one ever had any idea what he was going to do next. Least of all himself. Until suddenly he'd found that something had come into his head, and there he was, doing it already. Whereupon they'd laugh again. Or scream and run for cover, or phone the police.

'Oh, *no!*' the people he'd met would tend to cry. 'This time he's really gone too far!'

In the baggage hall here, of course, surrounded by fat holidaymakers who had never heard of him, there was no one but himself to be Oliver Fox for. He felt as if he were like the aircraft he had been sitting on for the past five hours, suspended over the void by his own bootstraps, with nothing in his head but nothingness.

So why was he like this? Why wasn't he doing a job of work like a normal human being? Something where you helped people. On a run-down council estate somewhere. In the third world. There were tens of millions of people in the world out there who needed help. He was too old to go on the way he was. He would change. He would put himself humbly at their service. Train as a doctor, perhaps. Specialise. Become a neurologist. He had always wanted to know how his brain worked, why and how he did what he did. He wasn't a fool, though – he knew how many years of study and hard work it would take. But he could still do it. He *would* do it. He would have applied for medical school this very moment, if only he could have found an application form.

Everyone would be astonished. 'Oliver Fox?' they'd laugh. 'A neurologist? We certainly weren't expecting *that*! How absolutely typical!'

On and on the mournful bags processed. Oliver's eye was caught by the sight of the man beside him, who had his phone in his hand and with his two thumbs was writing a text as long as a doctoral thesis. It reminded him to get his own phone out and switch it back on. Not that there would be any good news.

And no, there wasn't. The first of the waiting messages was from A. A was Annuka, Annuka Vos, with whom he had borrowed the villa, and who should have been standing here beside him at the carousel if she had not flown into a rage at his coming home with a donkey he had bought off the donkey-man in the park, or rather at his proposing to stable it in her flat, whereupon she had found herself abruptly unable to put up a moment longer with his being Oliver Fox, and he had been forced to leave, with nothing but the donkey and a handful of possessions, mostly his, in one of her rather elegant suitcases.

'U wont read this of course,' she wrote, 'because u r deaf and blind to everyone except yrself, but . . .'

He didn't read it, being deaf and blind at any rate to messages that started like that. He skipped down the list. The next four messages were also from A. Then came one from someone with only a phone number for a name. He couldn't remember anyone with a name that ended in 0489, but 0489 could evidently remember *him*.

'I know I am dealing with a moral lunatic,' he (or, more probably, she) began.

But before he had had time to find out what 0489's grievance was he saw his bag coming towards him. It was easy to spot, because he had had to borrow it from Annuka when he had moved out, and all her luggage had red leather address tags, like staff officers with red tabs on their collars. As he reached out to seize it he saw that the next message was from G. G was Georgie, of course, the woman he was meeting, A's replacement for the week in the villa. 'So sorry missed flight patrick trouble of course next flight is oh buggeration Ive just looked it up not until tomorrow.'

Of course. He could have guessed. The whole adventure had gone off the rails already, before it had even started. He lifted the bag off the carousel and touched her number. 'Hi! This is Georgie,' said her number. But it was lying. It wasn't Georgie – it was a few kilobytes of information stored on a server somewhere that were merely pretending to be her.

So he was going to spend the next twenty-four hours sitting on his own in some dreary villa, which would turn out to have cockroaches and no working sanitation. If, that is, the owners had remembered to arrange the taxi they had promised. Probably they hadn't. And probably he hadn't remembered to write down the address anywhere. So he wouldn't be in a villa at all – he would be stuck here at the airport. Then Georgie would miss the flight again tomorrow, or be unable to get on it. Change her mind, give up, fail to arrive at all.

He should never have come. He should have started his medical studies. He felt a lump in his throat, as if he were eight years old and going back to school again. A whole day – two days – a week – a term – stretching in front of him with no company but the cockroaches and an invisible answering machine with only the same half-dozen words to say for itself.

And himself, the apparently inescapable Oliver Fox. It was funny. Everyone thought it was so wonderful, being Oliver Fox. Everyone but himself.

7

It was an example of the ever-renewed triumph of hope over probability, thought Nikki, trying to keep the skin round her mouth and eyes soft and amused. Whenever you were waiting for someone and you didn't know exactly what they looked like, *everyone* seemed to be them. Fathers with small children. Grandfathers in ill-judged shorts. Women, even . . . Fat women . . . Fatter women still . . . Just for a moment, as each passenger emerged from the baggage hall and hesitated, not knowing where to go, Nikki tensed very slightly with the onset of charm. Then they would spot a familiar word – 'Polkinghorne,' 'Whispering Surf' – and they would raise an acknowledging finger and cease to have any possible resemblance to Dr Norman Wilfred.

More potential Dr Wilfreds at once took their place. She should have looked at the picture in his CV again before she came out. She tried to recall it. Nothing came to mind. He had looked, well, pretty much as she would have expected him to look.

She felt a little leap of the heart at the sight of one particular candidate, a rumpled young man with muddled, extraordinarily pale blond hair. His soft rueful eyes swept slowly over the waiting drivers and reps. He didn't look at all as she would have expected him to look. My God, thought Nikki nevertheless, it *is* him!

Except that it obviously wasn't.

Except that just possibly . . .

She went on watching him. The rueful gaze jumped unhurriedly from sign to sign, closer and closer.

For an instant she was eight years old again. If I think hard enough that it's him, she thought, perhaps it will be.

*

'Carling ...' 'Pleather ...' 'Spoon ...' Oliver looked carefully at the hopefully uplifted names, trying to make each in turn read 'Fox'. None obliged. Just as he had feared. As soon as one thing went wrong so did everything else. He was on his own in the world. 'Wertheimer ...' 'Begby ...' 'Budd ...' All these people with solid and convincing names! With someone to meet them, with lives to live, with friends and lovers, with happy days ahead full of laughter at taverna tables. Why was he not Begby? Why was he not Budd? Even as he looked, 'Begby' and Begby were shaking hands and laughing.

'Johanssen ...' 'Cholley ...' 'Dr Norman Wilfred ...'

He stopped. Dr Norman Wilfred ... Yes. That would have been a good name to have. There was something wholesome and down-to-earth about it that suggested a general practitioner in a country town. Someone with ruddy cheeks and a twinkle in his eye, beloved by his patients. If only he had been called Wilfred. With a name like that he, too, could have been a doctor already. He could have been leading Dr Wilfred's decent, useful life, and taking Dr Wilfred's well-earned summer holiday – could even now have found himself being met by whoever it was Dr Wilfred was being met by.

He looked up a little to see who it was.

Oh, *yes*! he thought, as he took in the soft openness of her eyes, and couldn't help but smile.

*

Oh, *no*! thought Nikki, as Oliver's soft melancholy smile rested on her. It *is* him!

And of course she smiled in her turn.

*

Good God, thought Oliver, as he saw the smile. She thinks I'm him!

And all at once he knew it was so. He *was* Dr Norman Wilfred. He saw his life as Dr Norman Wilfred stretching in front of him like the golden pathway into the rising sun. He had no choice but to walk along that pathway, towards the warmth, towards the light.

So he did, pulling his suitcase behind him.

*

She watched him approach. He was still smiling. She was still smiling herself, she realised.

'Dr Wilfred?' she said.

'I cannot tell a lie,' said Oliver. No – said *Dr Wilfred*.

*

She plainly wanted him to be Dr Wilfred, he could see. She would probably be disappointed later, of course, when he turned out not to have been Dr Wilfred after all. But later was later. The immediate priority was not to disappoint her now. In any case, there was some truth in what he had said.

He was not good at telling lies, and he never did. Not if he could manage without.

She went on smiling, and the warmth of that smile made her almost as beautiful as he was going to tell her she was, as soon as a suitable opportunity occurred. She tucked her sign away on top of the clipboard she was carrying and shook his hand.

'I'm Nikki,' she said. 'The name on all those e-mails.'

'Nikki,' he said. 'Of course. Though I couldn't have guessed from the name that you'd look like this.'

She managed to frown and took the handle of his suitcase. He could see, though, that her frown was a frown in the same way that he was Dr Wilfred. He felt the familiar jolt of joyous excitement. Here we go again!

'Anyway,' she said, 'welcome to Skios.'

8

Dr Norman Wilfred touched the Send button of his phone and his intercontinental ballistic missile departed in the direction of Manitoba. For something composed with two thumbs in a strange airport it was a remarkably powerful piece of writing. There would be body parts scattered over a wide area of Canada. He could resume his visit to Skios with a calm mind.

Now, where had he got to . . . ? Flight bag! Yes, still safely between his feet. So, suitcase . . .

The dark spate of luggage on the carousel, he discovered, had become a drought-stricken trickle, and, even as he looked, the one remaining fellow-passenger claimed his bag and departed. Dr Wilfred was left on his own in the baggage-hall, like the last boy at school to be picked for the football team. A disintegrating cardboard box came wearily into view . . . a ten-foot-long camouflaged canvas holdall . . . and yes, his suitcase with the familiar red leather tag. But even as Dr Wilfred reached out to take it he saw that the suitcase itself wasn't familiar at all. There was something subtly but unmistakably alien about it. Somebody else, evidently, had hit upon the idea of a red address tag. He opened the flap on the tag. Yes. Someone called Annuka Vos.

He let the suitcase go on its way. The cardboard box shuffled slowly back round the track, ashamed that no one wanted it . . . the ten-foot-long holdall . . . the alien suitcase . . .

That seemingly endless spring of luggage behind the flaps had finally dried up.

Box again . . . Holdall . . . Alien suitcase . . . And suddenly all three of them became motionless, as if they had at last given up hope of ever finding owners. A great silence fell over the baggage hall.

The bastards had lost his suitcase. Of course. First you see your entire life's work mocked by some nasty little nobody in Manitoba, and then the airline loses your bag.

The waiting glass of chilled white wine beneath the stars, the lightly tanned skin and the discreetly blonde hair, had vanished as if they had never been.

Skios! He'd somehow always known it was going to be a disaster.

*

'I'm sorry,' said Nikki. 'I had a great speech of welcome prepared, but somehow it all went out of my head.'

They were walking side by side to the car park through the beautiful heat of the night and the hot smells of sub-tropical flowers and herbs.

It wouldn't last very long, this wonderful new life of his, realised Oliver. He would only need to say one wrong thing. How many bright paths he had seen opening in front of him before! How many times he had then suddenly found himself falling into the darkness! Sooner or later he would once again be talking himself out his embarrassment. People thought he didn't feel the embarrassment, but he did, he did! Did the climber not mind falling or the sailor drowning? Of course they minded! They dreaded it! That was the point – the risk! There was nothing that made you relish every moment of being alive so much as knowing that at the very next you might be dead. Or might somehow still, even as you fell, find some overhanging plant to grab, some passing piece of flotsam to cling on to. 'I got a bit confused, etc. etc. Possibly by your being the most beautiful woman I have ever, etc. etc. I really thought for a moment that I actually *was*, etc. etc.' There was always some faint hope that it might work. It never had, so far as he could remember. But there was no logical reason why the future should always have to be like the past.

On the other hand, though – oh God! – she might suddenly realise that he was Oliver Fox! Had Oliver Fox's reputation reached Greece yet?

And even if he got away with it, he had perhaps only one night before Georgie arrived. He was going to have to live this short new life of his with single-minded intensity.

Nikki unlocked a car with the body of a bus and the wheels of a giant excavator. She laughed.

'You don't look at all the way I imagined!' she said.

The familiar first twinge of disequilibrium passed through Oliver as bracingly as a gulp of vodka.

'Why?' he said. 'How did you imagine I looked?'

'Well . . . the way you do in your photograph. The one in your CV. But you're much more . . . I don't know . . .' She was going to say more surprising, more handsome, more wonderful. '. . . *Younger*,' she said.

He thought about this. 'Yes, well, that's because I am,' he said. 'Younger. Than I was then.'

She laughed, not understanding. He laughed himself. He couldn't understand, either.

9

It was obvious what had happened. The owner of this single alien suitcase left on the carousel had taken Dr Wilfred's by mistake.

Yes, explained Dr Wilfred to the third official he had been passed on to, his bag looked rather similar, it was also black with a red leather address tag, and no, he couldn't precisely describe what the difference was, except that inside the tag on *his* suitcase it had *his* name, which was Wilfred. Dr Norman Wilfred. W-I-L-F-R-E-D. Not 'Annuka Vos', which is what it said on *this* bag. There was also a flight label with his destination written on it.

Which was?

Which was . . . Yes – what? He hadn't filled out the tag himself, it had been done by his personal assistant. It was the Something Centre. Or the Something Institute. The Something Something. The Something Something for the Something of Something. He hadn't thought he needed to have the address about his person, since he was being met. If he could just go through Customs and find the person who was meeting him . . . Yes . . . ? But he wouldn't be allowed back . . . ?

It was ridiculous. He knew perfectly well what the place was called, or he had until all this business had started. Everyone in the entire civilised world knew! It was what people came to Skios *for*! He had come to give a lecture there! Look – here was the lecture! But, as he explained patiently to the man, he had had a very stressful day, and he had quite a number of other things to remember, and in the past few months he had been in quite a number of other Somethings for the Something of Something.

It was his personal assistant who had made all the arrangements. He was phoning her now, look. She would tell them at once.

There was no answer from Vicki. Unbelievable how she was never there when you needed her. So did he perhaps have it written down? Of course he had it written down! It was on the label of the suitcase! It was also written down about fifteen times on all the documents they'd sent him! Where were the documents? He had explained this several times already: the documents were inside the suitcase.

But never mind what it said on or in *his* suitcase. Whatever it was, it wasn't 'Annuka Vos', because Annuka Vos was not his name!

No, she hadn't put her destination on it, so they couldn't get in touch with her on Skios. And yes, she had put her home address in London, so they could write to her there, certainly, but it might take a while to get a reply, particularly since she was presumably not there in London but here on Skios.

And no, he was not getting excited. He was perfectly used to losing his luggage. It was an inherent part of the way of life that he seemed to have committed himself to. This is why he always carried the text of the lecture with him. Here – in his flight bag. He did his best to promote the international exchange of ideas. He spent half his life sitting on planes and the other half gazing down at the dim faces gazing up at him, knowing that most of them were unable to understand

English, or were asleep with their eyes open, or were plotting hostile articles about him in obscure journals. For days on end he would be stuck in places where no reasonable person would ever want to go, in Manila or Minneapolis or Minsk, while his one clean shirt was in Manaus or Manchester or Murmansk. So he took the loss of his luggage very much in his stride.

On this occasion, however, his bag was probably not in Manaus or Murmansk. It was almost certainly still here on Skios, not more than a dozen or so miles away, since the island seemed to be only a dozen or so miles long. He supposed that all he had to do was to walk up and down the island calling out 'Annuka Vos'.

Unless some further clue to Annuka Vos's whereabouts could be found *inside* the bag. A possibility which could be empirically tested, since it appeared not to be locked.

The official gazed at him distrustfully. The only thing that he had understood was that Dr Wilfred was making trouble. He went away to have a cigarette.

Dr Wilfred leaned over the counter and undid the straps on the bag. Then zip . . . zap . . .

The first thing he took out was a batch of brightly illustrated tee-shirts. For a moment his mood changed, as he suddenly saw Annuka Vos almost as clearly as if she had been standing in front of him – in her thirties, lightly tanned, with discreetly blonde hair. They would meet at her hotel to exchange suitcases. Laugh about it together. She turned out to know who he was. Had read his books. They would have a drink . . . Dinner . . .

He rummaged further. There seemed to be no indication of her destination in Skios, however.

Only swimming trunks, men's underpants, and a bottle of aftershave.

His picture burst like a soap-bubble. Ms Vos was evidently a transvestite. Which might perhaps make her easier to find. He pushed the bag back across the counter.

Though whether its owner was a man describing himself as a woman, or a woman dressed as a man, Dr Wilfred couldn't quite understand.

*

The air conditioning inside the high palace of the four-by-four was discreetly chill. Oliver lowered the window and let the hot scented air of the Greek night blow over him instead.

'We're all so excited!' said Nikki. 'We're all so looking forward to it!'

Who the others were who were so enthusiastic he couldn't guess. But Nikki herself certainly did seem to be excited. She did seem to be looking forward to it, whatever it was. He could hear it in her voice. He could see it in her face as it was lit up by the headlights of an oncoming car.

'So am I!' said Oliver. Because yes, he was excited. What could be more wonderful than this – driving through the Mediterranean summer night with a woman who was happy to be with you, and all the possibilities of the world open in front of you? He felt intensely alive, like a mayfly with only one day to enjoy it all. And yes, he too was looking forward to it, all the more intensely because he had no idea what it was he was looking forward to, and because it was so likely to be snatched away from him again even before he had discovered.

'You've got all the literature I sent you,' said Nikki. 'But if there's anything else you want to know . . . ?'

'Nothing,' he said. Always before, so far as he could recall, he had known who he was. He was an undertaker, a visiting Danish parliamentarian, the new son-in-law. Perhaps this time he was a general practitioner in a country town – but then again perhaps he wasn't. Probably not, in fact; he was unlikely to have patients so excited to see him, or living so far from the surgery. Perhaps he wasn't even a doctor of medicine.

Well, he would work it out for himself as he went along, he wouldn't be able to stop himself. Sadly. Because for the moment he was a living metaphor of the human condition. He knew not whence he came nor whither he was bound, nor what manner of man he was, nor why he was here at all. He was being taken somewhere for some purpose, but of what that purpose was he remained in innocent ignorance.

'I'll tell you one thing, though,' said Nikki. 'You're *my* idea! It was officially Christian who invited you, of course. The director. Which is why it said "Christian Schneck" on the letter you got, but it actually came from Mrs Toppler's office, so technically it was her idea. I'm Mrs Toppler's PA, though, so I'm the one who suggests the ideas for her to have.'

'I see,' said Oliver, though he was not being quite as truthful as he aspired to be.

'I should perhaps just explain that there's a bit of a power struggle going on here. As in any institution. Well, you don't want hear all this. But just so as you know when you meet Mrs Toppler . . . And in case you run into Eric, and he says something . . . Eric Felt. Christian's assistant. Christian has rather retreated into himself. As you know, it was Dieter Knopp, Christian's predecessor, who made the foundation what it is. It's hard for Christian to live up to someone like Dieter Knopp.'

'I can imagine,' said Oliver, though this was another untruth. The flow of incomprehensible Knopplers and Schnopplers through his head was as soothing as the flow of dark wind through his hair.

'You were a pretty obvious choice, of course,' said Nikki. 'You do have a worldwide reputation. And your CV is just amazing. You seem to have done everything!'

'Have I?'

'Except get married, apparently!'

So he wasn't married. He was as free as the warm summer wind.

'I'm sorry,' she said. 'How rude of me! But women can't help noticing the personal things.'

'Even men sometimes notice whether they're married or not,' he said.

'Not always,' she said. 'In my experience.'

The headlights fell on a pole, striped in red and white, across the road in front of them. The car stopped and a uniformed security man emerged from the shadows. 'Security have taken on four extra staff for the occasion,' said Nikki to Oliver. 'All for you!'

'ID,' said the security man.

'Giorgios! It's me!'

'ID,' said Giorgios.

Nikki laughed. 'If only all our staff were so thorough!' she said. She showed Giorgios her pass. Oliver watched him as he carefully studied both sides of it. It was only too clear what was coming next. Yes. Giorgios gave Nikki her pass back and held out his hand towards Oliver.

'It's all right,' said Nikki. 'He's with me. Just open the barrier.'

Giorgios went on holding out his hand. 'No one come in,' he said, 'only he have ID.'

'This gentleman doesn't need ID. He's a guest.'

'Guest? So – he got a invitation? No staff, only he have ID. No guest, only he have invitation. Mr Bolt tell me. "No one," he tell me. "No one but no one."'

Nikki spoke to him in Greek.

'No one,' he replied in Greek. 'No one,' he repeated in English.

'I'm so sorry,' said Nikki to Oliver. 'Just show him your passport. That'll keep him happy.'

Oliver made a performance of feeling his trouser pockets. 'Oh my God!' he said. 'I think I've lost it!' Even the flimsiest twig was worth clutching at, if you were falling off a cliff.

'It's in your shirt pocket,' said Nikki. 'I can see it.'

'Oh, yes.' He took it out and looked at it, still reluctant to bring his little adventure to its inevitable end quite so soon. It had lasted rather longer than he had originally expected, but he had begun to build up considerable hopes for it. Also he needed a moment to prepare a variant of his usual exit speech, adjusted to local circumstances. Most beautiful woman he had ever, of course. Also confused by the time change. Overcome by the heat. New medication. Recent bereavement.

But already she had taken the passport out of his hands and was turning to the page with the name and photograph.

Was it too much to hope that she would at any rate drive him back to the airport?

She was laughing again. 'I shouldn't have recognised you!'

she said. 'But then of course in the photograph you're not allowed to smile.'

She handed the passport to Giorgios. 'Fox,' he read out slowly. 'Oliver.' But just at that moment a hand emerged from the darkness beside him and took the passport out of his hand. 'I'll look after this,' said a British voice. 'You ask Elli to get the bar up, lad.'

A red British face appeared in the open window of the car. 'Sorry, Nikki. I tell him not to let anyone in without ID, and bugger me, he goes and does what I tell him! So this is the great man himself, is it?' He leaned across Nikki to shake Oliver's hand and give him his passport back. 'Reg Bolt, Director of Security. Welcome to the Fred Toppler Foundation, sir! Nice to see a British passport doing the honours for once!'

The barrier swung up into the night and they drove in. 'You see what good care we take of you?' said Nikki. 'You wouldn't believe how many crooks and lunatics a place like this attracts. Though actually all this security is really not just to protect you but all the people who are coming to hear you. Various VIPs from Athens, of course. Also Mr Papadopoulou. Our great patron.'

She looked sideways at him. 'Mr Vassilis Papadopoulou? I don't have to tell you who *he* is!'

'You certainly don't,' said Oliver, as he put the passport back into his shirt pocket. 'He's Mr Vassilis Papadopoulou.'

'Exactly. And he's invited a number of his business associates. So you can see why they might all need a little extra security.'

Oliver laughed. Koffler Schnoffler. Papadopoulou Schnapadopoulou. And he was still on the tightrope!

[45]

At the sight of Dr Wilfred emerging from the baggage hall the solitary driver still waiting raised his little placard.

ΣΚΙΟΣ ΤΑΞΙ, it said, SKIOS TAXI.

'I'm sorry to keep you waiting,' said Dr Wilfred. 'Someone took my bag.'

'No problem,' said Skios Taxi. 'Fox Oliver?'

'What?'

'Fox Oliver?'

Phoksoliva? Dr Wilfred was too tired to start struggling with a strange language at this time of night. Surely they could have found someone to meet him who spoke English! And who was a little more personable than this. Skios Taxi's belly hung over the top of his trousers. His bald head was gleaming with sweat. He had a black wart like a fly on the end of his nose. Dr Wilfred found him quite disrespectfully unprepossessing.

'I'm sorry,' he said. 'I don't know what you're talking about. If you would be kind enough simply to take me where I'm going.'

The man didn't move.

'You Fox Oliver?' he said.

Dr Wilfred make a great effort to accommodate him. *Euphoksoliva* . . . The first syllable was familiar, anyway. *Good* something, as in 'euphemism' or 'euphoria'. 'Good day,' perhaps. 'Good evening.' Except it sounded like a question. 'Good flight?' perhaps.

'No,' he said.

'No?' said Skios Taxi.

'No. Someone took my bag.'

[46]

Skios Taxi gazed at him. '*Eunophoksoliva?*' he said.

Dr Wilfred surprised himself by how patient and polite he managed to remain.

'I'm extremely sorry,' he said. 'I have had a very bad day, which has culminated in discovering that my suitcase has been taken by someone else. So, until they find it and send it on to me, I have no clean clothes, no pyjamas, not even a toothbrush. And tomorrow I have to give a rather important lecture. Here, look. Lecture, yes? Lecture! So I think that what I should now like most to do is simply to get to my destination and go to bed and have a good night's sleep and hope that when I wake up everything will seem a little less horrible than it does just at the moment. All right? Am I making myself clear?'

'No problem.'

'Good. Thank you.'

'So – Fox Oliver?'

Dr Wilfred gave in.

'All right,' he said. '*Phoksoliva*. Certainly. *Phoksoliva*. Why not? *Phoksoliva, Phoksoliva, Phoksoliva!*'

Skios Taxi smiled and held out his hand.

'Spiros,' he said. 'OK. No problem. You got a bag?'

'No,' said Dr Wilfred. 'I have *not* got a bag. Someone has *taken* my bag. And before you say "No problem" again, please don't, because there *is* a problem, and the problem is, *that I don't have my bag!*'

Spiros made a calming gesture and ushered Dr Wilfred towards the car park.

'No problem,' he said.

10

'You're not allergic to lilies, are you?' said Nikki as she moved about Parmenides, turning on lights and putting Oliver's bag on the rack. 'Though I did already check with your PA person, because of the onions. I'll close the windows, though I don't *think* we've got any mosquitoes here.'

She stood looking round the room for any imperfections she had missed, and glanced at her watch.

'Supper in the taverna? Or shall I ask the kitchens to send something up?'

He shook his head and stood looking at her. She continued looking round the room.

'Well,' she said. 'I'll leave you to settle in.'

Still she lingered, though.

'You can just shut yourself away here and work if you want to . . . Of course, we hope you'll mingle . . . Or swim, or just sit somewhere . . . We like to think that the keynote here is civilisation. Civilised conversation in civilised surroundings . . . I think you'll find most of the people here pretty receptive. Though not, of course, specialists . . .'

She adjusted a cushion on the sofa.

'You're having lunch with Mrs Fred Toppler tomorrow, as you know. She likes to talk. I should just let her . . .'

She readjusted the cushion.

'And then of course there's your lecture. In the morning I'll show you where you'll be speaking. We can discuss all your requirements then. Just phone me if there's anything you need in the meanwhile. I've put my card on the desk. Or you can find me very easily. I'm in Democritus. Straight along the path and first on the left. The veranda on the right. There's champagne in the fridge, by the way.'

And she had gone. She had left clear enough directions, though. Champagne. Then straight along the path, first left, and . . .

She had come back.

'Not the veranda on the left! That's Mrs Toppler's part of the house!'

This time she really had gone. Oliver looked at himself in the mirror. The man in the mirror laughed. 'So,' he said to Oliver, 'you're at a foundation. And you're giving a lecture. I wonder what's it about.'

'Don't worry,' said Oliver to the man in the mirror, 'we'll both find out when I give it. If by any chance we ever get that far.'

First things first, though, since the lecture was tomorrow and tonight was tonight and might never become tomorrow. Have a bath, put on a clean shirt, take the champagne out of the refrigerator, and then – Democritus. The veranda on the right.

*

The swaying of the taxi on the bends in the dark and the thumping over the potholes suddenly ceased. After a moment the unaccustomed stillness and quietness penetrated Dr Wilfred's consciousness and he opened his eyes. He had no idea where he was. He had a feeling it was Malaysia, or Costa Rica. There was nothing to be seen but the narrow tunnel of bushes and unmade-up road created by the head-lights, and the back of a head silhouetted against it.

'Thirty-two euros,' said the head.

Oh, yes. The taxi. No bag. *Phoksoliva*. Skios . . . Dr Wil-fred opened the car door and struggled stiffly out into the blackness. He felt automatically for his wallet and then stopped. Thirty-two euros? But all expenses were paid! All expenses were always paid! Before he could protest, though, he realised that his getting out of the taxi had changed everything. The night had been transfigured. He turned round. A fairy palace of light had come magically into being. Olive trees with delicate silver undersides. Wavering reflec-tions on ancient stone walls. A flickering of bats. At the same moment, now he no longer needed it, the name of the establishment that all this was part of lit up inside his head: the Fred Toppler Foundation. Of course. For a moment he just stood and gazed. The foundation's reputation for its treatment of visiting speakers was more than justified; never in all his travels had he ever come across guest quarters quite like these. His own swing-seat . . . and parallel bars . . . and weather station . . . Around the side of the house he could just see what appeared to be his own pool . . . It all looked like a tastefully converted and very expensive holiday let.

He gave Spiros forty euros and waved the change aside. As the occupier of premises like these he could scarcely do less.

'Have a good evening,' said Spiros.

'Even without my bag,' said Dr Wilfred genially.

'No worries. They find it. I bring it.'

Bag, though! *Flight* bag! Still in the taxi . . . ! No, here, hung round his neck before he went to sleep just in case he did exactly what he for a moment thought he had done.

The luxury of the accommodation made up even for the appearance of the man they had sent to meet him, not to mention all the 'No problems' and 'No worries'. He rewarded him, as he turned to go, by repeating the man's own demotic salutation. 'Yes, and . . . what was it . . . ? *Phoksoliva!*'

The front door key was in the lock. As he pushed the door open the interior of the house sprang softly into being.

No, never before had he been in guest quarters like these! Dark traditional furniture, peasant pots and earthenware plates. Everywhere there were little civilising touches that made it seem more like a family home. Dolls, amateur water-colours, scattered books and magazines. The almost inaudible reassurance of the air conditioning. On the counter in the spacious kitchen a handwritten note: 'Help yourself to anything you can find. Pool towels etc. in the changing rooms outside.'

The foundation had more than made up for the shabbiness of its welcome at the airport. He felt as if he had wandered into the enchanted castle in a fairy-story. The bed was hung about with swagged white mosquito netting, like the curtains around a sleeping princess. Many of the cupboards and presses were locked. Perhaps the bodies of earlier lecturers who had been lured here were hidden inside them.

Now what, though? He should probably stroll along to wherever it was that the guests of the foundation gathered and introduce himself. But when he got to the edge of the silver world at the end of the garden path the blackness beyond looked impenetrable, and the soft, welcoming nest behind him even more enticing. He went back and ran a bath, with purple crystals from an old-fashioned pharmacist's jar. He found a bottle of local white wine in the refrigerator and a corkscrew waiting with glasses on the worktop. He undressed and folded his clothes carefully – he was going to have to put them on again in the morning – on top of the flight bag beside the bed . . . Lecture! Yes.

He lay back in the foam and sipped the wine. It was good. The day had gone some considerable way towards redeeming itself.

He dried his hands on one of the soft towels scattered about the marble counters around the bath and phoned Vicki. She was back on duty again.

'Me . . . Here, yes. Suitcase, however, not . . . I know, I know. Not the airline this time, though – some idiot woman at the carousel . . . All my papers, yes . . . Not the lecture, no. I've got the lecture . . . You're not in the office now . . . ? No, of course not, but you might e-mail me all the bumf in the morning. All I need now is a phone number. Make contact, set their minds at rest . . . Not too fast – I'm putting it on the phone . . . 00 30 – yes, go on . . . Wonderful . . . Bless you . . . However should we live without these magical little things?'

He pressed the new number.

'Fred Toppler Foundation,' said the voice at the other end. 'How my dreck your call?'

'I just thought I should let you know I'd arrived safely. Your lecturer. Dr Wilfred.'

'Oh, Dr Wilfred, yes, good, thank you! You had a good flight, you found your room, is everything OK, nothing you want, sandwiches, whatever?'

'Fine,' said Dr Wilfred. 'No, nothing I want. Except my suitcase, which some idiot at the airport seems to have taken.'

'Not a problem. Leave it to me. I fix it in the morning.'

'Anyway, it's very nice accommodation. Thank you. I thought I'd have an early night. Say hello to everyone in the morning.'

'OK. Great. Pour yourself a bath. Run a glass of wine.'

'I already have, thank you.'

'And in the morning, OK, you come out your door, you walk down the path in front of you towards the sea, there is breakfast by the water, everyone is so pleased to see you. Sleep well.'

'I will. *Phoksoliva*.'

'How was this?'

'*Phoksoliva*. No?'

'*Phoks* . . . ?'

'. . . *oliva*. Yes?'

'Oh . . . OK . . . *Phoksoliva*? You too.'

*

Oliver rose like a god, refreshed from the last of the bubbles in the bath, and wrapped himself in the waiting bathrobe. Straight, then left – veranda on the right. He unzipped his bag to find a clean shirt.

Except that it wouldn't unzip. Something was jamming it. A padlock.

A *padlock*? He'd never padlocked a bag in his life!

This *was* his bag, wasn't it? Or, to be pedantic, Annuka Vos's bag? He lifted the cover of the red leather address tag. 'Dr Norman Wilfred'.

Good God! He had Dr Norman Wilfred's suitcase! He had taken over not only his identity but the physical fabric of his life! Was now possessed of everything, probably, that Dr Norman Wilfred owned on the island of Skios! Had found it put into his hands, without any conscious effort on his part, by fate! The heavens had noted his initiative, and smiled upon it!

Perhaps he really *was* now Dr Norman Wilfred! Had actually *become* him!

The flight tag told the same story. 'Name:' it said, 'Dr Norman Wilfred. Destination: Fred Toppler Foundation, Skios.' And when he looked in the mirror this time it agreed. The man looking back at him was, yes, Dr Norman Wilfred.

All he needed was the key to his own suitcase. Which was where? And for the first time the obvious thought came to him – one he should have thought before, but somehow, in the onrush of events, hadn't: that somewhere in the world there must be another Dr Norman Wilfred. A Dr Norman Wilfred with none of Dr Norman Wilfred's worldly possessions, it was true, except the key to the padlock that secured them. A Dr Norman Wilfred sustained by the dangerous belief that he and no other was Dr Norman Wilfred, and that his rightful place in the world was precisely here, in this very room.

Where was he at the moment, this former Dr Norman Wilfred, whom the gods had so decisively rejected?

On the island, presumably, arrived on the same plane as the new and improved edition of himself. Not more than a dozen or so miles away, since the island seemed to be only a dozen or so miles long. Still at the airport, perhaps, waiting patiently for someone to collect him. Or, more likely by now, impatiently. Phoning furiously to ask where his car was. Being told that some confusion must have occurred. Finding himself a taxi. *In* a taxi already. On his way. Raging. Almost in sight of the foundation . . .

At any moment now the usual embarrassments would be beginning. 'I was somehow confused,' the new Dr Norman Wilfred, already fading back into Oliver Fox, would be saying. 'Can't apologise enough . . . A moment of inexplicable aberration . . . Nothing like this has ever happened to me before . . .'

So, no time to waste. Straight along the path at once, left, veranda on the right, before the superseded incumbent arrived. No time to put on his clean shirt – and no clean shirt to put on, anyway. Go just as he was, in his snow-white bathrobe.

He was out of the door so fast that he almost forgot to take his room key – *did* forget the champagne! – ran back to get it – and was out of the door again in a flash. Heard his phone ringing – realised he'd left it in the pocket of his dirty shirt – couldn't go back for it, because the door was already closing behind him, and the key was where he had put it down in the kitchen while he'd got the champagne out of the refrigerator.

Bridges burnt, then. No retreat.

Georgie Evers came down the steps of the plane into the hot Mediterranean night, her phone to her ear, waiting for Oliver to answer.

'Hi!' he said at last.

'Hi!' she said. 'It's me! I suddenly saw there was a flight to Thessaloniki! I thought "Thessaloniki? My God, isn't that in *Greece*?" So I ran all the way to the ticket desk, I ran all the way to the gate! And at Thessaloniki – I don't believe this! – there's a flight just boarding . . .'

She stopped, because she had become aware that Oliver was talking at the same time. No, he'd stopped as well.

'So here I am! I'm in Skios! I'm just getting off the plane . . . ! Oliver? Are you there?'

Because now there was a disconcerting lack of any further response from Oliver. She pressed End and dialled again.

'Hi!' said Oliver.

'Hi!' she said. 'We got cut off.'

But he was still speaking.

'*Sounds* like me,' he was saying. 'But it's not me. It's just my phone, pretending. Tell it your troubles, though, and it'll listen patiently and pass them on to me as soon as I remember to press the button.'

Of course. The announcement was only too familiar. But this time it really was a bit of a bugger. She had scarcely expected him to be waiting for her at the airport, since he hadn't known she was coming. But at least he might have been waiting at the end of the phone. Because otherwise she had no idea where she was supposed to be going. He'd borrowed a villa from someone. But what villa? Where? What was the name of the people he'd borrowed it from?

She tried once more to phone him as she waited for her bag, and again after it had arrived, but there was still only the answering machine. She felt suddenly lost and lonely. Most of her fellow-passengers from Thessaloniki were Greek, and when she emerged from the baggage hall even the signs that the waiting chauffeurs and taxi drivers were holding up were in an unwelcomingly incomprehensible script. Among them, though, was one that had an English translation with it: SKIOS TAXI. It was being held up by a man with a bald head and a large belly. In the middle of his bald head was a black wart like a fly.

'Do you speak English?' she asked him.

'*Eustrabolgi*?'

'Oh, hello, yes, sorry, *eustrabolgi*, only I wonder if you could help me . . .'

'I wait Strabolgi,' he said. He turned round and said something to a man sitting on the bench behind him, who heaved himself to his feet and ambled slowly over. He had a large belly, a bald head, and a black wart like a fly on the end of his nose. He held out his hand.

'Spiros,' he said. 'Stavros he don't speak English good. Where you like to go?'

She explained to him about how she was supposed to meet a friend here, only she had missed the plane thanks to the difficulties made by another friend, etc. etc., and then she had suddenly seen there was a flight to Thessaloniki, etc. etc., and her friend's phone was, etc. etc., and all she knew about the villa they were staying in was that it belonged to some people, only she didn't know their name.

'No problem,' said the man with the wart on the end of his nose. 'What?'

She had missed the plane, she explained again, thanks to the tiresomeness of her friend Patrick, with the result that another friend of hers who was supposed to be meeting her here, and who was called Oliver—

'Wait!' said the man. 'You want Mr Fox Oliver?'

'*Mystaphoksoliva?*' she repeated blankly. And suddenly she realised how easy it was to understand Greek. 'Yes!' she cried. 'Mr Fox Oliver! Yes, yes!'

'No problem,' said Spiros. He took the handle of her suitcase and ushered her towards the parking. 'I know where. I drive him. Mr Fox Oliver. Already now he have the bath waiting you, glass of wine on the table.'

*

Straight along the path and then left.

It had sounded so easy when Nikki said it. But in the darkness, as the new Dr Norman Wilfred groped his way around in his white bathrobe, with the bottle of chilled champagne tucked under his arm, he found it difficult to make any sense of the world he had invented himself into. Straight along the path, yes, but none of the paths *was* straight! They were all elegantly landscaped into the complex contours of the hillside. Then left. But when was a left a left, and when was it a winding straight with a right turning off it?

Here and there small lights kept their eyes modestly downcast upon the ground, or half-concealed behind veils of sweet-scented vegetation. Every now and then he heard a snatch of conversation or laughter, but lights and sounds alike only made the surrounding darkness and silence seem deeper. He caught occasional glimpses through the trees of some kind of life – of people moving about, or sitting at tables – but it was way down the hillside below him, and there seemed to be no possible approach.

His surroundings became stranger still when the moon rose above the hills in the east, silvering some of the darkness, plunging the rest into yet deeper shadow. There was something maddening about the timelessness of it all when he was so short of time himself. Somewhere in this great peacefulness those welcoming eyes were turned towards the veranda window that she had left open. But where, where? Already the smile in the eyes was beginning to fade, and at any moment the other Dr Norman Wilfred would come raging out of the shadows and shoulder him aside. The embowered bungalows were a long way from each other, and even in the moonlight he had to get very close to see the names carved in the stonework. Xenocles, Theodectes, Menander . . . Leucippus, Empedocles, Anaximander . . . He realised that he had forgotten the name of the one he was looking for. Demosthenes. No – Damocles.

He would have to give up. Go back to his own room, get a good night's sleep, and hope that somehow, somewhere, the old Dr Norman Wilfred was as lost as he was himself.

But he couldn't go back to his room. He didn't know the way and, even if he could find someone to ask, he'd forgotten the name of it. In any case he hadn't got the key.

He was beginning to feel nostalgic for the old days, when he had still been Oliver Fox. As so often in life, though, there was nowhere to go but on, and nothing to do but what you had so recklessly started doing.

*

At last, as the taxi swayed and rocked on the dirt road through the mountains, Georgie's phone rang. She was holding it in her hand, ready and waiting.

'Hi!' she said joyfully. 'I'm here! Where are you?'

'On the boat,' said Patrick. 'Where you left me.'

It took her no more than a quarter of a second to reconfigure herself.

'Oh, it's you,' she said.

'Obviously. Who did you think I was?'

'I thought you might be Nikki. My old schoolfriend. The one I'm staying with. I told you! She was supposed to meet me at the airport. At Zurich.'

'You're in Switzerland already? You said you missed the plane.'

'I found another one. Via somewhere . . . Belgrade.'

Silence from Izmir. She wound down the window and felt the hot scented night air flowing over her face. She was aware that the man with the wart on his nose was watching her in his rear-view mirror.

'What's the weather like in Switzerland?' said Patrick.

'Oh, you know. The usual. Bit cool.'

'So you're still in Zurich? Still at the airport?'

'I'm in a taxi.'

'What happened to your pal?'

'Nikki? Busy at her foundation thing. Tied up with her skiers.'

[60]

'Skiers?'

'I told you.'

'In June?'

'They go very high.'

'I thought this was some sort of cultural institute?'

'It is. Culture and skiing.'

Another silence.

'Yes, well . . . Just checking you're OK.' A special strangulated note came into his voice. 'I love you, you know.'

'I know. Me, too – me you.'

She pressed the red button. She tried not to catch the taxi driver's eye in the mirror.

'Spiros,' he said, and handed a card over his shoulder to her. 'You want taxi? Spiros. Not Stavros. Stavros he's my brother. He drive very bad. Kill you for sure.'

She wasn't thinking about Greece, though. She was thinking about Nikki, at her foundation thing high in the Alps. She couldn't remember now what Nikki had said about it. Only something about there being skiing there, or skiers. She thought about the skiers swooping across the whiteness of the high snowfields through the sparkling cold mountain air. And Nikki, up there with them, leading her clear, white, well-organised life. If only she could have been like that!

She pressed a number on her phone, then turned sideways to get away from Spiros, and hid her mouth behind her hand. There were some conversations that even she felt a little self-conscious about.

'Also electrical,' said Spiros. 'Also genuine antique amphorae. Also smell by septic tank. Send for Spiros. You don't like Mr Fox Oliver? No problem. You phone, you ask for Spiros.'

12

Nikki was getting slowly undressed in the darkness. She was undressing slowly just in case Dr Wilfred phoned and needed help of some sort. She had turned all the lights off and left the veranda windows open in order to breathe the natural air of the night for once. Every now and then the net curtains would stir and shift, or the plumbago sway in the security lighting. She didn't look round. She wasn't worried about intruders. And when finally her phone did ring she jumped out of her skin, she was so surprised. She let it ring on for a while before she answered.

'Nikki Hook,' she said, in a voice that went with pleasantly open eyes and crisply ironed shirts.

'Nikki!' whispered the voice at the other end. 'It's me!'

She couldn't think of an answer. Whoever me was, it wasn't the me she'd for one wild moment thought it was going to be.

'Georgie!' said the voice. Georgie? Oh, yes, Georgie. 'Hello, Georgie,' said Nikki.

'Nikki, listen. I'm doing something rather silly.'

Of course. The only times Georgie ever phoned was when she was doing something rather silly. Nikki waited.

'I know, I know!' said Georgie. 'Oh, Nikki! Why do these things happen to me? But listen, listen. I've got something dreadful to ask you. Now I know this is awful, but—'

'You've told Patrick you're staying with me.'

'I'm so sorry, Nikki! I know I should have asked you first.

I'll *never* do it again! I promise, I promise, I promise! He *won't* call you, I'm sure he won't, he hasn't got your number, but he might look it up somehow, it would be just like him, and if he does . . . It's just that he sounded a bit, you know, *scrungy* when he rang a moment ago. What was the weather like here, and so on. He might start ringing up the weather people to check.'

'So what *was* the weather like?'

'I told him cool. Is it?'

'About thirty-three degrees.'

'Oh, no! Not very good for skiers!'

'For Skios? Oh, about usual. Don't worry, though. If anyone asks, it's cool. I'm thinking cool thoughts.'

'Oh, bless you, Nikki! What should I do without you?'

'It's cool where *you* are, is it?'

'Actually it's about thirty-three degrees here.'

'Which is where? Or I suppose I shouldn't ask.'

'Well . . . I think it's a secret. There's this woman who keeps phoning him.'

'He's married, is he?'

'Married?' There was a pause. Nikki could hear the distant sounds of a car driving over an unmade-up road. Also of Georgie thinking. 'Probably, now you come to mention it.'

'Georgie! Don't you even *know*?'

'He won't talk about it! He just kind of smiles!'

'Oh, no! Remember the last one!'

'I know. Oh, Nikki! If only I were like you! All sensible and snow-white, and running foundations and things!'

There was another pause, this time because Nikki was looking at the net curtains stirring and the plumbago beyond them swaying. And thinking. Wondering whether to say.

'Nikki?' said Georgie. 'Are you still there?'

'The thing is,' said Nikki, in a suddenly small voice, 'I think I may be, too.'

'What? You've gone a bit quiet. I'm in a taxi. It's crashing about a lot. I can't hear. May what?'

'Also be doing something silly.'

There was a colossal shriek down the line.

'Oh, *no*! Not you! You don't do silly things!'

'I know.'

'You're the head girl! You're supposed to be setting us all an example! Oh, Nikki! Even you! So tell, tell! What's he like?'

'Well . . . he's rather wonderful.'

'No, he isn't! Don't be silly, Nikki!'

'I know. But actually he *is*. Tremendously distinguished and famous, and he knows everything, and he's done everything, and he's just so . . . *ordinary* about it all!'

'Mine's terrible. A total no-hoper. You don't know where you are with him from one moment to the next. How long have you known yours?'

'About two hours.'

'Well, there you go. Wait till you've known him for two weeks, like me. Is yours married?'

Now Nikki was silent.

'I don't think so,' she said finally.

'Nikki!'

'I did actually ask him. But he's like yours. He just smiles.'

'He's married! Of course he's married! Oh, Nikki! Head girl! Remember? And he's famous? Nikki, you're going to end up in the newspapers! So, what, he's nice-looking?'

'Very. Like a kind of blond dish-mop.'

'So's mine! Exactly! How funny!'

'Two hours, that's all, and I've only got him for one day more, and I'm sitting here in the dark because I've left the veranda window open just in case, and it's all absolutely ridiculous, and I'm so ashamed of myself, and if I put the phone down suddenly you'll know what's happened.'

Georgie laughed and laughed.

'I know,' said Nikki.

'And is he Swiss?' said Georgie.

'Swiss? No? Why – is yours?'

'Mine? No. Only since you're in Switzerland . . .'

But Nikki's attention had been distracted. There was a noise coming from somewhere like an unoiled door being swung back and forth. Then shouting, and running footsteps.

'Sounds like someone screaming,' said Georgie. 'What's going on up there?'

'Sorry,' said Nikki hurriedly. 'I've got to go.'

'Have fun!' said Georgie, as Nikki put the phone down. 'Just don't start being *in love* with him.'

*

The screaming, Oliver saw in the confused moment as the lights came on, was emerging from a woman who was cowering away from him on the bed above him as best she could while she kept her finger jammed down on the bedside panic button. She was richly and commandingly tanned and blonded, skin-creamed and silk-nightdressed. Oliver could see, even from where he was lying on the floor, even shocked and confused from having fallen off the bed with his foot caught in his bathrobe, that she was not Nikki.

There seemed to be three other people in the room, though it was difficult to see from where he was lying, and all of them in various states of social disarray. Coming through the open veranda window, where he himself had entered a few moments earlier, was the security guard who had been so eager to see his ID earlier, now struggling to conceal a lighted cigarette. Lowering above the woman on the bed was a bloated dark thundercloud of naked stomach. From the dense black bush beneath the stomach dangled a long male member. Above the thundercloud were piled more storeys of hairy flesh, and looking out from on top of it all, like Zeus from high heaven, was a boldly featured face framed by a trim grey beard and a luxuriance of billowing grey locks, raining down thunderbolts of excited and incomprehensible Greek.

In the doorway to the corridor was the only familiar face – Nikki, as discreetly tanned and blonded as ever, still struggling to do up her skirt and tuck her shirt into it.

Oliver disentangled his foot and got himself upright. 'I do apologise,' he said, when the screaming and shouting had subsided enough to make himself heard. 'I've lost the key to my suitcase.'

Nikki was the next to recover her social poise.

'Oh, Mrs Toppler,' she said, 'this is Dr Norman Wilfred. Our guest of honour. Dr Wilfred, this is Mrs Fred Toppler, who is of course your hostess.'

'I saw the window open,' said Oliver. 'I thought that just possibly I might find some wire-cutters . . . Or a hacksaw . . .'

'Fetch some wire-cutters from the tool-room, Giorgios,' said Nikki to the security man. 'Then show Dr Wilfred the way back to Parmenides, and get his suitcase open for him.

I'm so sorry about this, Mrs Toppler. I should have checked that Dr Wilfred had everything he needed.'

'Welcome to the Fred Toppler Foundation, Dr Wilfred,' said Mrs Toppler, recovering at last the use of words. 'We're all so excited.'

Mr Papadopoulou got his vast mass down from the bed and picked up the bottle of champagne that had rolled away out of Oliver's hand.

'Oh, and this is Mr Vassilis Papadopoulou,' said Nikki. 'A great patron and benefactor of the Fred Toppler Foundation.'

'Thank you,' said Oliver.

'Change from the guy we got last year, anyway,' said Mr Papadopoulou.

*

'You said the veranda on the right,' said Oliver quietly and reproachfully to Nikki in the corridor outside, while the security guard waited.

'It *is* on the right. If you're inside.'

'I see,' said Oliver. 'It is if you're *inside*. That's where I went wrong, being outside. Perhaps we could just take a look at it together, from the inside, so I've got it absolutely straight in my mind.'

She hesitated, and then became aware that the door of Mrs Toppler's room was open a crack, and that Mr Papadopoulou was watching them.

'You'd better go with Security, Dr Wilfred,' she said. 'You'll be at breakfast, perhaps?'

*

'She tells me she's getting me this great star,' said Mrs Fred Toppler. 'And all the time it's her boyfriend!'

'She hooks you a big fish – who cares?' said Mr Papadopoulou, his hand under Mrs Fred Toppler's nightdress in the dark, squeezing the spot that she liked to have squeezed, for medical reasons, just below the small of her back. '*She's* happy, *he's* happy, *you're* happy.'

'"Oh, Mrs Toppler," she says, "he's world famous! Oh, Mrs Toppler, he's going to be so much better than the one last year!" And all the time they're doing it right across the corridor!'

'Relax. He never got there.'

'No, this great intellectual, and can't even find his girlfriend's fanny!'

'Boy, did you scream!'

'The little tramp, though! That white shirt, that kind of stuffed English muffin look on her face. And inside it all she's a tramp like everybody else!'

Mr Papadopoulou suddenly laughed. 'You know what? She looks out the window for him. She says, "Darling, it's the window on the right!"'

Mrs Toppler thought about this. Mr Papadopoulou was kneading her buttocks. She was almost ready for the oven. Suddenly she laughed in her turn.

'He is rather cute, though,' she said.

*

Nikki lay wide awake, trying to calm herself with her cool thought. Christian will be going. The foundation will be looking for a new director . . .

But before she could finish thinking her cool thought it had been overtaken by a hot one: had the scene in Mrs Toppler's bedroom cast doubt on the suitability of her choice of lecturer? Hard on the heels of this hot thought came another one, even more hotly embarrassing, even more hotly tormenting: Mrs Toppler couldn't possibly have suspected, could she, in whose bed Dr Wilfred had really been trying to find wire-cutters or a hacksaw . . . ?

She got up and checked once again that her veranda window was now closed and bolted.

13

Perhaps there was more to Oliver than she had supposed, thought Georgie, as she opened the front door of the villa and the lights revealed the cavern of relaxed wealth within. He certainly seemed to have rich friends.

'Oliver!' she called softly. There was no response but the ghostly murmur of the air conditioning. And something else . . . Some elusive sense of a human presence. A faint sound, perhaps, that merged with the air conditioner.

She pulled her suitcase inside and closed the door. After all her adventures she had finally arrived.

She opened a door at random. 'Oliver?' But the sound in here was the purring of a vast steel refrigerator. Silhouetted against a discreet glow of light on the draining board sat the remains of a pizza, a single wine glass, and a three-quarters-empty bottle of wine.

She tried another door, and there in the darkness beyond was the sound. It was breathing. The deep, rough breathing of a man asleep, coming from behind the mosquito net around a wide bed. She had entered a fairy-story, though it was the wrong way round from usual; she was the princess awakening the enchanted prince from his hundred-year-long sleep. 'Oliver!' she whispered. The sleeping prince snorted and turned away. The rough breathing became snoring. She felt a moment of dismay. She somehow hadn't foreseen that the soft words issuing from that gently rueful face when it was awake might become coarse grunts when it was asleep.

Her heart sank as she thought of all the other disconcerting little things she was going to find out about him in the next few days. 'Oliver!' she said, rather more sharply.

On he snored behind the white gauze. By the pale shine from the doorway she opened her suitcase and took out her washbag. She fell over his shoes as she felt around for the bathroom, and still he didn't wake. The bathroom was all soft lighting and soft towels. She was tempted to have a bath, but settled for cleaning her teeth very carefully, and rubbing various creams into her face. She inspected herself in the mirror. Yes, only a few more years and she wouldn't be doing silly things like this any longer. She would have settled down without any effort on her own part.

She went back into the bedroom. The snoring had become more profound. She closed the door. Complete darkness. She thought for a moment. Snoring or no snoring, this is what she had come all this way for. This is why she had made so many arrangements and told so many lies. She got undressed, and then stood for a moment shivering, though whether from anticipation or simply the chill of the air conditioning she didn't know.

Carefully she found her way through the mosquito netting. Carefully she drew it closed behind her.

He was as naked as she was, she discovered as she stretched herself out behind him. His back was a surprise – it was covered in coarse hair. So was his chest, as she put her arm round him. She slid her hand down through the thickets. He was much fatter than she would have guessed; a rounded droop of flesh rested sideways on the sheets like the hang of a heavy swagged curtain. She reached an even denser thicket, and there, hidden in the midst of it, a creature as small

[71]

and soft as a piglet. All the tender excitement that had been gathering inside her over the past two weeks stirred again.

So did the piglet. So, at last, did the great father pig in whose fur it was nestling.

*

Dr Wilfred slowly surfaced from sleep to discover himself in a most delightful world, though it took him a few moments to realise exactly what the delightfulness of it was. Sometimes before on his travels he had found himself involved in a rather agreeable interlude of some sort. Someone would have approached him after his lecture. Something she hadn't quite understood, something she wanted to discuss further. A drink or two. Perhaps some exchange of revelations about tastes and feelings . . . backgrounds and home towns . . . aspirations and disappointments . . . Then usually a certain awkwardness over undressing . . . But never before had he woken up to find himself in the midst of things, with all the tedious preliminaries short-circuited. The sumptuousness of the Fred Toppler Foundation's guest quarters had already justified its good name in the profession, but never would he have guessed that it also provided amenities like this. His misfortunes with his luggage and the offhandedness of his reception at the airport had been most handsomely made up for.

The unknown owner of that sweetly importunate hand pressed herself against his back and kissed his ear. 'You bad boy,' she whispered. 'Don't you ever listen to your messages?'

Dr Wilfred found the soft whisper as delightful as everything else, but the sense of the words hard to construe. 'What messages?' he said.

The magical hand stopped moving. For a moment it remained motionless. Then the long softness pressing against his back abruptly removed itself, the bed bounced violently, and there was the sound of the mosquito netting ripping as a body rocketed through it and away into the darkness.

He was too stunned to understand, then too blinded to see as a light came on, then too deafened to think as the room filled with screaming. It seemed to be coming, he slowly made out through the pink dazzle in his eyes, from somewhere in the midst of a scrabble of torn mosquito netting pressed back against the wall near the light switch.

He struggled to sit up, so as to think more clearly. At once the bundle of mosquito netting screamed louder than ever, picked up various pieces of clothing scattered around the floor, and ran into the bathroom. There was the sound of a bolt being slammed home.

He remembered that he had uttered two words, but not, in his state of shock, what they were. What could they possibly have been? Never, surely, in the history of travelling lecturers had two words produced such an abrupt and total reversal of fortune.

14

Somewhere in the world, perhaps in America or India, inside one vast electronic machine among a bank of others, an inaudible voice was saying, 'Hi! I know it *sounds* like me. But it's not me. It's just my phone, pretending . . .'

And then, inside perhaps the same machine, perhaps a different one, on a different continent even, another inaudible voice was saying in a desperate whisper, 'Oliver, will you *please* answer your phone! I'm locked in the bathroom! He's hammering on the door! I thought it was *you*! He nearly raped me! I don't know how to phone the police in this country! Oliver! Please help me! I'm all on my own! In the bathroom!'

And then, a minute or two later, perhaps inside one of the same machines, perhaps not: 'Hi! I know it *sounds* like me. But it's not me . . .'

Followed by a voice that had risen to a hysterical scream: 'Oliver! Where *are* you? He was in bed! He was pretending to be you! He hasn't done something to you, has he? Tied you up? Murdered you . . . ?'

*

And inside perhaps once again the same machine, perhaps another one in some completely different part of the world, two inaudible voices talking simultaneously. A man's:

'Listen, I don't know what's going on here – some woman has broken into the guest quarters – she's having hysterics

– she's locked herself in the bathroom – can you send someone – or call the police – or tell me what to dial—? What
did you say?'

And a woman's:

'You have reached the Fred Toppler Foundation. There is
no one here right now to take your call . . .'

15

As the night wore on Nikki's worries about the future of the directorship began to change their shape, in the way that worries so often do in the darkness. What was keeping her awake now was a memory of the past. A past only a few hours old, but as lost to her as childhood. Once again she saw that tousled blond head slowly turning, and those rueful dark eyes coming to rest on the sign she was holding up. Once again she saw the summer dawn of that slow smile. And the smile becoming the full sunrise of his laughter.

She kept hearing the name. Dr Norman Wilfred. She turned on to her other side and pulled the pillow over her ears, but the name spoke through it. 'Dr Wilfred. Norman.'

She might manage to go to sleep, she thought, if she could get some air into the room. She could quite safely unbolt the window now, surely. No one was going to be trying to get in at this time of the night. She jumped out of bed and had her hand on the bolt when her phone rang. She ran back and snatched it up. 'Yes?' she said breathlessly. Too late she remembered the tone of voice she used for answering the phone, the one that went with the pleasant expression and the crisp white shirts. 'Hello? Yes?'

'Nikki, I know I've woken you up,' said Georgie, 'and I'm desperately sorry, and I know there's nothing you can do where you are, and I've calmed down, I'm not in a panic, but I can't get through to anyone, and I've just got to talk to *someone*, because I can hear him outside the door, he's hammering, he's shouting threats, I'm in the bathroom, he's going to kick the door down.'

At some point, as Nikki struggled to understand what was happening, and grasped that the man Georgie had found herself getting into bed with was not the one she had expected, and sympathised, and calmed the now supposedly calm Georgie even further, and offered good practical advice about how to negotiate through a stoutly built door and calm the unexpected bedfellow in his turn, she thought she heard a scratching at the window. But by the time the battery in Georgie's phone had finally gone flat and Nikki was able to get across to the window and open it, there was nothing to be seen outside.

Except, just possibly, one or two little pools of water on the tiled floor of the veranda, already drying in the hot night air.

*

Now he was Dr Norman Wilfred, Oliver had discovered, once the security guard had unlocked his room and broken the padlock off his suitcase for him, he had an unexpected taste for pure silk underpants and pure silk pyjamas. He was a more substantial man than he had realised; the underpants and pyjama trousers were both forty inches round the middle. He was also the master of a pair of swimming trunks of the same size. They were decorated with a motif of smiling dolphins, and were remarkably difficult to keep on.

By the time he had swum fifty lengths of a small flood-lit pool he had found near his room to work off his undischarged head of energy, he was in a relatively philosophical frame of mind. After the first twenty lengths he had been seized by a sudden hope that Nikki might have forgiven his mistake and opened her window again. But when he got down to Democritus and crept past the (still open) right-hand veranda window, as it appeared to him to be from outside, with scarcely the sound of a splash or a wet foot on the ground, the left-hand veranda window was firmly closed. He had tapped and pushed at it and peered in. He had thought he could see her sitting on the edge of her bed in the darkness inside, but she had not relented.

Well, there was always tomorrow. The golden pathway still stretched ahead. Until the other claimant to his identity turned up he was Dr Norman Wilfred still. He knew everything, he had done everything, and he would be irresistible. And if by any chance his elusive fat Doppelgänger had still not arrived in time to give his lecture ... He laughed to himself at the thought as he swam. What would he say? He had no idea. Something would come to him, though. Something would turn up. Something always did. The world would continue to revolve, one way or another.

Forty-one lengths. Forty-two.

But how endlessly uncertain life was! Things might be like this, or might be like that, or might be like nothing anyone could imagine – and it all depended upon the endlessly shifting sands of who was who and when they were and where. Upon who was Oliver Fox and who was Dr Norman Wilfred. Upon whether you were outside the window looking in, or inside the window looking out.

16

When Oliver emerged from Parmenides next morning the confusions of the night landscape had been resolved, and the reasonableness of the world restored, only fresher, greener, lighter, happier than ever. The air was already hot, but still agreeably so. Prostrating itself at his feet, almost whimpering and wagging its tail like a dog begging to be loved and walked, was a neatly cobbled path zigzagging down to the perfectly composed picture laid out below him: translucent blue water, white boats, blue and white cottages. His kingdom, waiting only for him to enter upon it and claim it.

Down there by the water he could see blue umbrellas, with white mess-jackets moving among them and bending to take orders, offer trays, pour juice and coffee. Breakfast! Yes! He had eaten nothing since the economy-class sandwich on the plane, and he had swum fifty lengths in the darkness. He was suddenly seized by a huge hunger – for breakfast, for the world at his feet, for being who he had elected to be. He had a clean shirt on, white and perfectly laundered, even if it was a couple of sizes too big, and clean silk underpants under his chinos, slyly insinuating their luxurious softness, even if they were held up by the paper clip from the foundation's brochure. His hair, after his nocturnal swim, was more tousled than ever.

He swung down the path with long strides. Nikki had told him that he was expected to mingle. He was happy to oblige. He was Dr Norman Wilfred. Everyone would be pleased to see him. There might be people there who had known him in the days when he was Oliver Fox, or who knew a rival claimant to the title of Dr Norman Wilfred. He didn't care. He would face them down. And when the pretender to his identity turned up, Oliver would face him down, too. This morning he felt himself to be so solidly established as Dr Norman Wilfred that no other Dr Norman Wilfred, however freighted with passports and credit cards, could take the title from him. Somewhere in this shining blue world Nikki was waiting. Together they would laugh over the misunderstandings of the night. And even when things went humiliatingly, flesh-crawlingly wrong, as sooner or later they inevitably would, he would laugh about it, and she would laugh with him.

The easy gradient ushered him eagerly on down into the picture. The world was bright, the world was downhill, the world was good again.

*

When Dr Wilfred came out of the villa that morning the unsatisfactorinesses of the night had faded, and he stepped into a new and better world. Just beyond the road he found the promised path, zigzagging enticingly downhill into a pale green sea of olive groves, with the tiled roofs of the foundation's buildings like red-rocked islands among them, though from up here there was still no sign of the sea. He started down the path with long strides. The sun was already hot, but it was still perfectly bearable, and as the valley opened out below him, he felt his spirits begin to return.

He had found it difficult to get back to sleep after the incident in the night; he had been painfully aware that the woman, who seemed to be seriously deranged, was still concealed behind the bathroom door, only feet away from where he was lying. He was now also ill-prepared to face the day ahead. He had had to put yesterday's shirt, socks, and underpants back on. He was unshaven and his teeth were uncleaned, since he had no razor or toothbrush. In any case, the woman was still locked in the bathroom, so he hadn't even been able to have a shower.

He had done his best in the night, once he had recovered from his initial shock, to establish rational communication with her. He had suggested, as calmly and temperately as he could through the woodwork, that he would help her find her way to wherever it was she supposed herself to be, but there had been no response. He had tried once again this morning. He was going out, he had told her, to find some-one who could help her, though she might prefer to avoid embarrassment by slipping quietly away before he returned. Still no response, and a picture had come into his head of her lying dead on the bathroom floor with her wrists slashed, or an empty pack of pills clutched in her hand, followed by another picture of his name prominent in the resulting head-lines. He had very cautiously tried the door. It was locked, but he had been reassured to hear a little cry of alarm as the handle turned.

His problems, though, paled in the bright light of the Mediterranean morning. Sooner or later, obviously, normal-ity would resume. He had his flight bag on his shoulder, and his lecture inside it – that was the main thing. Someone at the foundation would get rid of the woman in his bath-room. Someone would take charge of locating his luggage for him, and in the meanwhile provide him with everything he needed. He would presently be sitting down, shaved and showered, at a table beside the water. Breakfast! Yes! Freshly squeezed orange juice, certainly, and sugary Greek croissants, with perhaps a crisp rasher or two of bacon. He had eaten only a pizza out of the guest-quarters freezer since he had got off the plane. His breakfast would be interrupted, of course, by people coming up to introduce themselves in the usual tiresome way. 'Dr Norman Wilfred? Such an admirer . . . so looking forward . . .' This, though, he would bear, philosophically, with breakfast in front of him and clean socks on his feet.

The path was rough underfoot, but so steep that he was striding towards the coffee and the socks with wonderful swiftness. It was a remarkably long way down, though. He had been going for twenty minutes or more before he reached the first of the foundation's buildings.

It was deserted. The windows were broken, and the front door leaned wearily forwards on its one remaining hinge.

The sight was curiously disheartening. The foundation was evidently less well endowed than he had supposed. The sun was getting noticeably hotter as he set out again down the path. He could see another glimpse of tiles among the trees below him, but ten minutes later, as he got a little closer, he discovered that they were a jumbled heap, with no walls left to support them.

He had allowed himself to be inveigled into lending his prestige to an organisation that was plainly on its last legs. Or could he possibly have taken a wrong turning somewhere? Perhaps he should retrace his footsteps to check. But at the thought of how much time and effort he had invested in getting to where he was, and how much more still he would have to invest to negate his initial outlay, and to do it uphill instead of down, he hesitated. He looked uphill. He looked down. He could feel the coffee and sweet croissants calling out most eloquently to him. But where was the voice coming from?

He caught a brief glimpse of people moving about among the trees below him. The decision had made itself.

He hurried down the path to catch whoever it was before they disappeared. He found himself going even faster than he had expected, because the ground had somehow alarmingly removed itself from under his feet and got itself bouncingly and painfully under his bottom and the back of his skull instead. His flight bag came tumbling down the hill behind him, like Jill after Jack. The people he had glimpsed lifted their heads abruptly to watch him, startled by the speed of his approach.

Except that they weren't people. They were goats.

17

Slowly and silently Georgie eased back the bolt. Slowly and silently she turned the handle and edged the bathroom door open a few inches.

No one. She tiptoed out into the bedroom and listened.

Nothing. She crept out into the corridor, and looked cautiously into each of the rooms of the villa in turn.

Yes, she was alone.

She went back into the bedroom to fetch the intruder's belongings and put them out in the garden, but he didn't seem to have any. She bolted the front door, and another door at the back of the house that gave access to the pool. She checked that all the windows were fastened.

She switched on her phone. It glowed a dull and recalcitrant red at her, but it seemed to have recovered its spirits a little all the same and managed to utter a grudging little acknowledgement when she pressed Oliver's number.

'Hi!' said his voice. 'I know it *sounds* like me . . .'

She ended the call before it taxed the phone's limited goodwill any further. At once it rang. 'Patrick,' said the screen. She ended the call. The phone rang again. 'Patrick,' it said. She ended the call. It rang again. 'Nikki,' it said.

She snatched the phone to her ear.

'Oh, Nikki, thank God!' she said. 'He's gone out, I've locked all the doors, I can't get hold of Oliver, I might have known it was going to be like this, I simply don't know what to do, where can he possibly be, what's happened to him, I'm so worried, I'll never speak to him again—'

She stopped, because Nikki was talking at the same time.

'. . . be able to do something if I only *knew where you were*,' she was saying.

'I don't *know* where I am!' said Georgie. 'I'm in some villa somewhere, it belongs to some people, only listen, this phone's going to run out again, I'll call you back as soon as I've plugged it in—'

But she was talking to no one and nothing, she realised. The phone had relapsed into a coma.

She fetched the charger from her suitcase, and found a convenient socket. Socket and plug, though, she realised as soon as she tried to introduce them, were not on speaking terms. Of course. It was Patrick who looked after things like adapters.

*

'No,' said Nikki, 'I mean what *country* are you in, because then maybe I could, I don't know, phone the local police or something—'

But she became aware that she was talking to herself. She had already tried four times that morning to phone Georgie, and now Georgie's phone had gone dead again. There was nothing she could possibly do to help her.

She would have to go back to her other worry. Four times that morning she had tried to phone Dr Wilfred. Five times she had gone to tap on his door. Four times she had abandoned the call before she had got through, five times she had walked away again.

All she could think of was wire-cutters. And the little pools of water on the veranda outside her window. And the night creams on Mrs Toppler's face. And Dr Wilfred's soft, lopsided smile. And the dark forest on the lower slopes of Mount Papadopoulou. And Dr Wilfred's long list of publications, positions held, honours won. And the wire-cutters. And the face cream. She had been thinking of these things all night. She would never forgive Dr Wilfred. She would never forgive herself.

Her career was over. She had made a disastrous mistake in her choice of lecturer. She hated him.

She was standing by the Temple of Athena, the phone still in her hand, looking absently down at the tables in the square on the waterfront, some of them under the great plane tree, some of them shaded by blue umbrellas. Breakfast was being served. She was waiting to see him come into breakfast, she realised.

Her attention was caught by a shifting straggle of people that had collected around one of the tables. They were all looking at something that was happening in their midst . . . It was him. It was Dr Wilfred that was happening.

Her heart gave an uneasy lurch. She hurried down the path towards breakfast to clear up any misunderstandings, and to make clear to everyone who might have got the wrong impression quite what an extraordinary human being Dr Wilfred was.

*

'The Fred Toppler Foundation,' said Elli, for the twelfth time that morning. 'How my dreck your call?'

She slid back the window in front of her little cell, trying with her left ear to hear what the postman was saying in Greek as he handed over the morning mail with various receipts that needed her signature, and with her right ear to make sense of the incoming confusion of English in her headset.

'Sorry, who is this, please . . . ? Oh, Dr Wilfred! Dr Wilfred . . . ? Yes, hello, good morning. You sleep well? You find breakfast . . . ?

'No? No breakfast . . . ? Oh . . .

'You're *where* . . . ? You don't *know* where . . . ? So, what, you don't want breakfast . . . ? Oh, sorry – you *do* want breakfast . . .

'OK . . . OK, OK, OK . . . So you just do like I told you. You go straight down the path and you see tables, chairs, people, coffee . . . No . . . ? Yes! Just by the sea! You can see the *sea*, I hope . . . ! You *can't* see the sea? No *sea* . . . ? Only trees . . . ? And what . . . ? *Goats* . . . ?

'OK, so now I understand. Here's what happened, Dr Wilfred. You went the wrong way! I told you, "Go down the path . . ." OK, sure, you went down the path . . . But, Dr Wilfred, you went down the *wrong* path!

'So here's what you do. You go back to where you started . . . Up the hill, yes . . . ? All the way back up the hill. And then you start again on the right path. OK . . . ? You're welcome.'

18

'Wilson Westerman . . .' 'Darling Erlunder . . .' 'Peter Comax . . .'

At every moment the cloud of names hanging about Oliver's head became more tangled and less attached to all the smiling faces and outstretched hands.

'Dickerson and Davina . . .' 'Chuck . . . Chuck who? Chuck nobody! Just Chuck . . . !' 'Chuck Friendly, in fact – he's too modest to say . . .' 'Kate Katz . . .' 'Kate Kurz . . .' 'Morton Rinkleman, and you may have met Kellogg Rinkleman, who is in fact my second cousin . . .'

'Hi,' said Oliver – no, Dr Wilfred, Dr Wilfred. 'Hello, there. How nice to meet you. Hi.'

'A great honour . . .' said the smiling faces. 'A real pleasure . . . We're all so excited . . .'

Dr Wilfred remained alert and braced. It would get harder than this, obviously. Sooner or later there would be questions put to him, and he would have to find answers.

'I believe you know Senator Hauptmayer, sir?' said one of the faces.

And here it was – a question. A perfectly easy one to deal with, however, even though he so rarely resorted to lies.

'How is the senator?' he asked.

'Poorly, as you know.'

'Give him my best regards.'

'I will, sir.'

Another face: 'I read your book . . . What was it called . . . ?'

Harder, but not impossible. Dr Wilfred spread his hands helplessly and smiled. He didn't know, either. Everyone laughed.

'Anyway,' said the face, 'you know the one I mean, and I wanted to ask you: when you wrote this book, what were you trying to tell us?'

He could put this one away in the same fashion as he had the last one.

'Heaven knows,' he said. More laughter. 'Only whatever it was I was trying to tell you, I obviously wasn't trying hard enough.'

Another hit. On the edge of the group, behind all the unfamiliar faces, was one that he knew. Pleasantly open eyes, watching him and smiling. He gave her a little wave, and a small special smile that she would be able to see was different from the smiles he was handing out to all the others. She did; she quickly looked away to hide how pleased she was.

Another face: 'Now, I've read that book, and I was somehow expecting you to be . . . well, I don't know . . . *different . . .*'

'No,' said Dr Wilfred. 'I'm pretty much the way I am.'

They loved it. Another face coming up, though: 'You won't recall this, Dr Wilfred, but we have met before.'

Ironical, obviously. Means he's met Dr Wilfred and it wasn't me. On the other hand . . . 'Where was it? Not at that thing in Mexico?'

'Montreal,' said the face.

'Montreal . . . In the bar?'

'In the hot tub!'

'I wonder you recognised me with my clothes on.'

'I never forget a face. Though, yes, you've changed.'

'Changed? Have I?' The dark depths waiting below the high wire. The audience watching expectantly.

'You've got younger, Dr Wilfred!'

'Hot tubs, obviously.'

Unbelievable, thought Dr Wilfred. You were who you said you were, even if they knew you weren't! And even as he thought this he realised that it was Dr Wilfred who was thinking it. He was Dr Wilfred not just for the people around him. He was becoming Dr Wilfred for himself.

It was all too easy! More danger, more danger!

'Just a quick question, if I may,' said a small man in a pair of spectacles held together by sticking plaster. 'Oh – Professor Norbert Ditmuss, Department of Applied Dynamics, University of West Idaho. Emeritus, but I like to keep in touch with the subject. Now, sir, you say in your book *Planned Innovation*, Chapter Seven, I think it is, page 179, am I right, in the footnote on your statistical methodology, that assigning a value of between seven and ten to the theta function in a Wexler distribution, given that lambda is negative and mu is greater than phi, will yield a solution remarkably close to Theobald's constant. Now, my question to you, sir, is exactly *how* close?'

'Oh,' said Dr Wilfred. 'As close as a dog and a flea.'

Everyone laughed respectfully. Except Professor Ditmuss. 'Yes, but seriously,' he said.

'Seriously?' said Dr Wilfred. 'An inch and a half.'

'I really do need an answer to this question, Dr Wilfred,' said Professor Ditmuss, 'because I am writing a paper that will reference your work, and I don't want to be unjust. So would you be kind enough to take us step by step through your calculation?'

'Well . . .' said Dr Wilfred.

There was an easy way round this question, just as there was to all the others, but for some reason Dr Wilfred couldn't see what it was. He seemed to have come rather suddenly to the end of the golden pathway that had stretched out before him.

Everyone around the table had turned to watch him. None of them had understood a word of the question, and they looked forward to the brilliance that Dr Wilfred would display in providing an answer not a word of which any of them would understand either.

'Well . . .' said Oliver, since Oliver was what Dr Wilfred was now rather swiftly subsiding back into.

'I hate to interrupt,' said a soft and welcome voice. Nikki had stepped forward. 'But I shall have to ask you two gentlemen to discuss technical questions at some other time. I'm whisking Dr Wilfred away for a rather important meeting.'

19

On the pergolas in the shade garden the plumbago was piled as high and blue as the sky above it. Nikki looked up at it and felt as serenely happy as the blossom. There were forty different things she should have been doing. But she wasn't doing any of them. She was strolling through the shade garden with Dr Wilfred.

'This is the important meeting I've got to go to, is it?' said Dr Wilfred.

'It *is* important,' she said. 'We've got to discuss your schedule.'

She couldn't get over the sheer lightness with which he wore his immense distinction. You would never have guessed from meeting him how much he knew and how much he had done. He was totally unlike any other guest of honour they had ever had. And everyone plainly loved him. Of course. How could they not? From the first moment she had set eyes on him at the airport she had known they would. And it was she who had suggested inviting him. He was her discovery.

She found herself telling him about her childhood. She had always wanted to be an artist, she said – she had had such intense feelings stirring in her when she was sixteen, and the longing to express them had welled up like the sap in spring pouring upwards through the plumbago. Somehow, though, she found herself doing a degree in arts administration instead. Then gradually, step by step, by way of jobs in provincial art galleries and touring theatre companies, she had made her way to where she was now.

'Actually,' she said, 'what I'm doing is not *totally* dissimilar to your job. I know you're dealing with billions of pounds, and decisions that are going to affect the whole future of the world. Whereas I've only got the odd few million dollars to play with each year for this place. But I have to say who gets it and who doesn't! I'm the one who has to provide some structure! Scientific research is probably a bit like the arts, isn't it? I mean . . . *messy*. You don't know really know what's going to happen until it's happened.'

'True,' said Dr Wilfred. 'Well, *I* certainly don't. Not a clue.'

'It's like kids messing around in the sandpit. Great fun for the kids. Very educational. But someone's got to look after the sandpit. Stop the cat from using it as cat-litter, and the children from walking it into the house. Wash the sand out of their hair and clean it out of their noses. Yes?'

'Science and scientists! A total mystery to me!'

'Arts and artists are the same. Some of the writers we've had here!'

'I can imagine.'

She brushed her hand through the flowers in the herbaceous border. A shower of sparkling drops still hanging on leaves and petals from the overnight sprinklers came cascading down. 'Orodigia,' he told her. 'Flowering pangloss. Jacantha. Smithia. Peloponnesian daisies.'

'My God, you're a gardener as well as everything else?'

'Of course not. I'm making it up as I go along. Like all the rest of it.'

They walked on in silence for a while.

'Anyway,' she said, 'I've got plans for the future. I can't do much at the moment. Christian's still in charge. The director. You haven't met him. No one ever sees him. That's the way he exercises his power – by being invisible, like God, and doing nothing. Some people don't even believe he exists. I have a feeling he won't be here for much longer, though. I probably shouldn't tell you this, but I think you may be the final nail I'm hammering into his coffin.'

She broke off a low-hanging spray of violet blossom.

'Jacantha?' she said.

'If you like.'

She put the spray in the buttonhole of his shirt.

'Now, your schedule. This morning it's simply more mingle, mingle, if you can bear it. Yes? Then at midday, you'll remember, you're having drinks with Mrs Fred Toppler. Lunch with the other guests. After lunch . . .'

'A little siesta? Check that it really is right-hand inside?'

'I shall be at the airport, meeting Mr Luft.'

'Mr Luft?'

'Wellesley Luft! For your big interview! It's in your programme!'

'Of course.'

'Then tomorrow you're on the 10.45 flight back to London. After which, I suppose, we'll never see each other again.'

'But first a good night's rest.'

'First, the lecture.'

'Oh, yes. The lecture.'

*

One after another, all over the newly carpeted piazza, white tablecloths flew up into the sunlit air, spread their wings, and settled on the battered caterer's tables like huge birds landing. The agency waiters and waitresses who had come off the overnight ferry from Athens pounced on them and wrestled them down. The whole square was turning into an open-air banqueting hall in front of Dr Wilfred's eyes.

'This is the agora,' Nikki told him. 'The old marketplace. You'll be sitting exactly where we're standing, at the same table as Mrs Toppler and Mr Papadopoulou and their guests. There's quite a number of Mr Papadopoulou's business associates coming.

'It will be getting dark as we eat. By the end of dinner the only light will be from the candles on the tables.

'And then those spotlights up there will come on, and Mrs Toppler will stand up and introduce you. I hope I've got everything right in her speech. She may read it out wrong, of course, because she doesn't like to wear her glasses.

'Then the maître d' will move the lectern and the microphones, and put them here, in front of you.'

He stood in front of the still imaginary microphones and lectern, almost too dazzled by the imaginary spotlights to see the imaginary candlelit faces gazing up at him from the imaginary darkness. He was in no hurry. He waited while the imaginary audience settled. And then . . .

'And then,' said Nikki. 'Scientometrics!'

'Scientometrics? What are scientometrics?'

'What you're talking about! Isn't it? That's what we've announced! *Innovation and Governance: the Promise of Scientometrics.* You don't want to change it, do you?'

'No, no. Scientometrics. Wonderful.'

'I can't wait to hear what you're going to say!' said Nikki.

'Nor can I,' said Dr Norman Wilfred.

'And then at last,' said Dr Norman Wilfred, 'after the lecture . . .'

They had left the agora and reached a belvedere overlooking the sea. He leaned slowly towards her, smiling his lopsided smile. She put her finger on his nose and pushed him gently away.

'Some of your audience arriving,' she said. She nodded at the waterfront below them.

A vessel that looked like a miniature cruise liner was backing towards its moorings. On the stern, in huge chromium letters clearly legible even from where they were standing: RUSALKA, SEVASTOPOL.

'Oleg Skorbatov,' said Nikki. 'You've read about him in the papers. Everything you've read is true. Rich and ruthless. What Mr Papadopoulou is to Athens, Mr Skorbatov is to Moscow. A lot more yachts still to come. From Sicily, from Egypt, from Lebanon. All the places that Mr Papadopoulou does business with. Also helicopters at the helipad down there behind the winter garden. Executive jets at the airport. And me, rushing back and forth all day from waterfront to airport, from airport to helipad. All so that people can hear you speak!'

'I'll try to think of something good.'

She laughed. 'I love your casualness about it all.'

'What I love is the way you take it all so seriously.' He leaned towards her again.

'Back to work,' she said. 'Go and be lionised . . . Excuse me one moment.'

Her phone was ringing. 'Thank God,' she told it. 'I've been

trying and trying to get you! Are you all right . . . ? You're lying *where* . . . ? Oh, in the sun. I see. So what's happened to this rapist person . . . ?'

She gazed at Oliver as she listened, and moved her head from side to side a little to indicate to him a detached and mocking attitude to what she was hearing. He smiled back at her, and for no reason at all suddenly remembered Georgie.

He was suddenly engulfed in a wave of panic. *When* had she said she was arriving? Wasn't it tomorrow? But that was yesterday. Tomorrow today was today.

'Me?' said Nikki into the phone. 'No. Not yet . . . I know, but things got in a bit of a tangle . . .'

She looked straight at Oliver as she spoke. She laughed. 'Yes, he is . . . Yes, more than ever. Never mind about me, though. Where exactly *are* you?'

She waited for a moment. The phone at the other end had obviously gone dead. She put her own back in her pocket and laughed. 'Old schoolfriend of mine,' she said. 'She's quite sweet, and I can't help being rather fond of her. But she is a total idiot. She spends her entire life getting herself into the most ridiculous situations.'

'A *rapist*, though?'

'Yes, well. My idiot friend has gone off God knows where on some wild fling with some other idiot she's only just met. The other idiot doesn't turn up, and then suddenly in the middle of the night he *does*, and he gets into bed with her, only it's *not* her idiot, it's some *other* idiot. And now this other idiot, who's not *her* idiot, has vanished again. I think. Only of course her phone keeps going dead, probably because it hasn't ever occurred to her to plug it in and charge it, and I still haven't heard the end of the story.'

Oliver's moment of panic had passed. He might well not have listened to her message yesterday, he realised. He might have listened to it only today. He *would* listen to it today, as soon as he got back to his room, where he had left his phone. If he listened to it today then tomorrow would still be tomorrow.

20

Georgie's phone had not, in fact, gone dead. Not, at any rate, when Nikki had assumed. The silence was simply because Georgie had stopped breathing. She had stopped breathing because she was suddenly paralysed from head to foot.

This was the problem:

As the morning had worn on and her assailant had not returned, her confidence had. He had evidently passed out of her life, as inexplicably as he had come into it, the way so many no less confused and unsought companions had in the past. Her life had returned to normal. Or to as near normal as it ever seemed to get.

So she had unlocked the garden door and sat on a canvas chair that she had found outside, to wait for Oliver in the sunshine. She had a good field of view in every direction, and she was ready to run back into the house and lock the door again, if by some chance any more uninvited non-Olivers turned up. After a while it had occurred to her that she would have an even better field of view if she moved away from the house and sat on one of the loungers by the pool. It was so hot, though, that she had gone back indoors and changed into a bikini. She could run at least as fast in a bikini as she could in shirt and trousers. She had not been sunbathing for very long, however, when she had begun to worry that she would end up with piebald breasts. So she had taken her top off, and then a little later turned on her front so as not have tomato red ones. Had tried the phone again and discovered that a little life had returned to it.

It was while she was deep in her conversation with Nikki that she had slowly become aware of . . . what? Something. Some kind of feeling in her back. An uneasiness . . . The faint clammy touch of an alien gaze resting upon it. She was not alone. She was being watched. This was when the freezing paralysis had crept through her, even in the heat of the mid-morning sun.

Very slowly she turned her head. Him. Of course. He had returned. As, she recalled now that her memory had been prompted, the lunatics she thought she had got rid of in the past had tended to do.

He had come round the corner from the front of the villa, and was leaning on the back of a bench. For some time nothing happened. They were both transfixed. He, apparently, by the sight of her. She by the awareness that she couldn't move to cover herself without offering up yet more to those vulpine eyes. Now that she saw him in daylight and dressed he looked even more sinister than he had in the night. The whiteness of his face was shadowed by a grey scum of unshaven whiskers. His balding head was sweating like an old cheese. His trousers were torn. There were large damp patches on his grubby shirt. He was clutching with an unnerving intensity the flight bag that was dangling round his neck. The phrase 'escaped convict' came into her mind.

He spoke. 'Water,' he said, and there was a harsh convict croak in his voice.

He vanished into the house. Georgie sprang up at once and wrapped herself in her towel, but now that the intruder had occupied the house her planned line of retreat had been cut off. She ran to the gate, but stopped at the sight of the unmade-up road because she'd left her sandals indoors. She ran back to the lounger and snatched up the phone to call . . . someone – Oliver, Nikki . . . But now it really was dead.

The only thing she could think of was to go on doing what she had been doing before, which was waiting for Oliver. Perhaps by some miracle he would choose this very moment to put in an appearance.

The appearance, however, was put in not by Oliver but by the intruder once again. He looked even more alarming than before. He had evidently not only drunk water but poured it over his head, and his fringe of lank grey hair trailed down from his gleaming bullet skull like seaweed from a washed-up mine.

'I assume that this is a genuine mistake on your part,' he said, 'and not some attempt to demand money, which I may say has happened to me before.'

He hesitated, and then said in a different voice, 'Or are you something to do with the foundation in some kind of way?'

The foundation? She gazed at him blankly.

'The Fred Toppler Foundation.'

Some kind of clinic, perhaps. Of course. He wasn't a convict. He was an inmate of a clinic, out on day release.

'You're not also a guest?' he said. 'Of the foundation?'

She risked shaking her head.

'Because, you see, this is the foundation's guest quarters,' he said. 'It is reserved for guests of the foundation. I am endeavouring to find someone in authority who will be able to help you to get wherever you are supposed to be. Unfortunately I set out in the wrong direction. Which is why I have come back. I apparently need to go in the opposite direction.'

He turned towards the corner that led to the back of the villa. But by this time Georgie had had time to recover a little from her alarm. He was a sick man who needed help and understanding. Maybe he'd forgotten to take his medication. Or was so full of it that he didn't know what he was doing. He certainly seemed to be deeply confused. Exposure to the midday sun had probably not helped matters.

'Hat!' she called after him. 'Sunblock!'

She waved her own hat and tube of sunblock at him, but he vanished round the corner. She waited, with the towel clutched around her. After a while her alarm began to fade. The sun, however, did not. She took off the towel, removed the rest of her bikini, stretched herself out on the lounger, and applied the sunblock to herself.

*

Mid-morning coffee was being served under the trees shading Alcmaeon's Walk. Everyone was reclining on the basket chairs around Dr Wilfred, but in ways suggesting that their ease was tempered by deference.

Dr Wilfred himself, however, was entirely at his ease. Among all the confusion of faces and names around him, the identity he was now most certain of was his own. His brief panic at breakfast, when for a moment he had slipped back into being Oliver Fox again, was long since over. He was Dr Norman Wilfred, and the long years of being Oliver Fox had receded into the past like the brief spells among them when he had been Ophelia and Father Christmas. In some ways he was more Dr Norman Wilfred than he had ever been Oliver Fox. He had had many negative feelings about his old persona; he had none at all about his new one. He enjoyed his distinction and importance. He was proud of his achievements, whatever they were. He felt as if he had moved into a spacious new house, where there was room for extra furniture and new pictures on the walls, where there were roomy attics and cellars in which the unwanted lumber of the past could be dumped. It was what estate agents called an imposing residence, and living in it was a perpetual adventure, a challenge that brought out the best in him. Ideas and opinions seemed to like it, too. They found the occasion to drop in on him in a way they rarely had in his old house.

Ideas about climate change, for instance; views about stem-cell research; thoughts about the genetic modification of crops. To none of these subjects had he ever in his old life given a moment's consideration. The faces around him had no sooner to mention them, though, and accord him a respectful silence for his reply, than a reply began to utter itself – and often one of an originality and oracular profundity that plainly took them by surprise. Himself, too. Dr Norman Wilfred, discovered Dr Norman Wilfred, believed that climate change would encourage the study of foreign languages. Stem cells were like the little silver balls that were used to decorate children's birthday cakes. Genetic modification reminded him of the attempts made by his eccentric Auntie Jane, of whom he had never heard before, to train her four cats to appreciate poetry.

For a moment, as people heard these simple but mysterious utterances, they seemed to catch a glimpse of a meaning, like a touch of gold appearing through a passing window high in the stacked and complex cumulus of the world. The meaning vanished again as swiftly as the shifting gold, and was as transcendent while it lasted.

The conversation moved on to the cosmological and the theological. What had preceded the Big Bang? Did he see a role for God in cosmology? Had God been constrained by the laws of physics, or had he made the laws of physics up as he went along? Were there other universes?

And here Dr Wilfred, since he seemed to be some kind of scientist, became a little more technical. Everything in his personal experience, he said, suggested that it was possible to make something from nothing, and to do it simply by deciding that it was so. What was there before the Big Bang? Nothing. God had simply said, 'Bang!' and bang it went. Bang – yes, and there among everything else were the laws of physics. Oh, and forty more universes. A million more. An infinity of them.

So now we came to the age-old chestnut: if it had taken a God to bring all this into being, how had God himself come into being? Simple, in Dr Norman Wilfred's view. He had done it in exactly the same way. With a bang. An even bigger bang, probably, though this was difficult to establish empirically. He had simply said that he was God, and he was.

– Just a moment – *who* had said that he was God? – *No one* had said that he was God. *Nothing* had. That was the beauty of the explanation. It was simply an extreme case of what Dr Wilfred was talking about. Of what he was bringing into being, as God had done himself, by his very act of talking about it.

There was a silence at the end of this section of the conversation, as everyone contemplated the profundity of what Dr Wilfred had said, and rejoiced in their good fortune in having him there in person amongst them. And the hair flopped over his soft brown eyes in such a fetching manner.

I can relate this to my own experience as a financial consultant, thought Chuck Friendly, the second-richest man in the state of Rhode Island. In just such a way have I, even without divine powers, created value where no value previously existed.

And he's still just a kid! thought Mrs Chuck Friendly, the second-richest woman. I wish I could take him home and look after him a bit. Show him around, introduce him to a few people. Choose him some shirts and pants that fit a little better than the ones he's wearing, which seem to be several sizes too big. Pamper him some. Feed him up. Give him his personal space, of course, to get on with his work . . .

*

Not everyone was quite so impressed by Dr Wilfred, though. K. D. Clopper, for example, who had made his money as a nationwide franchiser of golf-cart concessions, thought that it all sounded complete bunkum, but then almost everything he heard sounded the same, and he had learned to keep his opinions to himself if he didn't want to get a roasting from Mrs Clopper afterwards.

Wilson Westerman hadn't even thought it was bunkum. He had formed no opinion at all, because he was busy trying to decide whether to sell his Manganese Industries Preferred. Mrs Wilson Westerman, for that matter, had been worrying about whether to change her t'ai chi trainer.

The almost egregiously English couple, Cedric and Rosamund Chailey, had slipped quietly away when the conversation turned to God. It had not seemed polite to be present when anything so American was being discussed.

'Oddly enough,' said Cedric Chailey to his wife as they walked back to their room, 'Norman Wilfred and I were in college together.'

'You'll have something to talk about, then.'

'Year after me. I didn't know him well.'

'You should have reminded him.'

'I was going to. Only it's a funny thing. He's not Norman Wilfred.'

'*Not* Norman Wilfred?'

'This one. No. Nothing like him.'

'You mean this is *another* Norman Wilfred?'

'Same one, apparently. I looked up the biographical note in the brochure.'

'So it *is* him?'

'But *not* him.'

'Odd.'

'*I* thought so.'

He waited, because Mrs Chailey had stopped to inhale the scent of a low-hanging branch of deep blue blossom.

'Heavenly!'

'Heavenly.'

They walked on.

'Are you going to mention it to anyone?' said Mrs Chailey.

'I don't know. What do you think? Bit awkward. I don't want to cause trouble.'

Mrs Chailey had stopped again to stroke a cat that had emerged from the bushes.

'Anyway,' she said. 'Motes and beams, perhaps. Since I'm not Mrs Chailey.'

'That's true.'

He stopped and looked round. Mrs Chailey stopped as well and looked at him.

'What?' she said.

Mr Chailey took her hand and kissed it. She smiled at him.

'Also,' she said, 'you're not always Mr Chailey.'

'Hush, my love,' said Mr Chailey. 'You don't know that.'

21

High up in the villa called Empedocles, behind shutters forever closed and blinds forever drawn, Christian Schneck, the director of the foundation, sat cross-legged on the floor in his prayer shawl. His lank grey hair fell on his shoulders. His face, lit only by the little coloured sanctuary lights on the low table in the middle of the austerely empty room, was lined and emaciated. He listened in silence, expressionless, as his assistant Eric Felt reported to him on the foundation's guest lecturer.

'He's got a lot of blond hair,' said Eric Felt. 'He brushes it out of his eyes and smiles. He's always smiling. He's the kind of scientist who appears on television. A celebrity. A populariser. Is there a role for God in physics? That kind of stuff. Jokes. Paradoxes. Pseudo-profundity. Pretty much the sort of fraud that you'd expect Nikki Hook to pick.'

Eric Felt was not just Christian's assistant. He was his companion and his confidant. His ally in the fight to prevent Nikki from dismantling everything that Christian had fought for since he had taken over from Dieter: proper European intellectual standards, the seriousness that he had always silently embodied. Since Christian never spoke these days, it was Eric Felt who had to express to the world the concern he knew Christian felt. And since Christian never left his room now, Eric was his eyes and ears as well as his voice. This morning he had been lurking unnoticed at the back of the guests surrounding Dr Wilfred, because he knew how concerned Christian was about Nikki's choice. It was a testimony perhaps to Dr Wilfred's appeal that no one had noticed Eric, even though he bulged at people so aggressively. He bulged partly from indignation, partly from a high intake of organic noodles combined with the sedentary life that he and Christian led together in Empedocles. It was difficult to bulge inconspicuously, particularly if you were doing it as Eric was, in a plum-coloured tee-shirt and three-quarter-length orange skateboarding trousers.

He bulged much less when he was talking to Christian, because he was sitting cross-legged on the floor himself, and leaning forward to take the strain off his spine. With Christian, also, he was expressing not indignation but reverence. Christian had suffered and had mastered his suffering. The suffering and the mastery were recorded deep in the eroded dry limestone of his face. Once upon a time he had done things. Now he had gone beyond that. What was it that he had once done? No one could now remember, not even Eric. This was how far above and beyond doing he had gone.

'Another Brit, of course, Dr Wilfred,' said Eric. 'The whole place is crawling with them! It's all Nikki Hook's doing. Everything you have ever stood for is being Anglo-Saxonised! Trivialised! Ironised!'

Eric knew about Brits. He was one himself.

'I do my best, Christian,' he said. 'But I can't do it all on my own. Nikki Hook's got her claws into everything. She twists Mrs Toppler round her finger. And last week I saw her talking to Mr Papadopoulou. She's up to something with him as well.'

The whole future of the foundation hung in the balance. Dieter had made the foundation what it was, and Christian,

Dieter's companion and personal assistant, had been his chosen successor. When Dieter had faded quietly away, worn out by austerity and dedication, and been quietly laid to rest under the stones of the agora, head down towards the centre of the earth in accordance with his highly specialised private beliefs, there had been no question but that the Board of Trustees would appoint Christian in his place. In the fullness of time Christian in his turn had taken Eric as his companion and personal assistant, and it seemed that the foundation was developing a line of succession as part of its unwritten constitution. One day, many years hence, no doubt, when Christian faded away in his turn, Eric would assume his office as director. Wouldn't he? Eric himself wasn't entirely confident. If Christian failed to make his wishes clear . . . If he let his powers trickle away through his fingers, while brash newcomers with no sensitivity to the constitutional niceties thrust themselves forward . . .

'Perhaps the time has come,' said Eric, 'when you should at last emerge from your seclusion and strike. Suddenly – out of nowhere – there you are! At the lecture this evening! Like Christ driving the money changers from the Temple! Like God on the Day of Judgment!'

The tiny points of light in the pupils of Christian's eyes drilled incorruptibly on. The deeply shadowed fissures of his face retained their immobile integrity. Perhaps, thought Eric, he had gone beyond feeling as well as doing. Beyond thought, even. Perhaps he had transcended not only the physical but the spiritual as well, and achieved a state of total inanition.

But no. He slowly lifted his head a little, and those two bright, unblinking lasers struck straight into his disciple. His lips almost moved. He almost spoke.

Yes, the second coming was at hand. Eric could sense it. Christian would appear. And he would be terrible.

*

'I'm still not absolutely clear about one thing,' said the same small man in broken spectacles who had badgered Dr Wilfred earlier. 'Oh, Norbert Ditmuss. West Idaho. Emeritus. Yes, I'm still not clear in my own mind how you derive a solution to Wexler's equation that comes close to Theobald's constant.'

Dr Wilfred thought very carefully about this. The professor was evidently going to keep nagging away at whatever small dreary point it was that he was trying to make. Dr Wilfred considered invoking string theory or quantum entanglement. He had very little idea what either of them was but had deployed them once or twice before to good effect. But probably Professor Ditmuss did actually know about them. Better might be Colibri's conjunction, which the professor certainly wouldn't know about, since Dr Wilfred had only just in that very moment discovered it. He suspected, though, that Professor Ditmuss might be honest enough to confess his ignorance and ask Dr Wilfred to explain what it was. He would need to draw deeper on his intellectual resources.

His silence went on for so long that everyone became aware that something was up. Heads began to turn towards him inquiringly. Even Wilson Westerman stopped thinking about his investments.

'I'm sorry,' said Professor Ditmuss. 'I don't want to hold up the conversation.'

'Not at all,' said Dr Wilfred. 'I was trying to think how to explain in some non-technical way that everyone here can understand. Myself included.'

They all laughed. Except Professor Ditmuss.

Dr Wilfred looked around. Something would come to him. Something always did . . .

Everyone waited, even Professor Ditmuss.

Dr Wilfred's eye fell on the empty coffee cups on the table. Yes. Well. Empty coffee cups were certainly something. And something was better than nothing.

He picked one up and showed it to them. 'An empty coffee cup,' he said. 'All right? No problems so far?'

Everyone gazed respectfully at the cup and shook their heads. No, no problems so far. Except for Dr Wilfred, for whom the problem was what to do next.

'Now,' he said. He carefully smoothed the tablecloth and put the cup back in the middle of it. There was a slight rustling sound, as everyone leaned a little closer in their basket chairs. 'Now . . .'

'Just a moment,' said Suki Brox. 'Sorry . . .'

'Not at all,' said Dr Wilfred. 'All the time in the world.'

'I'm being very stupid,' said Suki Brox. 'But I don't quite understand. What does the coffee cup represent? Is that a very silly question?'

'Not at all,' said Dr Wilfred. 'It's a very good question. This empty coffee cup represents . . . an empty coffee cup. All right?'

'All right,' said Suki Brox.

All right for her. But not for Dr Wilfred. Because now what? He looked around. There seemed to be nothing else to hand but more empty coffee cups. He picked one of them up and placed it carefully beside the first.

'Another empty coffee cup,' he said. 'What does this one represent? It represents another empty coffee cup. So now we have two empty coffee cups, side by side. Yes?'

They nodded, and gazed at the two inscrutable white cylinders in the middle of the tablecloth. They looked at him, then back at the cylinders, waiting for them to reveal their hidden meaning. He gazed at them himself, also waiting.

And as he gazed the first faint foreshadowing of a meaning began to emerge.

'Yes,' he said. 'So. Now. I take a *third* empty coffee cup ...'

*

There in front of Dr Wilfred was the sea, certainly, just as How-my-dreck-your-call had said. It appeared to be at least a mile away, though, and about a thousand feet below him. He had long given up all thought of breakfast; it seemed to him unlikely that he would get there even in time for lunch. Though he realised that in the glare and heat of the midday sun his judgment of distance was panic-stricken and unreliable.

He sat down on the ground in a small patch of shade cast by a stunted umbrella pine and got out his phone. As he waited for his call to fly to England, then all the way back again to some spot he couldn't quite see in the hard brightness below, he thought about a table in the shade, with a pastel-coloured tablecloth on it and a gleaming place-setting. The sugary croissants and crisp bacon that he had envisaged before had been replaced by bread and olives, gleaming pink taramasalata, and chilled prawns. He also thought about his lack of hat and sunblock, and the friendly offer of both hanging unanswered in the air. For a moment, too, a suntanned back came into his mind, rippling softly with the movements of shoulder blades and spine . . .

'Fred Toppler Foundation,' began the now depressingly familiar voice at last.

'It's me,' he interrupted her, before she could get any further with her performance, or he himself any closer to dementia or collapse.

'Dr Wilfred?' said the voice. 'Everything OK at last? You got breakfast? You know where you are now?'

'No,' he said. 'I *didn't* get breakfast. I *don't* know where I am.'

'No?' said How-my. 'Something funny with your voice. You saying you *don't* know where you are?'

'Yes.'

'What – *still* don't know?'

'No.'

There was a pause. I am Dr Norman Wilfred, he thought. I am the guest of honour. These things cannot be happening to me.

'OK,' said How-my. 'Go back to the guest suite. Sit down. Don't move. I send the buggy for you.'

22

Nikki scarcely had time to think about Dr Wilfred more than twenty times in the course of the morning. She was running between the waterfront and the helipad, the helipad and the airport. There were the usual last-minute problems – a dead cat in the yoghurt vat in the kitchens, the lighting and sound truck stuck on a hairpin bend somewhere on the way from the ferry – and the usual last-minute cancellations and changes. His Excellency Sheikh Abdul hilal bin-Taimour bin-Hamud bin-Ali al-Said had decided to bring two more wives than he had previously said. The Bishop of the Hesperides Archipelago and Parts of Kronikae and Topikos was threatening to walk out if he found himself at the same table as the President of the Panhellenic Rationalist Association. It didn't matter too much that the Minister of Prisons had scratched because of a mass escape of convicts in Patras, but it would if the governor and the chief of police of the Hesperides Periphery felt they had to cancel as well, because Mr Papadopoulou greatly valued the seal of approval that their presence gave to the occasion, and the assurance against any misunderstandings or overzealousness on the part of the local police force.

And yet Nikki and her pale gold hair remained as calm and collected as ever, and her expression as pleasantly open to the world. In her present mood she could cope more effortlessly than ever with any problems that could possibly arise.

When she arrived at Alcmaeon's Walk to collect Dr

Wilfred for his noon engagement all she could see was a circle of backs, two and three deep, leaning intently forward in complete silence. One of the backs, she noticed at once, was topped by the blond mop she was looking for, and beyond it were his hands – so delicate, so careful – holding something up in the air . . . A coffee pot . . . Slowly, slowly they lowered it until it was resting on something else. Which seemed to be a sugar bowl. A sugar bowl floating in the air a foot or two above the table beneath. As she craned further forwards over the watching backs, though, she saw that there was something supporting the sugar bowl. Coffee cups? Yes – four of them, arranged to make a platform. And beneath those four more. And beneath those four another four. And beneath them . . .

But already Dr Wilfred's hands were slowly detaching themselves from the coffee pot. His back was gradually straightening. So were all the backs around him, with a kind of soft collective sigh.

Nikki couldn't bring herself to break the hush round the delicately teetering tower of chinaware. In any case Mrs Morton Rinkleman was already making a little speech.

'It's so inspiring,' she said, 'to find someone who knows about science – and who can explain it in a way that we can all understand! No figures, no equations, no funny business about extra dimensions or time going backwards! Just a few coffee cups, a coffee pot, and a bowl of sugar!'

There was a murmur of agreement, and a certain amount of clapping.

'But I still don't see,' said the same dogged pair of spectacles as before, 'what any of this has to do with Wexler's equation or Theobald's constant.'

'No,' said Dr Wilfred, 'because we haven't finished yet.

And for the next part of the explanation we need your help. Here – take hold of the edge of the tablecloth.'

'Wait a moment,' said Professor Ditmuss.

'No, don't wait! Never wait! Just do it! That's the first rule for getting anything achieved in life. Now, take a good firm grip on the tablecloth. All right? I'll count up to three, and on "three" you whip the cloth out from underneath it all. Ready? Here we go. One . . .'

'But . . .'

'Two . . .'

'Listen!'

They listened, as Dr Wilfred's 'three' was followed by a brief crescendo of breaking china. Nikki and the backs in front of her sprang outwards from the flying white fragments and dark splashes of coffee dregs. Something struck Nikki on her upper arm, then fell at her feet. It was the spout of the coffee pot.

'Exactly!' said Dr Wilfred. 'And that, Professor, is the answer to your question.'

Professor Ditmuss was still holding the tablecloth. He wiped the coffee off his shirt with it. He seemed dazed. He also seemed as if there was something more he wanted to say.

'I'm so sorry!' said Nikki, as he opened his mouth. 'Me again! I'm afraid I'm carrying Dr Wilfred off for his next engagement.'

*

'Brilliant,' said Nikki as she led Dr Wilfred towards Democritus. 'Though I arrived a bit too late to really understand what was going on.'

'So,' said Dr Wilfred, 'what's the next challenge?'

'Drinks with Mrs Fred Toppler.'

'Shall I do my demonstration with the coffee cups? Or just get into bed with her again?'

'Simply be your normal brilliant self. And remember that my future in this institution does rather depend upon you. Also her friend Mr Papadopoulou has something of a reputation in this country.'

'A reputation? Does he? For what?'

'In modern Greek philosophy one of the rules for a happy life is: never ask questions about Vassilis Papadopoulou.'

23

I might have guessed, thought Georgie, as Dr Wilfred appeared round the corner of the house yet again. She turned over on to her stomach and covered herself with the towel, but he vanished into the villa without a word or a glance. She kept the towel over her. He had seemed to be in a state of collapse. But you never knew, in her experience, with even the shakiest old gent.

After a while he emerged with water running off his head once again, and sank slowly down on to the edge of the other lounger, at some distance from her. She kept her head turned warily towards him, her left cheek pressed against the towel she was lying on, her eyes open.

'They're sending a buggy for me,' he said. 'It's too far to walk. I have to wait for the buggy. I am giving a lecture. This evening. At the foundation. The Fred Toppler Lecture.'

He dragged a scruffy binder out of the flight bag that he was still clutching and held it up for her to see.

'At least I still have the lecture. Everything else has gone. It was all in my suitcase. Someone took my suitcase.' He loosened the damp shirt around his neck. 'Clean clothes, toilet bag. I shall have to borrow things from the foundation.'

He wiped his hands on his torn trousers and extracted a phone from his sweaty shirt pocket. He wiped more sweat off his hands.

'So where's this buggy they're sending?' he said. 'It should be here by now.'

She watched him as he waited with the phone to his ear.

'Or have they forgotten about me?' he said. 'Do I actually exist? Or have I somehow vanished like my suitcase?'

For a moment he remained completely still and silent, listening.

'Engaged,' he said. He pressed a button to redial. Another patient pause. Then he let out a sudden howl of fury that made Georgie jump.

'Not in service!' He hurled the phone away from him to the other end of the lounger. It skidded over the edge and disappeared into the pool.

For a moment he sat there, watching the blue reflections of the sky in the water, which lapped gently back and forth, as serene and unconcerned as a lizard that has just swallowed a fly. Then he put his head into his hands and gazed for some minutes at his dusty shoes.

'I'm sorry,' said Georgie. 'You're having a bad time.'

Eventually he lifted his head, and sat gazing at something else. Her beach bag, she realised, and the things that had spilled out of it. One of them was her phone.

'I might be able to remember my PA's number,' he said humbly.

She switched on the phone and held it up to him to show him the blankness of the screen. 'Battery,' she said.

'Charger?' he said.

'But no adapter.'

He sprang to his feet, energised and reborn.

'*I've* got an adapter!' he said.

'In your suitcase?' she said.

He sank back on to the lounger and looked at his shoes again for a long time. Then he raised his head once more.

'The buggy's going to the guest quarters,' he said. He had become a different person, calm and quiet, like someone recovered from a fever. He looked at the house. 'This isn't the guest quarters,' he said. 'It's nothing to do with the foundation. It's somebody's villa. What – yours?'

She nodded. He bowed his head. 'I do apologise for my misunderstanding.'

He had become a normal human being. An abnormally quiet one, perhaps. She knew what particular aspect of his trespass he was thinking about, but was too embarrassed to specify: how he had taken possession of not only her house but her bed, and how close he had come to taking possession of her as well. Well, everyone made mistakes. She had made a slight mistake herself. She decided to forgive him, and to put him out of his misery.

'I'm waiting for my friend to arrive,' she said. 'I presume he'll be in a taxi. You can have the taxi.'

'Thank you,' he said humbly. 'I should be extremely grateful. Do you mind if I wait here? It's very hot out there.'

She picked up the wide flowered sun-hat lying beside the lounger and span it across to him. 'You're going pink,' she said.

He looked at the hat, and reluctantly put it on. She laughed. He took it off.

'Come on,' she said. 'You're going to look a lot sillier if you stand there giving your lecture and you're bright red.'

He put it on again, and she threw him the tube of sun-block. He obediently anointed himself, and they went on waiting.

'So when are you expecting your friend?' he asked.

'Yesterday,' she said.

24

Mrs Fred Toppler and Dr Norman Wilfred were getting on like a house on fire. They were sipping champagne cocktails in the loggia high up on the corner of Democritus, where it caught every slight breath of air from the sea. His nocturnal expedition into her bed in search of the wire-cutters seemed to have been forgotten.

'It's such a tonic,' she said, 'to have someone here who is not only so distinguished but so *young*! It sometimes makes me just a little bit sad that the people who share our passion for promoting civilised values are almost all past retiring age. I feel so young in heart myself! This is what brought the late Mr Fred Toppler and me together. He was eighty-one years old when we first met. "Baby," he said – he always called me Baby – "you make me feel young again." I was a dancer. A serious dancer. Nothing cheap. I had a beautiful body. I was happy to express myself with it. I was in a show in Vegas. I'm in my dressing room afterwards and the girl comes in and says, "Miss LeStarr" – I was Bahama LeStarr, second billing – "there's a gentleman to see you, and he's in a white tux!" A white tux, would you believe! Like something in an old movie!

'So he takes me out to dinner. Champagne, caviar, all the baloola. He was a gentleman. This was twenty years ago. There were gentlemen then. "Baby," he says, "you make me feel like I've never grown up. Will you marry me?"

'I say, "Mr Toppler, that is so sweet, I am so touched, but I have my career!"

'And he says, "You go right on with your career, Baby, because that's what I love, to watch you dance."

'So, OK, I'm on tour, I have a contract. Palm Springs, Houston, Honolulu. And, Dr Wilfred, Mr Toppler follows me! Everywhere! Ten cities in ten weeks! Eighty-one! And he's on the road!

'I say, "OK, honey, you win." We fly to LA, because I'm his fourth, and LA is where he always likes to get divorced. Sweet! We get married in New Orleans – it's Carnival – we dance in the streets! Then straight back to Lake Tahoe to start the next tour. And for the next six weeks I'm dancing all night and we're honeymooning all day. Never out of our suite from dawn to dusk! "Baby," he says, "you make me feel like I can touch the stars!"

'Six weeks of true love. And then – oh, Dr Wilfred, this is so sad! – in Fort Lauderdale I lost him.

'Heart. Just like that. He didn't suffer. You wouldn't believe the unkind things some people said. I took no notice. I knew I'd given him those six wonderful weeks.

'So there I am, a widow already. And the major stock-holder in TipToppler Beauty Products, plus a string of TV stations and industrial-refuse facilities. Plus also – and this Mr Toppler had never even mentioned when he told me about his will – a plot of ground some place in Greece where he was building a vacation home for his second wife – she was Greek – singer – bouzouki – only then he moved on to number three and he forgot about it.

'So I cry my eyes out for a bit, and then I think, How best can I honour the memory of that wonderful man? And I think to myself, When I was Bahama LeStarr I worked my butt off to give something back to humanity, and I did it by the only means I had to offer, which was my dancing. But how many cities can you dance in before your knees go and your boobs need some work on them and agents won't return your calls? And I see I have to stop thinking like Bahama LeStarr now and start thinking like Mrs Fred Toppler, because Mrs Fred Toppler is what I am, and as Mrs Fred Toppler I can do so much more to make the world a better place than I ever could as Bahama LeStarr.

'And it's a funny thing – if you're Mrs Fred Toppler you suddenly find there are a lot of other people out there who also want to make the world a better place, and all they need to do it is for you to come in with them, and maybe help them out with a dime or two. So this German guy comes to see me. Dieter. Pointy ears, no hair, looks like some creature on Planet Zog. Two minutes with him and I know he's the cat's miaow. Architect – thinker – everything. A true vision-ary – and don't worry, he's gay.

'He comes here, he looks at the site, he reads stuff in the library, and what do you think? This place was sacred to the goddess Athena! And what was Athena in charge of? – Wis-dom and civilisation! "Mrs Toppler," says Dieter, "together you and I will dedicate this beautiful property of yours to Athena again! We will turn it into a centre of wisdom and civilisation, a place of beauty where the finest minds in the English-speaking world can mix with the leaders of English-speaking society."'

She indicated the view out of the window.

'Every stick and stone that you can see we had to bring here. Where was the Temple of Athena? Gone. Vanished. We had experts out here from Athens, holes in the ground all over. Nothing. We had to fetch our own temple from

Zakynthos. It was dedicated to Aphrodite. We changed her name, the way I changed mine. Now she's Athena. The agora came from Pelion. The church from Samos. We built this place from the ground up. You know what was on this site when Mr Fred Toppler first set eyes on it? Two rusty iron sheds where they gutted fish.'

Dr Wilfred looked at the perfection that had grown out of those two iron sheds. Several more large yachts had backed up to the waterfront, he saw. Their crews were coiling lines and running out hoses, reefing and brailing.

'And all this because you stopped being Bahama LeStarr and became Mrs Fred Toppler.'

'All this,' she said, 'because I became Bahama LeStarr in the first place. And we're not finished yet. Up there on the hillside – behind the fences – they're still working. A new fifty-metre pool. Olympic standard. Mr Papadopoulou's pride and joy. He's taken the work over personally! He's crazy about that pool of his!

'Hey, it's so nice talking to you, Dr Wilfred, because you don't keep saying things yourself, like some of our other guest speakers. You know how to listen! What are you a doctor of, by the way?'

'Oh, you know . . . this and that.'

'I love it! You Brits! So, not medicine?'

'Aren't I?'

'You are? You're a doctor of medicine?'

'Why not?'

'In that case . . .'

She pulled her shirt out of her trousers, turned her back towards him, and touched a spot on the brown bulge that was struggling to be free of the waistband.

'Just . . . *there*. Like a drill was boring into me. I've been to specialists, I've been to chiropractors and faith-healers . . . Maybe *you* can feel something . . . No . . . ? Press it . . . Lower, lower . . . Wait . . .'

She undid her trousers, pulled them down an inch or two, and leaned over the back of a chair.

'There, yes . . . Harder . . . Harder! It doesn't hurt . . . Well, OK, it hurts, but it hurts in a way that feels kind of good . . .'

*

'Rub it in properly, then,' said the woman who had turned out to be the occupant of what had turned out to be someone's villa. She was lying on the lounger, face down, with a towel over her bottom. Dr Wilfred was spreading sunblock over her back. 'Use your thumbs. You might as well give me a massage while you're about it . . . The top of my spine . . . Yes, good . . . Take hold of my shoulder blades . . . One hand on each shoulder blade . . . Press your thumbs into the inside edges and slide them up and down . . . Harder! I won't break.'

Dr Wilfred had not thought about the injustice of his fate for several minutes now, he realised. He was still obediently wearing the flowered sun-hat to keep the sun off his own neck, and he was absorbed in seeing how the shiny whiteness of the sunblock gleamed in the sunlight, and then slowly vanished into the brown softness of the skin. The shoulder blades moved with a disturbing fluidity under his hands. The vertebrae, too, were leading a subterranean life of their own that he could only speculate about. There were two moles on the left shoulder which seemed somehow to emphasise its smoothness.

'That's good,' said the owner of the back. 'I'm Georgie, by

the way. And you're . . . ?'

'Wilfred. Dr Wilfred. Dr Norman Wilfred.'

'Oh, no! I hate names that you can never remember which way round they go! And you're a doctor, are you, Norman? No – Wilfred . . . Wilfred?'

'Norman.'

'Norman. I should have thought a doctor would have had more sense than to go around in the midday sun with no sunblock on.'

'I'm not a doctor of medicine.'

'No? So what are you a doctor of?'

'Management. Among other things.'

'Management? And what kind of things do you manage, Wilfred, apart from losing your luggage and getting into bed with people you've never met in houses that don't belong to you?'

His hands followed the lines of her ribcage, downwards and outwards.

'Scientific research,' he said reluctantly.

'What, atoms and things? Pollution and stuff?'

Pointless to attempt any reply to this. His hands were working their way round to the front of her ribcage.

'Not round there,' she said sharply. 'I can do the front myself. And the only reason I haven't got an adapter is because it's Patrick who looks after things like that.'

His hands started again at the top of her spine, and moved slowly downwards.

'Patrick's the one who's coming with the taxi?'

'Patrick? Why should it be Patrick? Patrick's in Turkey.'

Dr Wilfred's hands stopped short, somewhere around the third thoracic vertebra.

'If it was Patrick,' said Georgie, 'he *would* be here. With an adapter. And a spare one, in case the first one broke down. And water-purifying tablets. And an anti-mosquito thing. And a jar of Marmite.'

'But this person who *is* coming . . . The one with the taxi . . .'

'Oliver.'

'Oliver. You've really no idea when?'

'Not the foggiest.'

Dr Wilfred fell back into despair. 'I've got to get to this place I'm going and I've got to find some clean clothes to put on and I don't know when I'm supposed to be there and I don't know where it is and I don't know how long it's going to take me to get there. I don't even know where we are *now*! So where in fact *are* we?'

'Search me. Ask Oliver when he arrives. Look, are you putting sunblock on me or aren't you?'

His hands resumed their journey down her spine.

'Not down there,' she said. 'Don't get any ideas.'

*

'So clever of Nikki to find you!' said Mrs Toppler as Dr Wilfred worked away on a spot just to the left and up a bit from her coccyx. 'Magic fingers, as well as everything else.'

The doors to the loggia had opened, realised Dr Wilfred. A short, trim man in a naval blazer and a club tie had stopped in the doorway, and was gazing at the scene with expressionless blue eyes.

'Thank you,' said Mrs Toppler to Dr Wilfred. 'That really felt nice. We'll do that again.'

A thundercloud of flesh, now transmuted into piled summer cumulus by white shirt and chinos, was ushering the well-muscled blazer in. 'You remember Oleg?' said Mr Papadopoulou to Mrs Toppler. 'He was here last year also. Oleg Skorbatov.'

'Hi, Oleg!' said Mrs Toppler as she did her trousers up. 'And this is Dr Wilfred, who's giving the lecture this evening.'

'Big star,' said Mr Papadopoulou. 'World famous.'

'And you know what?' said Mrs Toppler. 'Dr Wilfred's a doctor. On top of everything else. You got any aches or pains, Oleg, you bring them to Dr Wilfred.'

Oleg Skorbatov's unblinking blue eyes fixed on Dr Wilfred for a moment. He nodded briefly.

'Oh, hi there!' said Mrs Toppler to a young woman with unnaturally long legs who was standing in the doorway in her turn, topped by a piled brass hair-do that brought her up to almost the height of the architrave. 'Svetlana! Great to see you again, Svetlana!'

'Tatiana, this one,' said Mr Papadopoulou.

'Tatiana,' said Mrs Toppler, as she kissed her. 'Oh, Tatiana, that hair of yours is so brave!'

'Don't trouble yourself,' said Oleg Skorbatov. 'She doesn't speak English.'

'OK,' said Mr Papadopoulou, steering Oleg Skorbatov back into the house. 'See you later, Dr Wilfred. I have to show Oleg how we do with the new pool.'

'Men!' said Mrs Toppler to Dr Wilfred. 'He shows Oleg the pool! He won't let *me* see it! No one! Not even our wonderful Nikki knows what's going on behind those screens! Wait there, Tatiana, honey, while I see Dr Wilfred out.'

'May I ask you something?' said Dr Wilfred to her as they

left the loggia. 'I've been thinking a lot recently about names. What were you before you were Bahama LeStarr?'

'Before I was Bahama LeStarr I was Apricot del Rio. You come back and give me another session, now. I want your advice about something.'

25

Georgie and Dr Wilfred were having lunch in the shade of an ancient olive tree. She had unfrozen the contents of the freezer – half a sliced loaf and a packet of peas. He had found a jar of peanut butter. There didn't seem to be anything else to eat in the house.

'That's this great lecture you're supposed to be giving, is it?' she said, nodding at the travelworn binder on the table beside his plate. 'You could read it to me instead.'

He looked at it distractedly. He had been thinking about the two moles on her left shoulder blade, which had now vanished, like so much else, inside a tee-shirt. He put out his hand to touch the binder, to reassure himself that his lecture at least was still here.

'No, no!' she said. 'Joke! Save it up for people who'll understand it! And they paid your fare to come here, did they, Wilfred? What – economy or business?'

'Business.'

'So you're someone important?'

He said nothing. Each time she called him Wilfred he felt less like someone important and more as if he were back in school again, stuck in timeless alphabetical order between Walters and Wilkins.

'I'm trying to get a conversation going,' she said. 'To keep you entertained, so you don't brood about your lecture.'

He sighed. 'Am I important?' he said. 'Yes. As a matter of fact. In my field. Among people who are interested in the scientific management of science.'

She rested her elbows on the table and her chin in her hands, gazing at him, apparently fascinated. He didn't really suppose that she was, but it was difficult not to respond when someone was staring open-eyed straight into your face at a range of about two feet.

'My area of expertise is the funding of research,' he said. 'I write books and articles about it. I advise governments and the UN. Since you ask.'

He looked at the view for some time, but he realised she was still gazing at him as expectantly as ever.

'Research is very expensive,' he said. 'Someone has to recommend what research should be supported. You probably think scientists just have sudden brainwaves, or they do experiments with two tin cans and a piece of string in their garage, or they find things they hadn't been looking for.'

She didn't deny it.

'But scientists aren't just a lot of mad professors,' he said. 'They're rational human beings, just like you and me, engaged in a rational human activity which is subject to rational human constraints. The results of scientific research are scientifically measurable. We have developed a discipline for this. It's called scientometrics. And on the basis of scientometrics science can be scientifically managed.'

'This is your lecture, is it?' she said. 'I see why you don't want people to miss it.'

Those two hidden moles had resurfaced in his brain, so to push them back underground again he went on.

'This is not actually my lecture,' he said. 'I'm giving you a little private tuition. I just want to make clear to you for your own benefit that the view some people have of scientists and scientific research is completely wrong. Scientists do of course sometimes have eureka moments, and they do of course sometimes find important results they weren't looking for. But it's all still perfectly rational. You can always find a clear causal chain when you look for it. If the answer to a problem suddenly clicks into place in someone's brain it's because they've already done all the thinking. They know there's a problem that needs a solution just like you know there's a space in the jigsaw that needs a piece to fit it. Scientists aren't poets! But then poets aren't irrational, either. Not that I know much about poets, but I'm pretty certain that they're subject to the same causal laws as all the rest of us. They come up with words that fill a gap in the market, or they go out of business, just like everyone else.'

'Fascinating,' she said. 'So you just thought all this up, did you, Wilfred?'

He was about to agree when he saw the trap he was being led into.

'No,' he said, 'I didn't just think it up. It emerged from my reading and observation, as processed by my brain. And my brain is structured the way it is not through any efforts of mine but through my genetic inheritance. You could trace that inheritance back through the generations and see how it was gradually shaped by the various selective pressures on my ancestors. And you could keep going back, through the structure of the cells of which those ancestors were composed, to the organic chemistry that had shaped the fabric of the cells. Then the inorganic chemistry from which the organic had arisen. Back again to the elementary particles whose physics determines the chemistry. Back to the radiation energy that the particles condensed out of. Back,

back, back to the tiny object which according to some cosmologists was only a few millimetres in diameter, and from which everything in the universe originated thirteen point seven billion years ago.

'All I have done is to allow events to take their course. I have simply accepted my inheritance. I've worked hard, certainly. I could have played around, and frittered my life away. In fact I chose to work. But that choice in its turn was determined, like everything else.'

The gaze she still had fixed upon him had become somewhat absent, he realised. He seemed to have exhausted her interest in the subject.

'The only trouble is, Wilfred,' she said finally, 'that you cannot stand up in front of people and give a lecture looking like that. Take your shirt off. I'll wash it out for you.'

'I'm fine,' he said.

'You're not fine, Wilfred. You're a total wreck. Take it off.'

He took it off. 'Thank you,' he said.

'Trousers.'

He put on one of the bathrobes and turned discreetly away. Wilfred, yes. She was right. He had for all practical purposes reverted to being mere Wilfred, an awkward schoolboy who always said the wrong thing to girls. He had almost forgotten that he had ever been Dr Wilfred. Dr Wilfred had faded to an insubstantial fiction, a creature who had never really quite managed to exist.

'Pants. Socks.'

She took the sweaty clothes into the house, holding them at arm's length, and he sank slowly back on to his chair. There were two last cold peas on his plate. As he contemplated them they seemed to dissolve into the two moles on

Georgie's left shoulder blade. He speared them on his fork, one after the other, and ate them.

*

It took Dr Wilfred a long time to get from Mrs Fred Top-pler's apartment in Democritus to lunch in the taverna, because people kept coming up to him on the way for a private word.

'I know this is a terrible intrusion,' said Kate Katz. 'And I know how many people must be begging you to support one good cause or another. But could I just have one moment of your time to tell you about a desperately important campaign of which I happen to be a patron . . . ?'

But somebody else was already taking him by the other elbow.

'I have been so impressed by your approach,' said Morton Rinkleman. 'Now, I am on the Board of Trustees of a small but vibrant liberal arts college in Tennessee . . .'

Already, though, other people had spotted him, and even before Kate Katz and Morton Rinkleman had finished with him more requests, proposals, and invitations were pressing in upon him.

'. . . expanding our European operation, and looking for a non-executive director . . .' '. . . to have you visit with us in Sausalito . . .' '. . . your advice on the Hong Kong copra futures market . . .' '. . . nothing less than the ending of national and racial conflict throughout the whole of sub-Saharan Africa . . .' '. . . our house in Montauk at your disposal . . .' '. . . the otherwise certain extinction of the Arkansas horned owl . . .' '. . . remuneration in the 300K range, though this would of

course be supplemented by benefits and stock options . . .'
'. . . some literature here on the habits of the horned owl . . .'

By the time he reached the taverna Dr Wilfred had agreed to be a patron of five campaigns and charities and president of two institutes of higher education. He had invitations to stay in six states and address seven lunch clubs and ladies' circles, was committed to charitable contributions of some fifty thousand dollars, but on the other hand had prospects of directorships and other appointments which would bring him an income of several million.

He had only just managed to sit down at the table before word of his most recent achievement in life had somehow overtaken him. 'I hear you can do miracles with back problems, Dr Wilfred! Now, I have a displacement of the fourth lumbar vertebra . . .' '. . . a red-hot skewer through the nape of my neck . . .' '. . . a pain just *here* . . .' '. . . just exactly *there* . . .' '. . . a strange buzzing in my left ear . . .'

As he helped himself to salad he discovered that he had also become a counsellor on childcare and spiritual values.

'. . . I of course understand the problems parents have with growing boys, but quite frankly Wade is now thirty-seven . . .' '. . . a sense that there must be something *more* to life than Puccini and clam linguine . . .'

He picked up his fork.

'I still don't see . . .' said Professor Ditmuss.

Dr Wilfred plunged the fork into the salad, but the salad suddenly disappeared from the table and the fork was snatched out of his hand. He looked round. Nikki was holding them both aloft.

'Onions!' she said. 'You're violently allergic to them!'

26

The two moles on Georgie's left shoulder blade kept disappearing and reappearing, like two bright stars among shifting clouds. She was slowly pursuing Dr Wilfred's phone around the bottom of the pool with the net for fishing leaves and insects out. She had only one hand free, though, because she had taken her tee-shirt off again to sunbathe, and was using her other hand to hold the towel round her. Every time she tried to get the net under the phone either the phone slipped away from the net or the towel slipped away from her shoulders and she had to hoick it up again.

Dr Wilfred closed his eyes, then looked at the view, then closed his eyes again.

'I shouldn't bother,' he said. 'The phone's not going to work.'

'No, it's just going to leak poisonous chemicals into the water. We're both going to end up radioactive.'

His eyes seemed to be open again, and the two elusive dancing dots were just re-emerging.

'So, this friend of yours,' he said. 'Oliver. Oliver? Where is he?'

'No hurry. Your things aren't dry yet.'

'Yes, but why isn't he here, if he's supposed to be?'

'*I* don't know!' She flung the net down and turned on him, suddenly furious. 'Why aren't *you* wherever you're supposed to be? Why don't you have a sun-hat of your own? Why's your phone at the bottom of the pool? *I* don't know! But you *do*, do you? There's some rational explanation for it all, is there? It all goes back to that thing that was half an inch wide twenty million years ago? It was all in there, all in that little thing, was it? Your head, your phone, you, me, you ending up in some place you're not supposed to be, me getting stuck with you?'

He said nothing. There was never any point in replying to this kind of nonsense. Except to make one small simple point. 'Thirteen point seven billion years ago,' he said.

He suddenly went blind. Something soft but stinging had hit him in the face. Her towel, he saw, as it fell off and the world returned.

'And *that*?' she said. 'You saw *that* coming, did you? Thirteen point seven billion years ago?'

He tried not to look at her as he threw the towel back to her. Or not for longer than was strictly necessary.

'And yes,' she said, 'why *are* you here? If you know so much, why didn't you know where you were going? And even if you *didn't* know where you were going, why didn't you park yourself on somebody else? Why *here*?'

Yes, indeed, now she had raised the point, why, out of all the places on the island that were not where he was supposed to be, had he ended up in this particular one? There was an answer to this, of course. It was because the taxi driver had brought him here. So why had the taxi driver brought him here? Because . . . And in a sudden flash of illumination it came to him. Everything fell into place at last. A eureka moment, though of course just as rationally prepared for as every other eureka moment.

'*Phoksoliva*,' he said. 'Fox? Yes? Oliver? Oliver Fox?'

'Oh,' she said, in a rather different tone, 'you know him, do you?'

For everything there was always a rational explanation, a perfect causal ancestry, if only you could find it.

'*Know* him?' he said. 'I *am* him.'

*

More tables had been dragged across to join up with Dr Wilfred's in the shade of the great plane tree. The faces around them craned forward over the coffee and green tea so as to catch every word he was saying.

And gradually, as he spoke, he felt the adrenalin beginning to drain out of his veins. It was all getting too easy. The insubstantial fingerholds and crumbling toeholds on which he had been balancing his way up the cliff so far were broadening out from one moment to the next. It was becoming more and more like walking up a staircase. He saw another route opening up to one side with intriguing new dangers.

'Why are you sitting here listening to all this? I'll tell you. It's because you believe I'm Dr Norman Wilfred. But *why* do you believe I'm Dr Norman Wilfred?'

There was a silence. They gazed at him, waiting to be told. Sitting waiting on her chair behind him, Nikki gazed at the back of his head, also waiting.

'Because it's in the brochure,' said Chuck Friendly eventually. '"The Fred Toppler Lecture will be given this year by Dr Norman Wilfred, the distinguished etc. etc."'

'But perhaps Dr Norman Wilfred, the distinguished etc. etc., is someone else. Perhaps I'm not Dr Norman Wilfred.'

Various people laughed.

'Nikki goes to the airport to meet Dr Norman Wilfred,' said Dr Norman Wilfred. 'She holds up her sign – "Dr Norman Wilfred". And I see it. I've just got off the plane. I'm looking for my taxi. I'm not Dr Norman Wilfred at all. I'm someone called . . . I don't know . . . Fox, let's say. Oliver Fox.'

'I'm confused,' said Morton Rinkleman. 'Who's Oliver Fox?'

'Oliver Fox is me,' said Dr Norman Wilfred. 'Only as I stand there, looking round for someone holding up the name "Oliver Fox" I see this sign saying "Dr Norman Wilfred". And the name catches my fancy. So I take a look at the person who's holding the sign . . .'

He looked round and saw Nikki.

'Oh, and here she is.'

She smiled at him.

'She seems to be smiling at me,' said Dr Norman Wilfred. 'So I smile back at her. "Dr Norman Wilfred?" she says.

'And suddenly I think it might be fun to be Dr Norman Wilfred for a bit. The idea just comes into my head. Out of nowhere.

'And next thing I know, I'm here talking a lot of nonsense, and everyone's listening respectfully and taking it all seriously. Why? Just because they think I'm Dr Norman Wilfred.

'So here we are – we're making it all up as we go along. It's like a random mutation in a gene. If I tell you the truth, that I'm Oliver Fox, then consequences follow from that. No one sits here listening to me. No one even lets me through the gate. So the world goes on its way without my being here saying all this.

'And if I say I'm Dr Norman Wilfred, then the world goes another way. Oliver Fox – Dr Norman Wilfred – what does it matter? Heads/tails. Strawberry/vanilla. But who knows what the consequences will be? It's like the famous butterfly in Brazil. It just happens to flap its wings, and that sets off an escalating chain of consequences that ends up with a tornado in Nebraska. I say this – you say that – someone says something else – and there are consequences. The consequences will have consequences, and in three weeks' time the Dow Jones will suddenly plunge forty-seven points.'

People laughed, and stirred uneasily in their seats.

'Or else the Nasdaq will gain fifty-three points.'

They laughed again, and looked happier.

'And it's not just me doing this,' said Dr Norman Wilfred. 'We're all in this together. I said I was Dr Norman Wilfred. But you believed me. So between us we have determined the whole future course of the universe.'

He sat back, and took a sip of coffee. Everyone around the table did likewise.

'That's so true,' said Mrs Comax. 'People take everything on trust.'

'Someone's only got to say, "Hey, guys, I'm an expert,"' said Mr Chuck Friendly, 'and next thing he's operating on the President's brain, he's running the space programme.'

'Or no one says anything,' said Mrs Chuck Friendly, 'but people just *think* someone's a genius, or whatever, and they don't even know why they ever thought so in the first place!'

'We're all such fools!' said Morton Rinkleman.

'How do you know I'm Harold Fossett?' said Harold Fossett.

'How do *you* know you're Harold Fossett?' said Morton Rinkleman.

'Hey, how *do* I know I'm Harold Fossett?' said Harold Fossett.

'Who, indeed, am I?' said a distinguished Indian guest whose name and job description nobody had grasped, and got no answer.

'Are any of us, in fact, anybody?' said somebody.

They all sipped their coffee and green tea, and looked at each other with new interest and respect, delighted with the idea that they might none of them be who they said they were, their delight rooted in their absolute confidence that they were.

'OK,' said Mr Erlunder. 'I'm *not* Mr Erlunder! I'm *Mrs* Erlunder!'

'That makes two of us,' said Mrs Erlunder. 'Unless I'm you.'

'I'm George Washington,' said Russell Pond. 'I cannot tell a lie.'

'I'm a freshwater crayfish,' said Alf Persson, the Swedish theologian.

'I'm a sunspot,' said Suki Brox.

'I'm Professor Norbert Ditmuss,' said Professor Norbert Ditmuss.

'And Wellesley Luft is Wellesley Luft,' said Nikki, before Professor Ditmuss could expand on this. 'And Wellesley Luft is waiting to interview Dr Wilfred for the *Journal of Science Management*.'

Dr Wilfred got to his feet and inclined his head. Some of the others also got to their feet, and everyone else got to his or her feet and applauded, apart from the curmudgeonly K. D. Clopper, who still thought it was all bunkum, and Wilson Westerman, who was worrying about what Frankfurt had been doing since he last looked at his phone.

'He's actually not arriving for ages yet,' murmured Nikki as she manoeuvred Dr Wilfred away from various people who rather pressingly wanted to continue the conversation.

'You were saving me from Professor Ditmuss again?' said Dr Wilfred.

'Just in case you really aren't Dr Wilfred,' said Nikki.

He felt a sense of triumph. He had climbed the most exposed pitch yet and survived. If he could do that he could do anything. Except that there wasn't anything left to do. Apart from the lecture. His sense of triumph began to fade.

'I'll send Mr Luft up to your room, shall I? You might want to have that little siesta of yours first while I'm fetching him.'

'You're going to be holding up your sign again? Just make sure he *is* Mr Luft, though, and not somebody else. One somebody else is quite enough.'

She stopped and looked round, then gave him a very swift kiss.

'Quite enough for me,' she said. 'Anyway, *you'll* know if it's not him. He's an old friend of yours. He's interviewed you three or four times before.'

'Has he?' said Dr Wilfred. The dark depths below him reached tinglingly up into his knees again. 'So let's see if *he* thinks I'm Dr Wilfred.'

27

'But you're *not* Oliver Fox,' said Georgie finally, after the shimmering hot silence of the afternoon had gone on and on. 'You're Wilfred somebody.'

She was on the lounger again, with the towel in place around her middle, but now she had turned on to her back. She evidently felt that after all this time she knew him well enough. He, likewise, felt that after all this time he knew her well enough to take an occasional look, particularly since she seemed to have her eyes closed behind her dark glasses, though her two breasts, sprawled softly outwards, had still not seized his imagination as strongly as those two small and now concealed moles.

'Take a good long look, if you're going to,' she said. 'You'll do something to your neck, twitching back and forth like that. Why did you tell the taxi driver you were Oliver Fox?'

'I *didn't* tell the taxi driver I was Oliver Fox,' said Wilfred.

'Well, *someone* did. He told me he'd driven you here. Oliver Fox. He said you were waiting for me.'

Wilfred tried to remember exactly how the conversation had gone. *Phoksoliva . . . Euphoksoliva . . .* Yes, of course.

'It was *him*,' he said. 'The taxi driver. *He* told *me*.'

'The *taxi driver* told you you were Oliver Fox? What, and you believed him? And you're a famous scientist, are you, Wilfred? What else have taxi drivers told you?'

*

The afternoon went hotly on and on. A small cloud was created out of empty air, moved slowly across the sky, and dissolved again, exhausted, before it got anywhere.

'What I don't understand,' said Wilfred – no, *Dr* Wilfred, he was *Dr* Wilfred – 'is that this pal of yours is supposed to be coming in a taxi. He's not renting a car? How are you proposing to get around?'

'What, to art galleries? Famous cathedrals and so on?' She laughed. Little soft trembles ran through her breasts, like almost imperceptible waves in a calm summer sea. 'I don't suppose he was thinking of getting around very much.'

No, of course not, thought Dr Wilfred. Art galleries and famous cathedrals were probably not what either of them had at the forefront of their minds.

'Haven't you got a girlfriend, Wilfred?' she said. 'No? What – just a wife? Or no wife, even?'

He was not going to get drawn into a discussion of his own domestic arrangements. In any case, what he was thinking about was the still unmade bed in the villa. They would get out of it sometimes, he thought. To sunbathe, perhaps. Take a dip in the pool. What else? Nothing. Back to bed again. Yes, why should we need a car? Or rather *they*. Why would they need a car?

'Food, though,' he said. 'Meals. Groceries. You weren't planning to live on a loaf of frozen bread and a packet of frozen peas all week?'

'I don't know what the arrangements are. I suppose Oliver's thought of something.'

There was a silence while they both thought about the possible contents of Oliver's thinking.

'Or probably not, actually,' she said. 'I don't think he

thinks. Not that sort of thinking. Just something comes into his head and – woof! – he does it.'

Woof, he does it. Of course. Woof, they both do it. Dr Wilfred suddenly found this feckless pair and their brainless pleasures profoundly distasteful.

'No business of mine, of course,' he said, 'but what about this other friend of yours?'

'Patrick? He's in Turkey.'

'He's in Turkey. Oh. So as soon as Patrick turns his back you're off with *this* one, are you?'

'What do you mean? It's not like it's, you know, a regular arrangement! I've only met him once! For about five minutes!'

You heard this kind of thing about young people these days, thought Oliver, thought Wilfred, thought Dr Wilfred, but you never really believed it until you actually came face to face with one of them.

'Only met him once?' he said. 'For five minutes? Oh, that's all right, then.'

'Well, you've got to be spontaneous, haven't you? You've got to go along with things. Anyway, we've sent each other lots of texts.'

Lots of texts. Of course. Plus sliced bread and frozen peas. Or rather, now, no sliced bread and no frozen peas.

Then back to bed.

*

There was another small cloud overhead. He closed his eyes. When he opened them there was no cloud.

'Now I come to think about it,' said Georgie, 'I see why he hasn't shown up yet. It's just like you said – there's a perfectly logical explanation. It's because he hasn't bothered to listen to his messages. He doesn't know I'm here. He thinks I'm arriving this evening.'

The two moles, the sliced bread, and the unmade-up bed all vanished from Dr Wilfred's head as he took in the implications of this. 'You mean . . . he may not come until *this evening*? But that's when my lecture is! I need the taxi *before* then! I need the taxi *now*!'

'You'll just have to relax and have a day off. I shouldn't worry. They'll think of something else to do. People often don't turn up for things.'

He saw the faces in the hall. Distinguished faces, important faces – people who had flown from Athens and even further afield for the Fred Toppler Lecture. He heard the eager anticipatory hum die away as someone stepped up to the lectern to introduce him. *Not* to introduce him, though. To explain that for reasons beyond their control . . . Or that Dr Norman Wilfred was unfortunately indisposed . . . Or quite frankly that no one knew where he was. He had simply failed to show up.

And where he would be was here, toasting sliced bread with some entirely irresponsible young woman who didn't seem to think it mattered whether people honoured their professional obligations or whether they simply sloped off and jumped into bed with people they'd only known for five minutes. Not that she would be jumping into bed with *him*, of course, because at that moment she would be jumping into bed with someone else, and what he himself would be jumping into, if anything, would be the taxi that had brought the man she actually was jumping into bed with; and he would be on his way to run into the lecture hall, even more embarrassingly than if he had never shown up at all, just as everyone left.

'Though of course,' said Georgie, 'now I'm thinking, *Why* hasn't he bothered to listen to his messages? And I know why – because he had to hang around for half an hour with nothing to do, and he went into a bar, and he saw some woman, and he brushed the hair out of his eyes and gave her his ridiculous grin, and now he won't be coming this evening, or tomorrow, or all the rest of the week.'

Dr Wilfred thought about this. He might not be running into the lecture hall just as everyone left. He might still be here. For the rest of the week.

'So you're in charge now, Wilfred,' said Georgie. 'Food, yes. Eating. You'd better start thinking how we're going to find something.'

He already was. He was looking at himself in the days ahead, roaming the hillsides. Bargaining with peasants for bread. Stealing fruit off trees. Strangling stray pheasants. Milking the wandering goats. He had an old song running through his head that he hadn't heard since he was a boy: 'If you were the only girl in the world, and I was the only boy . . .'

'It's probably only for a few days,' said Georgie. 'Sooner or later someone's going to notice you're missing. Your wife or someone. Send out a search party.'

Sooner or later, yes. In the meantime, though . . .

Already the disappointed owners of all those respectfully upturned faces had vanished from his head as if they had never been. So had the lecture, and his professional obligations and reputation. They had all been pushed into oblivion by the two moles. And the three condoms in the right-hand inside pocket of his jacket.

And the words of the song. 'If you were the only girl in the world,' they murmured to him, over and over again, as if they had taken on a life of their own, 'and I was the only boy . . .'

28

A fire bell was ringing. Oliver, instantly alarmed, looked out of the porthole of the theatre where he was just about to perform his juggling act and saw smoke and flames pouring out of the starboard outer engine. He struggled to sit up, terrified.

Late-afternoon sunshine was coming through unfamiliar curtains. He was in a bedroom of some sort, not a theatre or an aeroplane. But the fire bell was still ringing. Except that it wasn't a fire bell – it was the phone beside his bed. He scrambled the receiver up to his ear and managed to make a sound like hello.

'It's me,' said a woman's voice. 'Nikki.'

There was something familiar about both the voice and the name, but he couldn't quite place them. 'Um?' he said.

'That *is* Dr Wilfred?' said the voice.

'Wrong number,' he mumbled, and went back to sleep.

*

When the phone rang again the woman was laughing.

'So that *isn't* Dr Wilfred?' she said.

It was her laughter that at last woke him up and returned him to recognisable normality.

'Nikki!' he said. 'Nikki? Nikki . . .'

'Oh, so it *is* Dr Wilfred?'

'I was asleep.'

'You certainly were. I'm sorry to disturb you.'

'How long was I asleep?'

'Never mind. You obviously needed it. Not enough sleep last night, perhaps. Anyway, we've got here. He's just dropping his bag in his room and freshening up. Then he's on his way.'

'Who is?'

'Wellesley Luft! Your old friend!'

And now he was even more awake. I can do it, he thought at once. I can talk anyone into anything. Even my old friend Wellesley Luft into recognising me as Dr Wilfred. Bring him on.

As he put the foundation's phone down he saw his own lying beside it, neglected and forgotten, where he had put it when he arrived the previous evening. He turned it on. He had texts, he had voice messages. He opened the texts. There were five new ones from Annuka. He skipped quickly up through the little windows. She seemed to be softening somewhat. She was forgiving him for having allowed her to throw him out.

He turned to the voice messages. The most recent was from Georgie. Yes, he should listen to it again, as he had promised himself earlier today, so he could truthfully tell her tomorrow that when she had said she was arriving tomorrow he had quite reasonably supposed that it had been not yesterday's tomorrow she meant but today's. Which would give him another night in hand.

He tapped the screen. But what sprang into his ear was not the message about arriving tomorrow – it was incomprehensible, uncontrolled hysteria. Her voice was scarcely recognisable. 'Oliver! Where *are* you?' it screamed at him.

He snatched the phone away from his ear in surprise, but he could hear her raving on even at arm's length. He turned the phone off. He thought he might sit this one out.

He had committed a solecism of some sort, obviously. Failed to phone when he had promised, or forgotten her birthday. But what he had promised was *not* to phone while she was with – what was he called? – Patrick. And her birthday? When they'd only ever met for five minutes?

He had a pee and splashed cold water into his face. Then he sat down and concentrated his mind on being Dr Wilfred, on being so overwhelmingly, so immanently Dr Wilfred that he and Dr Wilfred's old friend would immediately recognise each other as such.

*

Georgie lay there on the lounger all afternoon in the shade of the beach umbrella, perhaps asleep, apparently entirely content to do nothing. Dr Wilfred, though, grew more awake as the hours went by. He lay on his lounger, his head turned away from the source of his trouble, unable to move. He felt light-headed and nauseous, as though he had a temperature. He hadn't had these symptoms for this particular reason for twenty years or more. A feverish shudder went through him so sharp that his teeth rattled.

All he could think about were the two moles. The two moles and the three condoms. She the only girl in the world, he the only boy. The question was what he was going to do about it. How they were ever going to get out of this situation, where she was lying on one lounger and he was lying on the other. He had to *do* something. He had to make some kind of move, or they would remain here for ever. The more he thought about it, though, the less he could see what it should be.

*

Dr Wilfred, thought Oliver, thought Dr Wilfred, as he waited for his old friend. I'm Dr Wilfred. Born wherever it was that Dr Wilfred was born. Went to school wherever it was that Dr Wilfred went to school. Am, in a word, two words, Dr Wilfred.

His concentration was disturbed, though, because he kept remembering that note of hysteria in Georgie's voice. An unsettling thought somehow thought itself. Maybe Georgie's outrage had reached such a pitch that she had by one means or another discovered where he was. Maybe she was even now pursuing him here. Impossible, of course. Wasn't it? There was no way in which she could have followed his sudden private sideways leap into the persona of Dr Wilfred. Dr Wilfred, Dr Wilfred . . . In any case, she was still waiting for a plane in Turkey. Wasn't she?

He picked up the phone and touched the screen. 'Oliver! Where *are* you?' she screamed again, but this time he kept the phone within screaming distance of his ear. 'He was in bed! He was pretending to be you! He hasn't done something to you, has he? Tied you up? Murdered you?'

And then silence.

He gazed at the phone in astonishment. He had quite often found it difficult to understand what women were complaining to him about, but never had any complaint been as totally incomprehensible as this one. Who was this man who was in bed, and who had done, or might have done, all these things? Patrick, presumably. But why should Patrick have pretended to be him? *How* could Patrick have pretended to be him, when he didn't know him, since he'd taken care to get out of his chair in that bar, and out of his life, before Patrick had returned from his smoke? And how could Patrick have tied him up and murdered him when he was in Turkey and he himself, whether he was Dr Wilfred or whether he wasn't, was in Greece?

There was an earlier unplayed message from Georgie.

'Oliver,' said the voice, this time not in a scream but in a desperate whisper, 'will you *please* answer your phone! I'm locked in the bathroom! He's hammering on the door! I thought it was *you*! He nearly raped me! I don't know how to phone the police in this country! Oliver! Please help me! I'm all on my own! In the bathroom!'

And then, again, silence.

He jumped to his feet, overwhelmed by alarm and anguish. He must do something, and do it at once! But what? He ran to the door, but couldn't think where to go. He ran back, picked up the phone, and tried to call her back. 'This number is not available,' it said.

So, she was trapped in a bathroom. By a potential rapist. Somewhere in Turkey. Phone the police, obviously. Phone which police, where? Which part of Turkey had she said she was going to be in? Or – yes – the British embassy! Look up Istanbul. No, Istanbul wasn't the capital of Turkey . . . What *was* the capital of Turkey? He'd forgotten the capital of Turkey!

As he gazed hopelessly at the phone he saw that there was an even earlier message from Georgie still waiting to be played. He pressed the button, bracing himself for the next horror. This time her voice was entirely different, though. Hurried and incoherent, but very pleased with itself.

'Hi!' she said. 'It's me! I suddenly saw there was a flight to Thessaloniki . . . !'

He found it difficult to take in all the circumstantial details. He got the general gist of it, though – that she wasn't in Turkey any longer. She had arrived. She was here, in Ski-os. At the airport already. He looked at his watch. How long to get to the airport? And when was he giving the lecture? No, forget the lecture, forget all this Dr Wilfred nonsense. Georgie was trapped by a rapist in a bathroom at the airport, and it was he who was responsible for her being there. This was serious. He hadn't so far in life had much practice in making moral choices, but in these circumstances even he could see what had to take priority.

He ran about the room, picking up things he might need for the task ahead and putting them down again. Cash, credit cards. Phone, passport. A bar of chocolate and a pack of soluble aspirin he had found in the suitcase. Phone, phone, where was his phone! He put everything down yet again. Oh, yes, in his hand.

He was aware that he had reached an epoch in his life. He knew that he had without warning found himself faced with the chance – the necessity – to become the kind of human being he had always wanted to be. He couldn't help noticing that he had risen to the occasion. Without hesitating for an instant he had given up the best adventure he had ever embarked upon. Not to mention his forthcoming hour upon the world stage and however many million dollars a year he was going to be getting for the various jobs he had accepted.

[155]

And Nikki. He had given up the prospect of Nikki. For a moment he hesitated, bar of chocolate and soluble aspirin in hand.

No, not even the thought of Nikki could deflect him from his duty. Anyway, there might perhaps be a chance to slip back for an hour or two at some point and explain.

As he ran out of the door with his eyes on his phone, trying to think who to call to get a taxi, he found himself dancing left right left right with a bald-headed man in a seersucker jacket who was coming in the opposite direction holding a notebook and a bottle of bourbon, and who was struggling so deferentially to get out of his way that he was perpetually in it.

'I do beg your pardon,' said the man, as deferentially as he was jumping from one side to the other, 'but could you tell me where I might find Dr Norman Wilfred?'

'Out,' called Oliver over his shoulder as he ran on down the path. 'Gone. Urgent business elsewhere.'

29

Dr Wilfred had finally summoned the willpower to raise himself from his sickbed, as the lounger beside the pool had become. He was going to make a first move, and he had at last decided upon a way to start. Or upon two possible ways. He was going to say either 'So!' or 'Well, then!' He hadn't yet decided which.

Before he could open his mouth, however, and see which emerged, he became aware of a faint sound. His own racing blood in his ears, perhaps. No, something outside himself. A scrunching sound, of the sort that the wheels of a car make on a dirt road. He turned his head towards Georgie. She sat up very suddenly, her breasts tumbling eagerly forwards.

'Oliver!' she said. 'He's here!'

She jumped up from the lounger and ran towards the gate, then ran back and pulled the towel around her. 'And I'll tell the taxi to wait and take you!'

She vanished round the side of the house. Wilfred sank slowly back on to the lounger. His fever slowly subsided. A long and dreary convalescence had begun.

*

A taxi drew up outside the front of the foundation just as Oliver came running out. He waited while three men and one woman, together with two violins, one viola, and a cello, very slowly and painfully extracted themselves.

'Airport!' he said as he jumped in. 'And fast, fast, fast!'

'No problem,' said the driver, putting the taxi into gear.

'No!' said Oliver.

'No? Not airport?'

'Not airport!'

It had just come to him. It wasn't a bathroom at the airport that Georgie was trapped in. If it was a bathroom at the airport she would have shouted. People would have come running. They would have noticed someone hammering on the door. The airport was in the past. She would have arrived at the airport, then left and gone to the villa they had borrowed. It was the bathroom of the villa she was trapped in.

'Villa!' he said.

The driver put the gear back into neutral. Oliver saw that he was looking at him in the rear-view mirror. He had a wart like a bluebottle on the end of his nose. He seemed to be waiting for something. Of course. He was waiting to know *which* villa, and where it was.

Oliver quickly reviewed the arrangements of the last few days, before he had become Dr Norman Wilfred. Got it! Of course! 'It's in my suitcase!' he said.

Still the taxi remained motionless. Still the driver watched him in the rear-view mirror.

'So, yes, where's my suitcase?' said Oliver. 'In my room! No!'

The suitcase in his room was Dr Wilfred's. He was not Dr Wilfred – he was Oliver Fox. And Oliver Fox's suitcase was presumably still at the, yes – 'Airport!'

'Airport?' said the driver. 'No problem.' He put the taxi into gear.

'No!' said Oliver. '*Not* in my suitcase!'

The driver put the gear back into neutral.

'They never gave me an address!' said Oliver. So how had he been going to get to the villa? 'In a taxi! I was going in a taxi! There was going to be a taxi!'

The driver thought. Then he raised his eyebrows speculatively. 'Fox Oliver?' he inquired.

'*Phoksoliva*?' said Oliver. 'Oh! Yes! Right! Fox Oliver! And fast, fast, fast!'

'No problem,' said Spiros, as he put the taxi into gear.

*

'You bastard!' cried Georgie, half in jest and half not, as she came running out of the front gate, then stopped. The taxi was backing and filling as it turned to go. But where was Oliver?

She detached one of the arms holding up her towel and signalled to the taxi. 'Wait! Stop!' she shouted.

The driver wound down his window. She knew him – it was Spiros. 'OK?' he said. 'No problems? Nice holiday?'

'Fine,' she said. 'But, Spiros—'

'Stavros,' he replied.

'Stavros. Where is he?'

'Where is he? There he is.'

He pointed. There was a suitcase standing beside the gate.

'Suitcase?' she said.

'OK?' The taxi began to move off.

'Wait! Wait! The person! The person *with* the suitcase!'

Stavros pointed at the villa. And suddenly she realised. What he had brought wasn't Oliver, it was Wilfred's missing suitcase.

'Oh,' she said.

'No?' said Stavros.

'Yes. Fine. Thank you.'

'Not a problem.'

The taxi began to move off again.

'Wait,' she said.

He waited. She lifted the suitcase back into the taxi.

'No?' said Stavros. 'Don't want?'

'Of course he wants it,' said Georgie. 'But he's coming with you.'

*

Slowly Wilfred took his underpants down from the clothes-line and put them on in the shelter of the bathrobe. They were still damp. But then so were his spirits. So, obviously, were Georgie's as she watched him.

'I'm sorry it wasn't Oliver,' he said.

'You must be pleased to get your bag back, though.'

Was he? He hadn't really thought about it. His bag had long lost its central place in his picture of the world.

'And to have a taxi. So you're going to be able to give your wonderful lecture.'

Yes, he was going to be able to give his wonderful lecture. He put his shirt on. It stuck around his armpits and across the back of his neck.

'It'll dry out as you go along,' she said. 'Anyway, you can put some dry things on in the taxi. Now you've got your bag back.'

A thought came to him slowly as he forced the buttons back into the damp buttonholes. If no Oliver . . .

'You wouldn't like to come with me?' he said. 'To the lecture?'

'What, about how it all goes back to some dot in the middle of nowhere ten thousand years ago?' she said, pulling the towel tighter round her. 'Thanks most awfully.'

He put his trousers on. They adhered to him in ways that made it quite awkward to walk.

'Thirteen point seven billion years ago,' he said.

30

'Oliver?' said Annuka Vos, putting her head into various rooms of the villa. In her impatience she had left her suitcase where the taxi driver had dumped it, outside the gate. There was no response, though, but the ghostly murmur of the air conditioning. She had thought for a moment that she could hear his voice somewhere . . . But no, nothing. He seemed to be out. Out where, doing what? Shopping, swimming? Unlikely. Causing trouble of some sort, more probably. It was entirely characteristic of him not to have answered any of her messages. She wouldn't have been surprised if he hadn't even read them. Hadn't known when she was arriving. Or even that she was arriving at all.

God, she was sick of the whole stupid business!

None of her friends could understand why she put up with him. She couldn't understand it herself. In fact she *hadn't* put up with him. She had thrown him out. Three times. And yet here she was, on one last holiday with him yet again. None of her friends could understand how she had got involved with him in the first place. Everyone knew what Oliver Fox was like. She didn't have to waste her life on people of that sort. She was dark and plump – with the sort of darkness and plumpness that men want to lose themselves in – and there was something fundamentally mysterious about her. No one knew whether she was Finnish or Brazilian. Some said Persian or Latvian, and she didn't comment, only smiled her dark smile. She could have had anything she wanted in life – a rich husband, six brilliant children, a career in banking. And what she in fact had was Oliver Fox.

Yes, she was a mystery, was Annuka Vos, and to herself most of all.

Still, the villa was everything she had hoped it would be. As her eyes got used to the cool darkness of the interior she began to make a more leisurely tour of inspection, appreciating each room in turn. This was another thing that people failed to understand about her. Unreadable, un-English, yes, but at the same time simple in her tastes and immediate in her responses. She had a natural aesthetic sense, she was a born home-maker. She loved the dark traditional furniture in the living room. Just the kind of thing she would have expected people like Petrus and Persephone to collect for their holiday home, of course. She loved the earthenware pots and plates thrown by Persephone, the water-colours painted by Petrus, the dolls hand-sewn by little Petal.

It was entirely characteristic of her relationship with Oliver, of course, that it was friends of *hers* who had lent them the villa. She shuddered to think where she and Oliver would have ended up if they had had to rely on *his* finding somewhere. But then if she hadn't booked the tickets and made all the arrangements they would never have gone anywhere at all. And if she hadn't happened to have an income from the Vos family trust, and a flat big enough for both of them, the whole thing would have been over months ago.

Which would have been a thoroughly good thing, of course. Everyone said so. She knew it herself. She had been pretty merciless about throwing him out, after all. You don't throw someone out three times without demonstrating a pretty cool-headed assessment of their shortcomings.

In the big country kitchen she found a note in Petrus's handwriting inviting her to help herself to anything she could find. Dear Petrus! Oliver had already helped himself, she saw. There, showing up very distinctly against the shining dark stone worktop, was a characteristic little muddle of used packaging and food scraps – a wine bottle left uncorked, the curling remains of a pizza, crumpled wrappings from sliced bread and frozen peas, an empty peanut-butter jar. She looked in the refrigerator. Nothing. Of course not. He couldn't even be bothered to go out and buy a few groceries.

She cleared away the mess, found rubber gloves and kitchen spray, and returned the worktop to the shining dark gleam that it would have had when Petrus and Persephone left it. This was another thing that people failed to understand about her. At the heart of her darkness was a simple housewife, who loved nothing better than getting the rubber gloves on and making everything unspoiled and new.

Again she thought she heard a voice. She stopped cleaning to listen. Nothing. But her heart had leapt up for a moment, she realised, and immediately her irritation returned. She should never have come. She had threatened not to often enough. She should have stuck to it.

She went into the bedroom. Bed unmade, of course, and his suitcase open on the floor, spilling out a muddle of tee-shirts and chinos. She gave a little hiss of disapproval, possibly Brazilian in origin, possibly Persian, that she knew would have particularly irritated him, if only he had been here to be irritated. She picked up a handful of the tee-shirts and sniffed them to see if they were clean. They smelt as if they had been washed, but not by her. And they certainly hadn't been ironed, either by her or by anyone else.

In the cupboard in the hall she found an iron and ironing board, and set to work.

*

'I've put your suitcase on the front seat,' said Georgie, 'so you can get at some dry clothes as you go along.'

Dr Wilfred hesitated. 'Well,' he said. 'Anyway.'

'Off you go, then.'

'Yes . . . I'd just like to say . . . Well . . . Thank you for everything.'

'What – the bread and peas?'

'Everything.' He wanted to mention in particular the two moles on her shoulder blade, but didn't quite have the nerve.

'So,' she said. 'You've had a nice little rest. You're not too burnt. We got your clothes washed and your suitcase back. Haven't left anything behind? Passport? Credit cards? Phone? The lecture! You've got the lecture?'

He unzipped the flight bag and showed her. She held the door of the taxi open for him.

'Or I could wait for a bit,' said Wilfred. 'Until Oliver gets here.'

'Wilfred!' She pointed to the lecture.

'Yes . . .' He took it out of the flight bag and looked at the first page. *It is perhaps particularly appropriate to find myself giving this address here, in the vibrant and bustling city of Kuala Lumpur.* No, that was deleted . . . *in the great open spaces of Western Australia.*

He looked at her. 'You really wouldn't like to come and hear it?'

'No, but you really want to go and give it!'

[165]

Did he? He heard the familiar voice issuing from some dull inaccessible place a couple of feet above the lectern. He saw the faces raised expectantly towards him. Most particularly the one directly in his eyeline in the middle of the front row that was beginning to close its eyes and sink helplessly into sleep. He saw the woman halfway along Row E who was struggling to get over people's feet and out, for reasons that everyone in the room was now trying to guess at. He heard the man who made strange little noises, and the woman with the whistling hearing-aid, and the man who laughed at every mention of hunger and disease. He saw the questioners at the end rising to ask him about the existence of God and the moral responsibility of scientists. He heard the never quite enthusiastic enough applause, and the never quite convincing enough 'Thank you for that stimulating talk.'

Then he thought about roaming the hillsides for game and fish, for fruit and olives. He thought about Georgie being the only girl in the world and him the only boy.

'I don't, actually,' he said. 'I don't want to give it. I'd like to make a new start in life.'

'Off you go,' she said, and pushed him towards the taxi. He bent down to get in, then suddenly straightened up at the last moment and gave her a kiss, just at the same moment as she suddenly bent down and gave him one, so that their foreheads collided.

'I bet you saw *that* coming, too,' she said, rubbing her head.

*

Five assorted tee-shirts lay neatly folded on the table by the ironing board. Annuka picked the stack up and felt it against her cheek. They were smooth, they were warm. They felt right. They still smelt alien, though; where had he got them washed? She couldn't recall any of the logos on them, now she came to look at them; where had he acquired them?

She held up the two pairs of chinos. She was somehow softened to see that his legs were shorter than she had remembered.

Yes, she thought, as she ironed the chinos, however had she got involved with him? She recalled a party. At Vaclav and Bianchetta's. A lot of noise. Impossible to hear what anyone was saying. Then out of the noise and the darkness, this lopsided smile had appeared, and handfuls of blond hair being brushed out of soft brown eyes. She had somehow got the impression as they talked that he was a writing the history of sixteenth-century Tibet.

And he had been so modest about it.

*

Georgie stretched herself out on the lounger again. The sun was beginning to decline, but at least she didn't have to cover anything up now.

She had the first premonitions of hunger for the next meal. She should have gone with Wilfred, she realised, at least as far as the nearest supermarket. Or asked him to buy something on his way and bring it back. She knew with a sudden absolute certainty that Oliver wasn't going to come. What on earth was she going to do?

She suddenly thought she could hear something inside the villa. Footsteps . . . No. Nothing. Or . . . ? No.

She felt the goose-pimples spreading over her skin, even in the heat and light of day. The night was coming. And she was going to have to spend it here alone.

31

Wilfred lay face downwards on the soft grass, watching his hand trailing in the stream in front of him. His fingers were softly undulating in time with the water-weed around them. Yes, and there was the trout, flicking lazily through the weeds. He watched it edge nearer and nearer. He could feel its cold scales on his quietly tickling fingers. And then, whoosh! It was in his fist! In the air above his head! In the keep-bag he had improvised out of creeper! In the hot ashes of the oven! On the table under the stars! On the fork he was lifting up to her smiling lips . . .

'So,' said Stavros, nodding at the suitcase beside him, as the taxi bounced along down the unmade-up mountain road, 'airport?'

Georgie's smiling eyes were shining in the candlelight. She moved closer and closer to him. The trout had vanished from the picture. 'Yes?' she whispered.

'Yes,' said Wilfred. 'Yes. Yes!'

'Not a problem,' said Stavros.

Not a problem. Wilfred slowly emerged into the light of day. Stavros. Of course. Taxi. And he himself was not Wilfred, sharing home-caught trout under the stars with Georgie, but Dr Wilfred, on his way to give the Fred Toppler Lecture at the Fred Toppler Foundation.

They bounced on down the hillside. He was flung sideways by the hairpin bends, and up against the roof by the potholes; he had presumably been flung around in much the same way ever since they had left the villa, but had been too involved with the trout to notice. Now that he was conscious of his surroundings, though, he realised that in the air-conditioned chill of the taxi his wet clothes were hanging noticeably dank upon him.

He dragged his suitcase over from the front seat. There was something subtly alien about it. And even before he had lifted the flap of the luggage tag to check he knew with a sudden dull certainty what it would say. It wouldn't be Dr Norman Wilfred. It would be exactly what it had been before.

Yes. 'Annuka Vos'.

Of course. Naturally. They had sent the same bag. The wrong bag. The transvestite's bag.

And all at once he was hit by a bolt of black lightning. Every single thing had gone wrong since he had arrived on this horrible island. He was Dr Norman Wilfred, for God's sake! Not a helpless victim of forces beyond his control, but a rational human being in a rational world! He was used to something better than this! And he had been mocked and humiliated! Led around like a bear on a rope by idiocy and incompetence, by chance and misunderstanding, by coincidence and two moles on a shoulder blade!

The suitcase sat there beside him, the visible embodiment of all his frustrations. He opened the window and heaved it out. It hit an outcrop of rock in the track with a satisfying crunch, rolled over and over in the wake of the taxi, burst open, and scattered a long trail of clothes in the dust.

The taxi stopped. Stavros turned and looked out of the back window, and then at Dr Wilfred. His mouth was slightly open. The carapace of apparent indifference that taxi drivers develop to the waywardness of their customers was visibly dented.

'Not mine,' said Dr Wilfred.

*

Annuka took the tee-shirts and chinos she had ironed back to the bedroom, hung the chinos in the wardrobe, and laid the tee-shirts away in the chest of drawers. There seemed to be no tissue-paper to fold in with them, but perhaps it didn't matter too much. It was only for a week.

She turned back to the still hopeless muddle of clothing on the floor. Men! She picked up a small tangerine-coloured garment. Underpants. Tangerine-coloured underpants. Also lime-green ones. Sky-blue. Black underpants so scanty that they were scarcely underpants at all. She looked at it all in surprise. None of the underwear that Oliver had left scattered around her floor had ever been anything like this. He had obviously been running a little wild since she last put him out.

She was about to iron them, but somehow the iron hung in the air above them. Tangerine underpants, lime-green and sky-blue ones, black underpants so scanty that they were scarcely underpants at all – they weren't things that she wanted to put an iron to. If they had belonged to her, or to some other woman, it would have been a different matter. But to a man . . .

She folded them all thoughtfully and put them away unironed.

*

Stavros had got out of the taxi and walked back to the long slew of clothing that stretched away up the track from the eviscerated suitcase. Dr Wilfred could see no reason to accompany him. He looked at his watch. They should be getting on. The adrenalin began to drain out of his bloodstream. What was Stavros up to? What business was it of his what his customers chose to throw out of the window?

He turned round in spite of himself and looked. Stavros was picking up random items of clothing and letting them fall again. In the sunlight their colours appeared brighter than they had at the airport. Now he was holding up what seemed to be a pair of high-heeled silver diamanté shoes.

Under the men's clothing that he had seen at the airport a layer of women's clothing must have been concealed. So was Ms Vos a double agent? A trans-transvestite? A woman dressed as a man dressed as a woman?

Stavros tossed the shoes down on the track with the rest of the clothes, walked slowly back, and got into the taxi again. His face was expressionless.

*

Annuka picked up the next heap of clothing on the floor to sort out. It wasn't clothing, though. It was gauze netting. Yards and yards of torn gauze netting.

Heap after heap of it she picked up. She shifted the heaps from hand to hand, gazing at them in bafflement. Why would Oliver pack half a suitcaseful of torn gauze netting to go on holiday? Or even half a suitcaseful of untorn gauze netting, and then tear it?

[172]

With a slowly dawning dismay, the truth came to her. It was a bridal veil.

She sat down on the bed, as if the floor beneath her feet had become all at once uncertain. The Oliver she had known for seven long and difficult months had sprung surprises enough on her. But this was something else again. What she now had to envisage was an Oliver with a secret penchant for dressing up in – yes, it was obvious, now she had found the veil – women's underwear and see-through bridal outfits. Which he then rent, perhaps in some sickening symbolic representation of defloration.

She looked round the room for any further evidence of ritual perversion. A whip. A crucifix.

From a rail above the far side of the bed hung more swathes of gauze netting, this time still intact. From the hooks on this side hung torn shreds and scraps of the same stuff.

Oh, yes. Mosquito netting.

Her outrage slowly began to subside. He had simply had a bad night. Had thrashed about in his sleep, or flailed wildly against a plague of invading mosquitoes.

As her outrage subsided her irritation returned. She angrily beat the undersheet smooth, thrashed the pillows against each other, and snatched up the duvet from where it was nervously skulking on the floor. How characteristic of him to offer her such a thrilling new cause for dissatisfaction, and then to snatch it away again.

Though there was still the underwear. Her outrage returned.

32

As Spiros swung the taxi at reckless speed, hairpin by hairpin and pothole by pothole, up the mountainside, Oliver was flung back and forth and up and down like a shirt in a washing machine. He was too busy thinking about the forthcoming encounter to notice, though. If the potential rapist was still camped outside the bathroom door he was going to have to confront him. He didn't fancy his chances of doing anything too egregiously brave; he was being quite brave enough by simply showing up. Calming words seemed a more plausible option. 'Perhaps we could sit down and talk about this over a drink.' It might help if he was a psychiatrist. He had done very well as whatever Dr Norman Wilfred was. There was no reason why he shouldn't go on to become some sort of mental-health professional.

And if the man had already broken down the bathroom door . . .

'Still faster, if you possibly can,' he said to Spiros. 'Life and death.'

And then, in either case, there was the question of the explanation he would have to give Georgie as to why he hadn't got her messages earlier. This needed a bit of work. Phone out of range, of course. Battery run down. But then how had he eventually managed to get the messages? Moved within range. Oh, sure. Recharged the battery. It was all a bit too plausible. In his experience an explanation really needed to have a touch of the outlandish, even the impossible, if anyone was going to believe it. Phone snatched by wild goat. Stolen by Albanian bandits. Yes, this might be one of those rare occasions when it was necessary to assist fairly actively in the encouragement of misunderstanding.

It was so unfair, though. Whatever explanation he came up with, it would be ungentlemanly to reveal what this dash to her rescue was costing him – the once-in-a-lifetime chance of delivering a learned lecture on a subject that sounded as if it might be important, and to do it before an audience consisting of some of the richest and most influential people in the world. Still less, of course, could he tell her that it meant giving up his one hope of a night with Nikki. Unless he could think of some good reason why he had to return to the foundation. Left his passport behind, perhaps. He felt his pockets. Yes! It was actually true! He *had* left his passport behind! There was another taxi coming down the mountain-side towards them. As it drew level both drivers stopped, wound down their windows, and exchanged a few words in Greek.

'Keep going!' said Oliver. 'Keep going, keep going!'

'Stavros,' said Spiros, as they resumed their climb. 'My brother. You thank God you got not him drive you. You go fast with Stavros? You're a dead man.'

Three hairpins and nineteen potholes later they stopped again.

'*Now* what?' said Oliver.

Spiros gestured at the roadway ahead of the car. An open suitcase lay face down in the dust, with a muddle of what appeared to be old clothes stretching away beyond it up the track.

'Yes, but don't stop!' said Oliver. 'Come on! Keep going!'

Spiros began to squeeze the taxi past the remains of the suitcase.

'*Stop!*' said Oliver. He was gazing through the rear window of the taxi. Something about the suitcase . . .

'Wait!' he said.

'Wait?' said Spiros.

Oliver got out and walked back. The suitcase had a red leather address tag on it. He lifted the flap. 'Annuka Vos', it said.

Yes. It was his. His missing suitcase.

*

Annuka had found needle and thread, and tried to repair the shredded mosquito netting. She was still too angry with Oliver to give the work the patience it demanded, though, and in the end she simply bundled all the stuff up to go in the dustbin. Which was presumably outside the back door.

She opened it, and there in front of her was the rippling, glittering blue you expected to see outside a Greek villa. Beside the pool a swing seat, a barbecue, loungers already spread with towels. And on one of them a naked brown body, face down.

She felt a familiar double shock of anticipation and irritation. How absolutely like Oliver not to have been here when he should have been, and now to be here when she had got used to his not being!

'Oh, so you *are* here,' she said. She held up the mosquito netting accusingly. 'You seem to have wrecked the place already.'

Oliver raised his head sharply. So sharply that two sub-

[176]

stantial breasts appeared, squeezed between the arms supporting him. Something very strange had happened to him. Even his face had altered out of all recognition. He was no longer Oliver. No longer even he. He was she.

But if not Oliver . . . 'Who?' said Annuka. 'You! Who are you?'

'So sorry!' said not-Oliver. 'I'm Georgie. We're staying here. Me and Oliver – me and Mr Fox. We've borrowed it from these people he knows.'

She nodded at the mosquito netting.

'Are you the cleaning person?' she said.

*

How his suitcase had got itself on to a dirt track halfway up a mountain Oliver couldn't easily imagine, nor why it was broken open, and all his possessions scattered. He hastily shovelled them back into the bag, guilty at delaying his mission of mercy by even two short minutes. Another thing he found difficult to understand was why, as he now noticed, he seemed to have brought a pair of silver diamanté high-heeled shoes on holiday with him. And a silk nightdress. And a long flowered evening skirt.

'We go on?' said Spiros. 'Life and death?'

'Wait,' said Oliver.

He was standing transfixed, gazing at the skirt. A horrible thought had come to him. When it said 'Annuka Vos' on the label, it couldn't possibly mean, could it, that this was a suitcase that belonged not to him at all, but to . . . ? Oh, no!

*

Of course, thought Annuka, as she stood there with the mosquito netting in her arms. Of *course*! This is why the house was full of discarded tangerine knickers! This is why Oliver had had a bad night! This is why he had been thrashing about in bed!

How could she not have seen it at once, at the first glimpse of tangerine? After she had had seven months to learn what he was like!

She flung down the mosquito netting, ran back into the house, and snatched up her phone.

*

And if, thought Oliver, as he stood there in the middle of the track, his hands full of flowered silk and his head full of gradually dawning implications, if there was a suitcase belonging to Annuka Vos on the island, then possibly there was also—

His phone rang. He looked at the name that had appeared on the screen. Of course. As if hypnotised, he pressed the button and put the phone to his ear.

'The cleaning person!' said the familiar voice. 'Yes! That's me! The cleaning person! I don't believe this! Even from you! Because it's so absolutely *typical*! As soon as my back's turned! And *here*, of all places! You bring her *here*! *I* borrow a place where we can quietly be together for a week! *I* borrow it, not you! Because it *doesn't* belong to some people *you* know! They're friends of *mine*, thank you very much! You've never even *met* them! And there you are, rolling around their bed with her great fat boobs flopping everywhere in her orange knickers! And before you know where you are you've smashed the place to pieces! And then you expect me to clean up after you! And you're not even here! So where *are* you? And don't tell me, because I don't want to know, I don't *care* where you are! Just so long as it's not where *I* am! Drop dead, all right? And show your face here if you dare! The cleaning person? Right, then, I'm going to finish the cleaning!'

Oliver had drawn in a good supply of breath for the reasonable and pacifying reply that he would surely find himself uttering as soon as he had thought what it would be, but before he could convert any of it into words the phone had gone dead.

He threw the long silk skirt back on to the track.

'OK?' said Spiros, getting back into the car. 'We go fast now?'

'Wait,' said Oliver.

'Wait?'

Oliver was thinking.

33

Georgie tried to go on sunbathing. But the sun was getting low in the sky, and she felt a bit guilty that her nakedness had obviously upset the cleaning person. She pulled the towel around her and went back to the house to put some clothes on. Just as she reached the door, though, it opened, and her clothes came out. They were in her open suitcase, which was being carried by the cleaning person.

'Oh, thank you!' said Georgie. 'How sweet of you! And you've even folded everything up and put it away for me!'

The cleaning person said nothing, and the clothes marched straight past Georgie without stopping. She turned and watched, still holding the towel around her. The cleaning person was taking the clothes back to the lounger for her to get dressed. No, to the pool . . . And was tipping them in . . . was shaking the bag over the water to make sure she had got every last item out of it . . . was throwing the bag itself into the pool . . . was wiping her hands on a towel . . . was turning back to confront Georgie . . .

For a moment they stood facing each other, both too surprised to move – Georgie by the fate of her clothes, the cleaning person by Georgie's renewed and even more brazen effrontery, because, as the clothes went into the pool, she had stretched out her hands in a remote and ineffectual gesture of dissuasion, which had let the towel she had been holding around her fall to the ground. The stand-off lasted only a moment. When Georgie took in the expression on the cleaning person's face she saw that the situation had somehow got beyond discussion or explanation, and that the only possible action was to get out of her way as fast as possible. She turned and fled. Back to the house, grabbing the fallen heap of mosquito netting on the way and dragging it round herself, the cleaning person right behind, shouting something in what was presumably Greek, was certainly abusive, and almost certainly obscene.

Georgie slammed the garden door in the cleaning person's face, which delayed her for a moment, and ran into the bedroom, eager to find some more suitable and dignified covering to replace the mosquito netting. Her clothes had gone, though. Of course. Every last stitch of them. She just had time to run into the bathroom and slam the bolt home as the cleaning person ran into the bedroom.

'Open the door, you filthy little slut!' said the cleaning person. 'Or I'll kick it in!'

Georgie sat down on the lavatory seat, where she had sat for so long during the previous night, and pulled the mosquito netting round her. She was shivering and her hands were shaking. Life seemed to be going round in circles.

*

Oliver stood in the middle of the roadway, still trying to adjust his plans to the changing situation. So, there were two of them at the villa now. Georgie was no longer alone to face the rapist outside the bathroom door. She had someone to protect her. She had Annuka. Against Annuka even the most violent attacker was unlikely to prevail.

It was one thing to rush to save Georgie if she was on her

own. He hadn't hesitated. He had been ready to sacrifice everything. But if she already had someone to protect her . . . And if that someone was Annuka . . .

Then again, if Georgie and Annuka were there together there would be other issues to be settled. But it seemed to him that they would be the sort of issues that his presence could only exacerbate. It might be better to let the two of them sort things out between them.

'So,' said Spiros, 'we go on?'

Oliver shook his head. 'Airport,' he said.

*

There was suddenly silence in the bathroom, and the door stopped shuddering so alarmingly in its frame. The house was solidly built, and the door had evidently frustrated the cleaning person's efforts to kick it in. Georgie held her breath, waiting to hear what the woman would do next, and perhaps also so as to make her own existence loom less objectionably large to her. Even through the thickness of the door she could hear her breathing hard enough for both of them.

'Right, then,' shouted the woman finally. 'I'm going to phone the police! I'm going to have you arrested!'

Silence. She had evidently gone off to fetch her phone. Her objections to nudity, even practised by her employer's guests in the privacy of their own garden, were astonishingly violent. Perhaps she had weird religious convictions of some sort. Unless she had bristled at being called the cleaning person. She looked Greek, but she sounded English. Maybe you had to call local English employees something different. Cleaning supervisors. Directors of leisure services.

[182]

Footsteps coming back, and another sudden volley of blows on the door.

'My phone!' the cleaning whatever-she-was was screaming. 'Give me my phone! You've got my phone in there!'

Georgie invisibly but involuntarily shook her head. She hadn't got *anything* in here! The woman had cleared out even the great muddle of creams and lotions that Georgie had left around the wash basin. They were all in the pool.

Oh, no. Lying where the creams and lotions had been was, yes, a phone.

Georgie picked it up. Her first thought was simply to unbolt the door and hand it to the woman. But then she hesitated. Getting her phone back might still not be enough to appease her. Unbolting the door might create more problems than it solved. Anyway, if the woman was really going to phone the police . . .

Also . . . Yes, why not? Now she had a phone she could phone someone herself. Nikki – yes! But without her own phone she didn't know the number. Oliver, then? She pressed the button, then realised that she had no idea of Oliver's number, either.

But there, unbelievably, was his name, on the screen of the cleaning woman's phone, waiting for her. She touched the number.

Even in Greece people had heard of Oliver Fox.

*

The airport, yes. Because Oliver could see that the whole enterprise was over. It was doomed. It had seemed to be working – it might even have gone on working – but fate had caught up with him. He might have guessed that Annuka would change her mind, since she'd done it three times before. Three times she had thrown him out, and three times she had phoned him with much the same kind of invitation to reopen negotiations as she had just issued.

Annuka Vos. The very name sounded like the dull tolling of some great bell. The leitmotif of heavy destiny. To find it announcing itself on the same island as he happened to be cast a grey pall over even the most hopeful of initiatives. He had only to think of her and he could feel his foot insecure on the high wire he was treading, his balance uncertain.

He had second thoughts for a moment, as Spiros turned the taxi round and drove down the mountain again. The sound of Annuka's name was blotted out by the applause of all those people gazing up at him from the dinner tables as he began his great lecture on whatever it was that his great lecture was about. And then, with the applause still in his ears, by the look in Nikki's clear blue eyes, and the freshness of the two crisp and trusting syllables in her name.

'Or rather . . .' he said to Spiros.

'No?' said Spiros. '*Not* airport?'

But then his phone rang, and there it was on the screen again: 'Annuka Vos, mobile'. He couldn't face listening to any more of her raging. He wiped the name away with the touch of a button, but a few seconds later it reappeared. This time he put the phone back in his pocket and left the name to bleat on unanswered. He could see what would happen. She would keep phoning. She would find out where he was and pursue him. She would have joined forces with Georgie by this time, their mutual antipathy overtaken by their mutual grievance against *him*. They would pursue him together –

hunt him down like two of the three furies. Into the lecture. Out of the lecture and into Nikki's room. And there they would explain their joint grievance to her and their joint grievance would become a triple grievance. They would recruit her to their cause. They would become all three of the furies. He was not Dr Norman Wilfred. He was Oliver Fox, and he was beaten.

Spiros was still looking at him inquiringly in the rear-view mirror.

'Airport,' said Oliver.

34

'Dr Wilfred?' said Nikki cautiously, tapping softly on his door. The interview couldn't still be going on, could it? If it was, if he had still not managed to get rid of Wellesley Luft, he might welcome an interruption. He would presumably want to freshen up and get changed before the evening began. She tapped again. Still no response.

The door was open a crack. She put her ear to it. Silence . . . and then a strange low sound, a kind of gathering deep groan.

She pushed the door open at once.

'Dr Wilfred!' she said in alarm. There was a sharp snort, and the bald head she could see over the back of the armchair jerked upright. The suddenly awakened face of Wellesley Luft appeared, trying to work out in evident confusion where its owner now was.

'I was at Junior Prom,' he said. 'I'd just got to dance with Jackie Kennedy. I do apologise. I was on the red-eye, as you know. Also I am seven hours out of step with Eastern Standard Time.'

'He's still not here?' said Nikki. She looked at her watch. 'I'm awfully sorry. He must have stepped out for a moment, and then . . . I don't know . . . got cornered by his admirers, perhaps. So many people who want to talk to him!'

'Everyone wants a piece of Dr Norman Wilfred!'

'He's going to be in a bit of a rush when he arrives. I'll try to find you a little time after dinner.'

'Even half an hour would be most deeply appreciated. Oh,

and I guess sooner or later he's going to be needing this. I found it on the floor.'

'On the floor? Oh, dear. He does seem to be a weensy bit disorganised.'

She opened the passport and glanced briefly at the familiar face. 'I'll put it somewhere safe for him. You go on down. Ask them to give you a glass of champagne.'

*

Nikki put the passport on the desk, where Dr Wilfred would be sure to see it. But as soon as Wellesley Luft was out of the room she picked it up again and resumed her study of Dr Wilfred's photograph. He was unsmiling, of course, as passport regulations required, and made strangely alien by his staring immobility. He was still Dr Wilfred, though, still chuckle-headed Norman Wilfred. Her eyes moved to the date of birth and other details beside the photograph. Good God, no wonder he seemed so young! He was only a couple of years older than herself! And he had already achieved so much in life! Her eye moved up to feast on his name for a moment or two . . .

Her phone was ringing, though. It was him! At once her eyes were more pleasantly open than ever, her shirt more crisply ironed. 'Nikki Hook,' she said.

It wasn't Dr Wilfred. It was a woman having some kind of hysterical breakdown.

'Sorry – *who* is this . . . ?' said Nikki. 'I can't hear . . . Oh – *Georgie*!' Of course. Georgie. Again. Who else? She stood, holding the passport in her hand, trying to make sense of the cascade of sound in her ear. 'Georgie,' she said, 'Georgie . . .

Georgie . . . ! Slow down a moment . . . ! Yes, but I can't . . .
Had to *Google* me . . . ? Fingers shaking . . . ? But why did
you have to Google me . . . ! The *cleaning person's* phone . . . ?'

She kept her eyes fixed on Dr Wilfred's sane and
untroubled face.

'Georgie . . . Yes, yes . . . But just tell me one thing: *where
are you* . . . ? The *bathroom*? You're back in the *bathroom* . . . ?
Oh, Georgie, no . . . !

'And this person outside the door . . . Is the *cleaning person* . . . ? And is he the same man as before . . . ?

'*Not* the same man . . . ? Not a *man* . . . ? *Her* . . . ? The
cleaning person is the cleaning *woman* . . . ?'

She looked out of the window. The yachts rode quietly at
anchor. Shirt-sleeved waiters hurried back and forth to the
Temple of Athena with crates of champagne and bags of ice.
The Fred Toppler Foundation was quietly, thrillingly, doing
what it had been founded to do: promote the civilising values of European culture. Meanwhile, out there in the rest of
the world . . .

'Georgie, let me just make sure I've got all this straight.
You were lying by the pool. Nothing on – no – of course
not – sunbathing – yes. And the cleaning woman came out?
Yes . . . yes . . . And threw all your clothes in the pool . . . ?
Everything . . . Emptied the suitcase . . .

'Of course . . . Yes . . . I understand . . . So, Georgie, have
you got any clothes on now . . . ?

'You've got *what* on . . . ? Mosquito netting . . . ?'

Nikki opened the passport again as she listened. Even
without his regular smile there was something calming
about Dr Wilfred's appearance. You looked at him and you
knew that the world could be a simple and straightforward

place, that it was possible to live one's life without getting besieged in bathrooms by cleaning women with insane religious convictions. He had been born in London, she discovered. He was a British citizen. And his name was somehow as reassuring as his appearance. She let her eye move up the list to savour it. 'Given names/*prénoms*: OLIVER.' Yes! It somehow suited him. So did his surname/*nom*: FOX.

'Georgie,' she said, 'you're in the bathroom, yes, but what *country* is the bathroom in . . . ?'

She didn't hear Georgie's reply, though, because it had just occurred to her that there was something odd about the spelling of Dr Wilfred's name.

*

In fact Georgie hadn't replied, because she hadn't heard Nikki's question. The cleaning woman had suddenly discovered a new grievance. Georgie had only just taken in what it was.

'My suitcase!' she was screaming through the woodwork. 'What have you done with my suitcase?'

Her *suitcase*? *What* suitcase? There *wasn't* a suitcase!

There *had* been a suitcase, of course. There had been her own suitcase, now floating in the pool. And, yes, there had been another suitcase before that. The one that had come in the taxi – Wilfred's suitcase.

A queasy, unsettling insight came to Georgie. She had jumped to conclusions, she realised, as she had done quite often in life before. Wilfred's suitcase *hadn't* been Wilfred's suitcase. It had been the cleaning woman's. The taxi had been bringing the cleaning woman. And her suitcase with her.

But why would the cleaning woman have been arriving in a taxi? Why would she have been bringing a suitcase with her?

And suddenly, in one lightning leap after another, everything became clear to Georgie. It was because the cleaning woman *wasn't* the cleaning woman. She was coming to stay in the villa. Just like Georgie herself. A fellow-guest. Of Oliver's. Like herself. She was some part of Oliver's notorious past. Or even, like herself, of his notorious present.

There seemed to be another ceasefire in the siege of the door. Instead there was the sound of the suitcase search moving through the house, of doors being flung open, of tables being shifted and chairs overturned. Georgie wondered whether to try shouting through the door that the suitcase was presumably still outside the gate where the taxi driver had put it. But then she remembered – it wasn't. She had picked it up herself, and put it back in the taxi. So now it was . . .

Wherever Wilfred was. Giving a lecture. Gone.

At any moment the woman would be back, still suitcaseless, and angrier than ever. It might be an idea, thought Georgie, to follow the example of the suitcase – to be out of the house and away from here.

*

Oliver rested his head against the side window of the taxi, absently watching a plane that had taken off from the airport just ahead of them. Up, up it soared, catching the early evening sun as it began a long climbing turn. He felt like that plane – light, unencumbered, free. As magically as a plane becoming airborne he had become Dr Norman Wilfred. As easily as a plane revolving the landscape beneath itself he had rocked the world a little on its axis. Had varied the great dullness of things, the vast yawning predictability of the planets going round the sun.

Then, just as easily, he had reverted to being Oliver Fox again and was off. There was nothing he had to drag through the airport and get airborne with him. His suitcase could stay where it was, in the room he had left. Nothing in it that he couldn't abandon as easily as the room. Nothing in it that belonged to him, in any case, now he thought about it. Not even the suitcase. Somewhere there must be another suitcase, full of things that actually were his. It was presumably in the keeping of that other Dr Norman Wilfred, the shadowy figure who was now free to step forth into the light again and resume his existence. Let him have both suitcases, whoever he was.

All Oliver needed in life he carried in his pockets. A little cash and a couple of credit cards. He checked his trouser pockets. OK. Fine. He checked his shirt pocket. He had his phone. Not essential, perhaps, but certainly useful. The bar of chocolate and the pack of soluble aspirin. Optional, but handy. Nothing else in the whole wide world did he require.

Oh. One thing . . .

*

Nikki sat down. Her legs had gone wobbly. She looked at the passport yet again.

No, there was no way round it. The spelling was definitely wrong. 'Norman' was not spelt O-L-I-V-E-R. 'Wilfred' was not spelt F-O-X.

35

'Thirty-two euros,' said Stavros.

He had to say it twice, because the first time Dr Wilfred was standing on a dark hillside somewhere under the glittering night sky, explaining to Georgie how the apparently random distribution of the heavenly bodies was entirely consonant with a causality fully determined by the pre-existing fundamental laws, and it was difficult to see how the sum of thirty-two euros came into the relevant mathematics at any point.

The stars faded. Oh, yes, Stavros. The taxi. They had arrived at the foundation. Dr Wilfred got out and hoisted his flight bag on to his shoulder while he fumbled for his wallet. He couldn't help being aware that there were gratifyingly large numbers of people arriving at the same time to hear his lecture. Over and over again the glass doors slid back to admit them. Surprisingly many of them were obese, and they were dressed in surprisingly informal ways, with bare bulging midriffs and sun-reddened knees and shoulders. A lot of them had brought their children, and they were all pushing baggage carts piled with suitcases.

The thirty-five euros Dr Wilfred had got out of his wallet hesitated in the air above Stavros's waiting hand.

'Hold on . . .' he said.

*

'Thirty-eight euros,' said Spiros, in the taxi pulling up outside Departures just behind Stavros's.

Oliver didn't get out, however. He checked all his pockets once again. No, he hadn't got it. For a moment he thought he might try to talk his way through passport control without it. If so many people were prepared, without any effort on his part, to believe that he was Dr Norman Wilfred when he wasn't, surely a few simple officials would take his word for it that he was Oliver Fox when he actually was . . .

'No,' he said finally. 'I'll have to go back.'

'Back?' said Spiros.

He had left his identity behind. Put it down in the guest suite somewhere, when he had been taking off Oliver Fox and putting on Dr Norman Wilfred, and forgotten to pick it up again.

They had to wait, though, because the man who had just got out of the taxi in front was also changing his mind and getting into it again.

*

Still Nikki sat gazing at the passport. Her first thought was that the passport office had made a mistake. It was so obviously Dr Norman Wilfred in the photograph! But then it started to seem not quite so obvious after all.

She became aware that she was also still holding the phone. She put it back to her ear. There was silence. Georgie had evidently calmed down a bit. Which gave Nikki a chance to tell her that their roles were now reversed.

'Georgie,' she said quietly, 'I think *I've* done something rather silly, too.'

Because *of course* Dr Wilfred wasn't Dr Wilfred. How could he be? Dr Wilfred would be somewhere in his fifties. She knew that perfectly well. He couldn't possibly be an amiable young idiot with an engaging smile and hair flopping into his eyes. He was a self-important celebrity with a bald head and a lot of expensive meals built into him.

How had she ever for one moment thought that Dr Wilfred was Dr Wilfred?

Because – yes – it had happened at the airport, in the very first moment that she had set eyes on him. He had looked at her sign and smiled. She had said 'Dr Wilfred?' and he had said yes. It was as simple as that.

No, he hadn't even said yes. She remembered exactly what he had said: 'I cannot tell a lie.'

He couldn't tell a lie. He *hadn't* told a lie. She had made Dr Wilfred into Dr Wilfred all by herself, single-handed.

'This person I told you about,' she said to Georgie. 'He isn't who I thought he was. You told me, didn't you. You said, wait till you've known him for a bit longer. Actually I suppose I really did know. Always. From the very first moment. Of course I knew. Everything about him was just too good to be true.'

There was no reply from Georgie.

'Georgie?' she said. 'Can you hear me? Hello? Are you there . . . ?'

'Yes, I am here,' said a voice which was not Georgie's. 'And your filthy little friend isn't, and nor is my suitcase. And if you were somehow also involved in stealing it then let me tell you that this is my phone and I now have the number of yours.'

Nikki put the passport carefully on the desk next to the suitcase and ended the call. Somewhat reluctantly. She felt so small and lonely that she was almost ready to confess herself even to the cleaning woman.

36

Down, meanwhile, the sun moved towards its nadir and its foreordained daily extinction in the ocean. On the foundation sailed towards its apogee, and its scheduled annual apotheosis in the Fred Toppler Lecture. Sun and foundation both were as complexly self-absorbed as a liner steaming towards its New York, or the world itself on its great journey towards whatever fate awaits it. Neither sun nor world, nor foundation either, were troubled by any small internal discrepancies.

The agency waiters who had arrived on the morning ferry from Athens were clipping on their bow-ties. The string quartet who would be playing inaudibly during the champagne reception in the Temple of Athena were setting up their music stands and squabbling about the mess that second violin had made of their booking the previous night at a funeral in Kalamaki. In guest villas among the greenery all over the headland wives were standing in front of mirrors, looking with dissatisfaction at themselves over the dresses they were holding up, and asking husbands for the reassurances they had uttered so many times before over the years; and husbands were reclining on beds, still sunk in their early evening torpor, gazing at the ceiling and murmuring sight unseen the well-rehearsed words yet again.

Around the boardroom table in Democritus the Bishop of the Hesperides Archipelago and other worthy trustees of the foundation were busy receiving apologies, adopting minutes, approving accounts, reappointing auditors, suppressing yawns, expressing thanks, offering congratulations, standing down, standing again, and looking forward to any other business, or rather the absence of it. Behind the closed doors of the conference suite in Aristippus Mr Papadopoulou was hosting a private meeting of his own with Oleg Skorbatov and various other business associates from Turkey, Lebanon, Egypt, and southern Italy, though exactly what their discussions had to do with European civilisation no one knew, since Mr Papadopoulou's people had swept the entire premises for bugs, and Mr Skorbatov's people, not trusting the Greeks, had swept them all again; and because now all the security people from the various parties involved were standing outside the doors watching each other.

Down on the waterfront Giorgios, the security guard, wandered slowly along the dock, yawning and scratching himself. There was little for him to do, since so many of Mr Papadopoulou's guests had brought their own security people – and since in any case the whole foundation seemed to be entirely secure without the help of any of them. A large wooden crate had appeared on the dockside, he discovered. 'Marine diesel spares', said the stencil on the side, in Greek and English. Curious. A useful addition to the facilities of the waterfront, though, because it was a good five feet high, and there was enough room behind it for Giorgios to sit on the edge of the wharf and lean against it, out of sight of any possible security cameras.

He took off his shoes and socks, and lowered his feet into the water. All around him the waiting crews of the visitors' yachts and cruisers were going about their traditional maritime business, hosing down decks and coiling ropes, throwing kitchen waste overboard and rattling crates of empty wine bottles. It was pleasantly relaxing to watch other people working.

Marine diesel spares . . . Still attached to the small crane that had presumably swung them ashore. From which of the boats, though? From *Why Worry*, of Dubrovnik? *Lady Luck*, of Istanbul? *Ciaou Ciaou*, of Brindisi? Their chrome fittings flashed in the sun. Their spotless white paintwork gleamed. None of them looked like the kind of vessel that might be shipping crates of marine diesel spares around the Mediterranean.

Giorgios smiled to himself. He had a pretty good idea what was in that comfortably placed crate, and it wasn't marine diesel spares. It was cash. Used banknotes from all over the eastern Mediterranean. Everyone knew that the function of the Fred Toppler Foundation for Mr Papadopoulou was to launder the proceeds from some of his other enterprises. Giorgios had no idea what money-laundering involved, but he liked the feeling that something useful was going on here, some clean and wholesome operation that made the world a better place.

He leaned back against the solid comfort of all that money behind him and lit a cigarette. He had scarcely taken his first long, consoling drag, though, than the world fell to pieces around him. He was sprawling on his back, his support gone. The currency had collapsed! It was flying in the sky above his head. He struggled to sit up. The crate was swinging away out over the water, and the crane it was swinging from was being operated by Reg Bolt, the Director of Security. Giorgios threw his cigarette into the water and scrambled to his bare wet feet.

Reg Bolt, though, was gazing at him as if it was not Giorgios but he who had been caught napping. He was offering some kind of explanation, but since it was in English Giorgios had no idea what he was saying, only that it referred to the crate, which was now heading away from the dockside on the deck of a trim white launch. The marine diesel spares were not imports – they were exports, and the launch was heading for the biggest of all the yachts out there – *Rusalka* of Sevastopol.

After Reg Bolt had gone, and Giorgios was left to drag his socks over his wet feet, he couldn't help wondering what it was that the Fred Toppler Foundation could be exporting to Sevastopol, in the personal transport of one of Russia's great oligarchs. Perhaps it was the finished products of the laundry operation. What was laundered money like? Perhaps it wasn't just figures written in a bank account, or zeroes on the screen of a computer, as Giorgios had vaguely supposed. Perhaps it was banknotes going back out again – hundredweights of them, crates of them, freshly pressed and starched, wrapped in soft tissue paper, to be laid out by Mr Skorbatov's valet for his personal use . . .

*

Nikki hurried blindly from one final check, one last-minute problem, to the next. Eric Felt appeared out of nowhere, bulging accusingly at her, and holding up a small grey object. 'A toe,' he said. 'I found it near the new swimming pool. One of your people has obviously bashed into something. I shall have to report this to Christian. He's going to be very upset.'

'Superglue,' said Nikki. But what she was thinking about was how Dr Wilfred had told her he had once been older than he was now.

'Salt-free onion-free,' said Yannis, when she went into the kitchens, showing her a single portion of mushrooms à la grecque in its own skillet. 'And it's also kosher veggie, because hey, what the hell?'

'Brilliant,' she said. 'Not that it matters any more.'

'Not matter?' said Yannis. 'If he's allergic? If he's gonna swell up and get red spots and choke to death?'

'Not any more, he isn't,' she said. 'Unfortunately.' But all she could see were the wet footprints outside her window.

And no sign of him anywhere. Not that she knew what she was going to say to him when she found him. Or what she was going to do about it.

She was angry, though. Angry with him for making her ridiculous. Angry with herself for letting him. He had looked around and picked her out to be his victim. He had destroyed her professional credibility and all her hopes for the future.

What kind of lecture was he going to give, anyway? Had he somehow got hold of the real Dr Wilfred's text? Or was he going to invent some lecture of his own? A mockery of a lecture? A hoax lecture, in the spirit of the masquerade he had been – was still – performing? Or would it be no lecture at all? Perhaps, when the moment came for him to stand up, he would remain sitting. Or stand up and say nothing. Or prove to have slipped away into the darkness a moment earlier.

But where *was* he?

And where was the real Dr Wilfred?

And which of them was going to be standing up to give the Fred Toppler Lecture in two hours' time?

And if neither of them was, then . . . ?

The first thing she had to do, obviously, was to tell Mrs Toppler what had happened. And to do it before she read out the eulogious introduction that Nikki had written for her to someone who wasn't Dr Norman Wilfred at all. Or even to someone who *was*, supposing he should suddenly turn up, if Mrs Toppler thought he *wasn't*. Or to no one at all.

But how *could* she tell her, when it would finish her career? Not that she wanted to become director of the Fred Toppler Foundation just at the moment. Or to remain there in any capacity.

Or to be anywhere else on this earth.

*

Behind the screens around the new swimming pool the contractors were still working, apparently oblivious of any aspect of European civilisation but the financial penalties for failure to complete on schedule. They were contributing to the intellectual life of the community, however, because Chris Binns, the foundation's writer in residence, gazing out of the window of his room in Epictetus watching the dump-trucks emerging from behind the screens, had at last had the idea for a poem.

He had been struggling to find a subject for some time. He obviously had to write *something* while he was here. If you went to be writer in residence somewhere you had to come back with more than just a suntan and a jar of the local honey. You were supposed to have written a poem, or prefer-ably a whole sequence of poems. Something that alluded to the local landscape, certainly. But not, obviously, just saying how blue the sky was and how nice the bougainvillaea looked. It had to be something that crept up on the place obliquely. Obscurely. Ironically. Something that referenced bits of the place's history and mythology that no one else knew about. That needed footnotes, and that would provide material for the thesis that a PhD candidate somewhere would one day be writing about you. He could see the thesis more clearly than he could see the poem. 'This haunting and elusive work was written during a summer that Binns spent on the island of Skios, and interweaves the crisis of creative barrenness and existential purposelessness from which he was at that time suffering with the vibrant local resonances of . . .'

Of what, though? This was the problem. Of blue seas and purple bougainvillaea? Of all the vibrant local resonances that had already been interwoven with his predecessors' spiritual crises each year since this place had been open?

Now, however, he seemed to have cracked it. The poem was going to revolve around the figure of Athena. His idea was that the contractors digging out the new swimming pool had hit upon the site of the temple that was supposed to have been dedicated to her, and in some kind of half-hinted, largely incomprehensible way disturbed the goddess's spirit. Since, as he had discovered from his researches on the inter-net, she was the goddess not only of wisdom but of civilisa-tion, which was what the foundation was dedicated to, he could see considerable ironic possibilities opening up here. Wearing her helmet and chiton (whatever a chiton was – he could look it up later), carrying her shield, and accompanied by her traditional attendance of serpents, she would emerge from behind the screens and join in the life of the foundation. She might go to a class on Greek mythology. Take off her chiton and sunbathe. Come to one of Chris's creative writing classes and read him some little epic or tragedy she had written.

This was the idea, but the actual words to express it he hadn't yet found. It was difficult to concentrate in this place when for so much of the time there was nothing going on. And then suddenly, just as you were getting used to that, there was. A bird flying past the window. Another dump-truck emerging from behind the screens around the construction site. The sun sinking ostentatiously towards the horizon. Right now, for example, here on the path below him Nikki was hurrying by, in her crisp white shirt, clipboard in hand, on her way from one mysterious importance to another. The sight of her reminded him of something. What it reminded him of most strongly and distractingly, of course, was herself. Or of Athena, perhaps, in her crisp white chiton, shield in hand. But also of something else. Something she had said.

A lecture? Someone giving a lecture? Someone asking a question . . . ?

*

In the Temple of Athena the two waiters by the buffet finished filling the hundred flutes with champagne. The string quartet picked up their bows. The head waiter ushered Mrs Toppler and Mr Papadopoulou to their positions facing the entrance. Mrs Toppler looked in her bag one last time to check that she had the texts of her introduction and her speech of thanks.

She closed her bag and nodded at the head waiter. The head waiter nodded at two of the under-waiters, who picked up heavy trays of charged glasses and took up their positions on either side of the entrance. First violin nodded at his colleagues.

Stream upon stream of tiny rising bubbles. Bar upon bar of serene singing notes. The endless pause before something happens.

Nikki, waiting in the shadows, settled a calm but concerned look on her face, and seized her chance. She stepped bravely forward.

'Mrs Toppler,' she said. 'Listen . . .'

But just at that moment the first guests walked into the temple. 'Dickerson! Davina!' said Mrs Toppler. 'I might have known you'd be the first!'

37

One by one and two by two the tall flutes of champagne vanished from the waiters' trays. One by one and two by two they wandered among the ruins in the gathering dusk, trying to find other glasses of champagne to talk to, keeping themselves pleasantly occupied by refracting in their pale sparkling depths the torches already flaring around the masonry, the riding lights on the yachts along the waterfront below, and the silently labouring right arms of the string quartet.

'So romantic!' said Rosamund Chailey to Darling Erlunder.

'You feel any moment you might see Agamemnon's fleet sail over the horizon!' said Russell Pond to Mrs Comax.

'Or Athena come round with the canapés!' said Mrs Comax.

'And here's Nikki, our very own goddess, instead!' said Chuck Friendly.

'Nikki, this is all *so* divine! But where is our Apollo? Our heavenly Dr Wilfred?'

'I'm just looking for him myself,' said Nikki.

'We all have so many questions we want to ask him!' said Morton Rinkleman.

'So have I,' said Nikki. She moved on.

'Poor Nikki,' said Mrs Comax. 'She looks just *desperate*!'

'Such a load she's carrying on those lovely young shoulders of hers!' said Mrs Friendly.

*

A flute of champagne and a plate of canapés sailed head-high through the guests still getting out of taxis and limousines in front of the lodge. 'Oh, Nikki!' said Elli. 'That's so sweet of you! I think everyone has forgot me, sitting here in my box like a doll in a shop and nobody wants her.'

'You haven't seen Dr Wilfred, have you, Elli?' said Nikki. 'Our lecturer? He hasn't phoned, by any chance?'

'Oh my God!' said Elli. 'He's not here?'

'I can't find him.'

'But it's nearly time!'

'I know.'

'He's got lost again! This great brain, and he can't find his way from the guest room to breakfast! He phones me. "All I can see is goats," he says.'

'Anyway, if he phones now, or if you see him . . .'

'I call you at once, Nikki. Oh my God!'

Yes, oh my God, thought Elli, as Nikki hurried away again. She loses the great man just before his lecture – she never gets to be director! And what happens to me? I never get to be Mrs Fred Toppler's PA, and I'm stuck here in this glass box for ever!

*

'Sixty-three euros,' said Stavros. 'I take a credit card. Not a problem.'

There were no overworked glass doors here, only a striped barrier pole and uniformed security staff. No obesity, no sunburn, only slim and distinguished-looking people presenting gilt-edged invitation cards with raised italic print. Dr Wilfred had finally arrived at his destination.

'Invitation,' said the security man.

'I'm your lecturer,' said Dr Wilfred. 'Your guest of honour.'

'No invitation?' said the security man. 'No admission.'

*

'Sixty-nine euros,' said Spiros. 'I accept Visa and Master-Card. No problem.'

'Wait here,' said Oliver. 'I'm coming back. I'm just fetch-ing my passport.'

'Invitation,' said the security man.

'You're Giorgios, right?' said Oliver. 'You saw me before. Nikki's guest, remember?'

'No guest come in,' said Giorgios, 'only he have invitation.'

*

The first security man looked dubiously through Dr Wil-fred's passport, and then through the text of his lecture.

'I haven't got an invitation to the lecture,' said Dr Wilfred, 'because I am the lecturer. It's me who is giving the lecture for which the invitations have been issued. This is the lecture I am giving.'

He was surprising himself once again by the patience and politeness he was managing to display. The security man turned back to the beginning of the lecture and began slowly to turn all the pages over again.

'I know it says I am in Kuala Lumpur,' said Dr Wilfred. 'Or Western Australia. But they are deleted. I am here, in Skios. I shall put that in before I start.'

He couldn't help noticing that there was someone else

who was also being refused admission by one of the other security people. Also no invitation, and in his case no passport or lecture to offer in lieu.

'Come,' said the security man. Still holding Dr Wilfred's passport and lecture he led the way towards some kind of lodge or gatehouse. Dr Wilfred kept very close to him, never taking his eyes off the lecture.

*

'I'm so sorry, Dr Wilfred!' a familiar voice called out to Oliver from the darkness. 'We're going to miss your lecture!'

Mr and Mrs Chuck Friendly, the second-richest couple in the state of Rhode Island, were emerging from the pedestrian gate beside the barrier, on their way out with a couple of companions.

'We were really looking forward to it!' said Mrs Friendly.

'I have to fly back to the States,' said Chuck.

'A sudden summons!' said Mrs Friendly. 'Right out of the wide blue yonder!'

'So, Dr Wilfred, why aren't you in there drinking champagne with all the rest of them?'

'No invitation,' said Oliver. 'They won't let me in!'

Mr and Mrs Friendly both laughed. 'I love it!' said Mr Friendly. He fetched out his wallet. 'Here's his invitation,' he said to Giorgios and slipped something into Giorgios's shirt pocket.

Giorgios shrugged and waved Oliver in.

'Let's hope we meet again!' said Chuck Friendly to Oliver. 'I have a number of ideas about the possibility of creating something out of nothing that are remarkably consonant with yours, and I greatly look forward to exploring them with you!'

He raised his arm to wave goodbye, and Oliver couldn't help noticing the gleam of the handcuffs that connected him to one of his companions.

*

The young woman behind the screen inside the lodge finished the phone call she had been making and looked at the passport and the lecture that the security man was holding.

'Dr Wilfred!' she said. 'It's you! You're here! Hi! I'm so happy! We talk, talk, talk on the phone, but I never see you! Where you been? You get lost again? You get eaten from goats? Nikki's going crazy! I call her.' She dialled as she talked. 'You just got time to change! You know where to find your room? No, you don't! You're going to get lost again! You're going to phone me – "Where am I?"'

'Wait – I get you a buggy . . . Nikki! He's here!'

38

'Dr Wilfred!' cried Mrs Comax. Oliver was trying to slip past the Temple of Athena unobserved, since he was no longer Dr Wilfred, but merely Oliver Fox on his way to recover his passport and go. Everyone, though, was just at that moment beginning to emerge from the temple to move on to the agora for dinner, and now Mrs Comax had spotted him he was caught and surrounded.

'Oh, Dr Wilfred!' The name pressed in upon him from all sides. 'We've all been looking for you, Dr Wilfred! We thought you'd despaired of us poor simpletons, Dr Wilfred, and abandoned us!'

Oliver wondered whether to confess the truth to them, now the game was over, but no one had believed him when he had tried before, and it scarcely seemed worth the effort of trying again, or the social disruption it would entail, since as soon as he had fetched his passport he would have vanished from their lives. And since, after all, at any moment the real Dr Wilfred would almost certainly show up and do the job for him.

*

There was a young man just coming out of Parmenides as Dr Wilfred approached it. He was wearing three-quarter-length orange skateboarding trousers and a plum-coloured tee-shirt that bulged obsequiously at Dr Wilfred as he passed.

All thought of him went out of Dr Wilfred's mind, though, when he opened the door of the guest suite. Another guest was obviously already in occupation. There were clothes scattered everywhere – shirts, trousers, underwear. On the luggage rack a suitcase lay open, with more clothes tumbling from it like fruit from a cornucopia, so profusely that it took Dr Wilfred a moment to see that it had a red leather address tag.

He stood stock-still for a moment, then put his passport and the text of his lecture carefully down on the desk and opened the flap of the luggage tag. 'Dr Norman Wilfred', it said. The name smiled up at him like a reflection in a mirror. It was *his* suitcase. He picked up a handful of the scattered shirts and underpants. The patterns on the shirts were old friends. They were *his* shirts. The underpants were pure silk. They were *his* underpants. He and his lost luggage had been reunited. It was not some other guest who was occupying the room. It was himself.

Presumably the airline had somehow found the address and sent the suitcase on. But why was it open? Why had the contents been taken out and thrown around? Someone must have come in and opened it. He looked at the padlock. Yes, it had been forced. That unsavoury-looking young man who had been leaving as he approached . . . He had been ransacking the room when he had heard the buggy outside . . .

Never mind. The important thing was that he had clean clothes to change into. His evening lecturing trousers. Yes, crumpled, but still with creases in them. His clean soft silk underpants. He rubbed them between finger and thumb, and sniffed their cleanness. He pressed them affectionately against his cheek to feel their softness. The silk snagged against the unshaven whiskers on his cheek. Yes – first, a shave.

Where was his razor, though? And his toothbrush, for that matter, and all the rest of the stuff in his toilet bag? Where was the toilet bag?

He pushed open the bathroom door. And there it all was, scattered around the basin. There was a chef's toque of lather on the shaving brush. Someone had been using his shaving things! The cap was off the toothpaste. They had even used his toothbrush!

That young man with the obsequious stomach. He hadn't been stealing Dr Wilfred's things – he had been using them. He had been *living* in the room!

Dr Wilfred felt the lather on the shaving brush. It was dry. The toothpaste spilling from the open tube was caked hard. The young man had been here all day. He looked at the bed. The man had slept here. He must have arrived the night before. In fact he must have been on the same plane as Dr Wilfred, since he had stolen his bag from the carousel. And then been met by whoever was meeting Dr Wilfred. And persuaded them *he* was Dr Wilfred!

Everything was at last becoming clear.

And if the man had been shown to Dr Wilfred's room . . . if he had been allowed to remain in it all day . . . he must have continued to pass himself off as Dr Wilfred . . . Was presumably *still* doing so.

He had taken over Dr Wilfred's identity. He had stolen his life.

And where was he now? He was out there somewhere having pre-dinner drinks, being introduced to scholars and millionaires. As Dr Norman Wilfred. Some young delinquent in skateboarding trousers!

It suddenly came into Dr Wilfred's head what the impostor was intending to do. He was going to give the Fred Toppler Lecture.

No – not possible! Dr Wilfred had the lecture here, on the desk in front of him. He picked it up and glanced through it: '. . . the challenges facing us today . . . the hopes and fears of mankind . . .' He put his arms round it and pressed it against his chest. How right he had been never to let it out of his sight!

But perhaps the fake lecturer had a fake lecture? Perhaps he was planning to deliver a text of his own invention? Some thesis that blithely ignored the challenges, that mocked and derided the hopes and fears?

No, it was ridiculous. He was simply having one of those moments of panic that you laugh at afterwards. In any case, the imposture was now over, since he himself, the real Dr Wilfred, had arrived.

Perhaps he should quickly shave and change, then get out there and make absolutely sure that everyone understood that it was he who was he.

No, not even shave and change. He could do that later. Even unshaven and unchanged he was who he was.

*

'Oliver Fox,' said Eric Felt for the tenth time, as if repetition might somehow tease a little more meaning out of the name. 'And he *told* everyone! That's the ridiculous thing! I was there! I heard him! "I'm Oliver Fox," he said. But he said it in a kind of funny way, so everyone thought it was a joke. I knew it wasn't. That's why I went and searched his room.'

He and Christian were sitting in the shuttered darkness of Empedocles, with the passport that Eric had found in Dr Norman Wilfred's room lying on the low table between them. Christian was bent over it, trying to catch what little light there was from the tiny sanctuary lamps, almost concealing it behind his drizzle of lank grey hair. Dr Norman Wilfred gazed back at him from under his own blond mop. But the face was not the property of Dr Norman Wilfred. It belonged to someone called Oliver Fox.

'So poor Nikki's made a complete laughing stock of herself,' said Eric. 'This is the speaker she landed Mrs Toppler with, and it turns out to be someone who's just walked in off the street! She's been leading Mrs Toppler round on a piece of string! Nikki thought she was going to get her to push you out and make her director!

'And now this. They've put a knife in our hands, Christian! The time has come to use it.'

39

Dr Norman Wilfred couldn't even get into the Temple of Athena, because the guests were already spilling out on their way to dinner. They all had their backs to him, concealing something or someone they were surrounding like swarming bees. It was difficult to think how to make people know that their lecturer had at last arrived.

'Hello!' he said. 'Excuse me.'

No one turned. The bees seemed to have been deafened by the sound of their own excited buzzing.

There was one woman standing a little apart from the others, as absorbed in whatever it was as everyone else, but holding a clipboard, which suggested some kind of official standing.

'I beg your pardon,' he said. He waved his hand about in front of her. 'Hello . . . Excuse me . . .'

Her eyes flicked briefly towards him, up to the fringe of unwashed and uncombed hair around his sunburnt pate, then down over the grey stubble on his chin to the daytime travelling trousers dried awkwardly around the contours of his legs.

'Dr Norman Wilfred,' he said, holding out the hand he had been waving in her face.

She ignored his hand, and nodded at the backs of the people in front of her.

'There,' she said. 'If you can see him through all his worshippers.' She turned on her heel and walked away.

Dr Wilfred felt the sensation of sand being sucked away

from beneath his feet by the receding tide. Perhaps his ridiculous moment of panic earlier was not so entirely ridiculous after all. What people were saying so excitedly, he realised, at various pitches and with various intonations, was his name. 'Dr Wilfred! Dr Wilfred? Dr Wilfred, may I ask you . . . ? Dr Wilfred, what is your view . . . ?' They were saying it not to him, though, but to someone he couldn't even see in the press of people around him. 'Dr Wilfred, this is the Bishop of the Hesperides Archipelago . . . Mr and Mrs Oleg Skorbatov . . . His Excellency Sheikh Abdul hilal bin-Taimour bin-Hamud bin-Ali al-Said . . .'

For a moment Dr Wilfred believed that he was having the kind of out-of-body experience he had read about in which someone looks down upon himself dying. Concealed by all these people, like the discarded body on the operating table concealed by the doctors and nurses so desperately bending over it, was himself. Not himself as he actually was, but as he might have been in some other life. Younger, pot-bellied, in skateboarding trousers. And not dying – living. Living the life that belonged to *this* Dr Wilfred.

Yes, that was what was so wrong – precisely that the himself in there *wasn't* himself. It was someone else. The author of all his misfortunes and the thief of all his labours.

Another of his black bolts of rage went through him. He ran after the crowd of duped sycophants as they began to move up the roadway, hardly able to wait for the moment when he publicly exposed and humiliated the trickster, when he reclaimed the kingdom that had been stolen from him.

'Hey!' he said. 'Wait! Stop!'

No one waited, though. No one stopped. No one even noticed.

'Not him!' he screamed. 'Me!'

A man at the back of the crowd turned round to look.

'Me, me, me!' said Dr Wilfred, but found it difficult in his fury to find any form of words that articulated comprehensibly the monstrous injustice he had been subjected to. 'Dr Norman Wilfred! Me! *I* am!'

The man smiled and nodded and looked away. He was embarrassed to have been picked upon by some wandering schizophrenic.

At this even more immediate insult the focus of Dr Wilfred's rage shifted to the more accessible target who had offered it. He grabbed the man's arm.

'I *am*! I *am*!' he shouted. The man snatched his arm away, terrified. Various people in the crowd turned round to see what the disturbance was. Dr Wilfred waved the text of his lecture about in front of their faces.

'My lecture!' he cried. 'Mine! *I* am Dr Norman Wilfred! Not him! Me!'

The people looked not at the lecture but at each other, and then anywhere but at each other, embarrassed at even having been seen to be seeing this outburst.

Dr Wilfred stopped still and watched them all getting further and further away from him. Public opinion in the matter of his identity was overwhelmingly against him. He was in a minority of one, and there was nothing he was going to be able to do about it.

He sat down on a bench beside the roadway, feeling for the third time that day suddenly weak and strange, as if he were recovering from yet another bout of delirium. He looked at the text of his lecture in the last of the fading daylight. *He* was Dr Norman Wilfred, though! He *was*, he *was*! It said so on the binder!

He opened it, and found himself once again in the vibrant and bustling city of Kuala Lumpur . . . or rather, in the open spaces of Western Australia . . . no, on the green and tranquil island of Skios. He read the paragraphs he had written specially for the present occasion, about the parallels between, on the one hand, the patrons who had guided and nurtured the European civilisation that the Fred Toppler Foundation existed to promote, and, on the other, the business enterprises and government departments that commissioned and financed scientific research. Now all this specially composed material was going to waste.

He turned over more pages. '. . . Challenges . . . hopes and fears . . .' Somehow, though, they didn't seem quite as compelling, quite as real, as they had before. Here was a good bit, though – 'A concerted and imaginative response is required from governments and leaders of industry alike . . .'

Or was it so good after all?

He turned over more pages, but his mind was wandering. Two dark spots had appeared in the air between him and the page like importunate flies. He brushed them aside. He turned back to the section about the overall framework of social responsibility. The two dark spots reappeared. They were two moles, he realised. They had become detached from the shoulder blade on which they lived, and taken up residence inside his brain.

He tried to focus his eyes on the overall framework and the concerted response, but the virtue had gone out of them. The whole lecture had turned to dust before his eyes. He felt relieved that the prospect of reading it aloud to an audience now seemed to have receded so far.

It was not only the two moles that were now coming between him and the text, he discovered. There was the whole shoulder blade on which they lived, gleaming with the oil he had rubbed into it. There was the little gleaming hillock beside it that marked the top of the spine, and the gleaming ladder of vertebrae that led down, down to the little hollows on either side of the coccyx . . .

He remembered how encouraging Georgie had been to him. How she had believed in him. How she had accepted unquestioningly what no one else on this island would: that his name was Wilfred. Or at any rate that one of his names was. But since, when she called him Wilfred he heard it as his surname, it was like being back at school. It was like being young again.

And she had believed in his lecture. She had wished him well with it. Had kissed him goodbye . . .

He had been mad to leave! And by now her boyfriend would have turned up and claimed her.

No! He wouldn't! It came to Dr Wilfred, in the second rare eureka moment he had been granted in the course of a single day, who Georgie's boyfriend was, and why he was not with Georgie. The whole story at last fell into place. The narrative at last made sense.

Yes. It was Georgie's boyfriend who had taken his suitcase, his taxi, his room, his life. And who was now taking the place he should have had at dinner – who was sitting there in his skateboarding trousers, surrounded by admiring faces and attentive microphones, stuffing his bulging stomach with one specially prepared onion-free course after another.

While poor trusting Georgie waited up there in her lonely mountain retreat, abandoned and forgotten.

And, if her boyfriend was here, then she still had nothing to eat. Dr Wilfred could feel the nagging emptiness inside her, the uneasy lassitude, almost as painfully as Georgie would be feeling them herself. The sheer wrenching injustice of it overwhelmed him.

The more Dr Wilfred thought about it, the more serious Georgie's situation appeared to him. Not only was she hungry now – she had no prospect of ever eating again. Or any way of communicating her plight to the outside world. By the time she realised that no one was ever going to come she could conceivably be too weak to struggle to some other settlement for help. It wasn't possible that a fit young woman could actually starve to death at the height of summer on a Mediterranean island. Or was it?

Anything was possible. In the last twenty-four hours that horrible bulging impostor in the skateboarding trousers had proved it over and over again.

He jumped to his feet and walked back to the now-deserted Temple of Athena. Among the empty glasses and overturned bottles were platters still scattered with uneaten canapés. On one of the platters he assembled a reasonably representative selection: soft-poached ortolans' eggs, anchovies in absinthe, and tiny baskets, woven out of sea-grass, filled with lobster tartare and fouetté of shark fin. He covered the platter with a tablecloth, clamped the lecture under his arm, and hurried back towards the outside world.

If he's me, he thought, then I'll be him. He lives my life – I live his.

*

In the sky above the agora lingered a frescoed ceiling of pink and golden cirrus. On the tables the flames of the candles swayed languidly as the diners moved about, finding their places, and then stood behind their chairs, waiting for the Bishop to say grace. There was a bright murmur of people introducing themselves to the neighbours on either side. 'Hi!' the wealthy and socially adept guests of the foundation were saying to each other, extending welcoming hands and smiling welcoming smiles. The wealthy and socially wary business associates of Mr Papadopoulou unsmilingly inspected the outstretched hands, and nodded, and gave nothing away.

In the centre of the top table, at the focus of everyone's attention, stood Dr Wilfred. He had surrendered to public opinion. Dr Wilfred he would have to remain.

On his left stood Mrs Fred Toppler, the candlelight flashing points of fire back from her hair, her neck, her bosom, her fingers; on his right Mrs Skorbatova, with richly tanned full breasts struggling to be free of her décolletage, and a construction of brass-coloured hair on her head that would have been proof against small-arms fire. In front of Mrs Toppler was a table lectern and various microphones. Before these would be moved to stand in front of Dr Wilfred, though, there were four courses of dinner, four fine wines, and surely also time for some idea to come to him about what he would do when the moment arrived.

Mrs Toppler picked up a gavel made from local olivewood, and struck its olive-wood base three times. The murmur of conversation died away. The candle flames settled and stood as still as the diners themselves behind their chairs. From the further end of the table came a mumble of Greek, incomprehensible but recognisably liturgical. 'Amen,'

[220]

agreed all but the most committed atheists and the most taciturn businessmen, and there was a slithering of rented gilt chairs being drawn back from the tables over rented oriental carpets as everyone sat down.

The dinner that marked the triumphal finale of the Fred Toppler Foundation's annual Great European House Party had begun.

40

Nikki stood on the steps at the edge of the agora, in the darkness of the gathering night, looking out over the world she had created. Candlelit eyes sparkled. Candlelit lips talked and smiled. Candlelit heads bent forward to listen, were thrown back to laugh. Candlelit hands lifted soup spoons, broke bread, made charming gestures. More faces emerged from the shadows as waiters leaned into the light to serve and pour, to lay plates and clear them. A reassuring music of incomprehensible social noise rose into the night. Everything was going well.

All Nikki could see, though, was Dr Norman Wilfred, as she still couldn't help thinking of him, smiling his lopsided smile at Mrs Toppler as she talked to him – talked and talked to him, leaning close to him, her hand resting on his arm. He couldn't tell a lie, he had told Nikki at the airport, but he could smile a lie and he could listen a lie. He could look a lie as he brushed the lying rumpled blond hair out of his soft brown lying eyes.

Who was he, this Oliver Fox?

Why had he done it?

What was he going to do next?

And, most important of all, what was she going to do about it?

She knew what she was going to do about it. She was going to stop it. She was going to tell Mrs Toppler. She was going to tell her now.

How, though? She would have to approach her on her right side, away from Dr Wilfred, and interrupt her even as she spoke to him. Then do her best to whisper over the noise of the dinner.

But what whispered words could she find that could possibly make Mrs Toppler understand something so incomprehensible? And even if she could find the words, how could she ever make Mrs Toppler believe them?

All around Nikki the world continued on its allotted course. The forks went back and forth between plates and mouths. The first faint stars overhead moved westwards. She was alone with her problem in the midst of it all.

She was going to do it, though, and do it precisely now. The decision was made. Somehow, though, the decision failed to reach the appropriate muscles. Still she stood watching.

*

'I must stop monopolising you!' said Mrs Fred Toppler to Dr Wilfred. 'I get so nervous, though! Every year it's the same! Dance, yes, no trouble at all. I could get up on the table right now and dance my heart out, and I'd love every second of it! I have to make a speech, though, and all I want to do is get *under* the table and *die*! So of course I just keep talking! It's terrible! I should be listening to you!

'So where was I? Oh, yes. Christian. I shouldn't be criticising our own director to you. But why isn't he here? Why is he never anywhere? What does he do all day? We don't know! We never see him! OK, he's an elf, like Dieter. But even an elf has to come out of Elfland sometimes!'

Dr Wilfred gazed at her, nodding and smiling his soft

sympathetic smile as she went on and on about whatever it was she was going on about. But he was thinking uneasy thoughts. He had succeeded in climbing the impossible climb. Only now he couldn't get down again. He was stuck on the mountain top. He had made himself Dr Wilfred by his own individual act of will. He remained Dr Wilfred by the will of others.

'So,' said Mrs Toppler, 'Christian's days here are numbered. Only he doesn't know it yet. How are we going to do it? Mr Papadopoulou's going to fix it. Cut off his supply of lentils. Under-age boys on his computer. Concrete boots. I don't know. I don't want to know. Tell me after it's all over.

'I shouldn't be saying all this to someone I only met this afternoon. But I feel I know you really well! I feel I can talk to you!'

He had pulled a face, thought Dr Wilfred, and the wind had changed. He had created a monster, and his creation had risen from the laboratory bench and walked. And talked. And been listened to. And had quietly killed off its creator.

'So, OK,' said Mrs Toppler, 'this is what I wanted to talk to you about. This is where I need your advice. Who do we get to succeed Christian?'

She stopped. She was looking round the side of Dr Wilfred's head at the guest on his other side.

'Oh my God!' she said. 'Mrs Skorbatova! She looks as if they just dug her out of the permafrost! You better talk to her. I can pick your brains later. If she has a bad time here she takes it out on Mr Skorbatov – Mr Skorbatov takes it out on Mr Papadopoulou – we don't get this great new deal the boys are talking about. What great new deal? I don't know. I don't want to know. Tell me when we got it.'

Dr Wilfred turned his head. Mrs Skorbatova was gazing into space, her face as expressionless as her piled blonde hair and her naked brown shoulders; an ice goddess, inhabiting some freezing world of her own in the midst of the warm Mediterranean night.

'She doesn't speak English, though, does she?' said Dr Wilfred.

'Not a word,' said Mrs Toppler. 'Say anything you like. Just so long as she sees someone making the effort. Tell her the ten times table. She won't know. A mouth opening and shutting. That's all most people here want, when you come right down to it. Plus one of your nice smiles. I'll just read through my speech again.'

41

'Imagine it's you,' Dr Wilfred told Mrs Skorbatova as he ate his mushrooms à la grecque and she ate her rump steak. 'You're standing here at the lectern. A few last coughs and rustlings as the audience settles. You wait until there's absolute silence. You look out into the darkness, and there are all these faces gazing up at you, waiting to hear what you're going to say.

'And you don't *know* what you're going to say! You may be about to say anything! Things you never knew you knew! Things you can't understand! And all the time the real Dr Norman Wilfred may be out there somewhere. May be about to get to his feet and humiliate you in front of the entire world.

'Now, don't you feel a kind of horrible, wonderful tingling running up your arms?'

He had already told her that she was perhaps the most beautiful woman he had ever set eyes upon. She had slowly turned and looked at him, but her face had remained as unflawed as ever by any trace of an expression. He had been encouraged enough by this response to confide in her completely. He had confessed to her that he wasn't Dr Wilfred. He had told her about Georgie and Nikki and Annuka Vos. About how he had climbed the climb and couldn't climb down, performed the magic spell and couldn't reverse it. And still she had gazed at him with her eyes apparently focussed on something about two inches beneath the surface of his forehead. It was difficult to know whether she was doing it out of the same sense of social obligation as everyone else, or whether, in the great sea of meaninglessness on which she found herself cast away, even the sight of a particular mouth meaninglessly moving, particular eyes meaninglessly crinkling, and a particular hand meaninglessly brushing at its owner's hair, was a piece of flotsam worth clinging to.

'Well, there we are,' he said. 'Our hostess told me to talk to you, and now I have. So, if you'll excuse me, I'd better resume my conversation with her. I don't think I ever actually introduced myself, though. My name is really Fox. Oliver Fox.'

And now at last her expression changed slightly. She was still gazing at him. But her eyes were a little more widely open, and they seemed to have come into focus. Her lips had softened a little, as if she were contemplating the possibility of a smile. He was taken aback. She seemed to have understood something he had said. But what?

'The name?' he said. 'You've heard of me? Oliver Fox?'

She raised her eyebrows. She was expressing something. Irony, perhaps. And she smiled. Definitely smiled.

'Good God,' he said. 'You haven't heard of me when I'm Dr Norman Wilfred? And you have when I'm *Oliver Fox*?'

She rested her elbow on the table, and her chin on her hand. She looked straight into his face and raised her eyebrows again. Then started to laugh.

*

Nikki felt a sour acid around her heart as she watched them. He was making Mrs Skorbatova laugh just as he had made her laugh. And what a deceiving manipulative cow Mrs

Skorbatova was! Refused to be able to understand a syllable of English when it was spoken by anyone else. A few flattering words from Dr Wilfred, though – no, from Mr Oliver Fox – and she understood them perfectly. As well as Nikki herself had.

This is why he'd done it, of course. This is why he'd put Nikki in this impossible situation. For a laugh. He'd seen the name she was holding up at the airport and simply decided on the spur of the moment to have a bit of fun at her expense. He'd told everyone so this afternoon. He'd been speaking the truth for once. So of course nobody had believed it.

Or *was* it quite as simple as that? Her eye moved from Mrs Skorbatova and Mr Fox to Mrs Toppler. She was reading yet again through the speech that Nikki had written for her, then glancing yet again at her watch, making herself more and more nervous. Nikki's eye moved on to Mr Skorbatov, on the other side of Mrs Toppler. He was cutting himself some grapes from the bunch on the table in front of him with a tiny pair of silver scissors. There was something about the way he was holding the scissors, about the single-minded concentration with which he was using them, that made Nikki uneasy.

Her eye moved back to Mrs Skorbatova and Oliver Fox. He was still talking to her. She was still laughing. What was he telling her? Was it something that Mrs Toppler had just been telling *him*? Is this why he was here? To find out about the foundation for Mr Skorbatov? She knew, of course, about Mr Papadopoulou's money-laundering, though she was careful not to know about the details of it. But what else was he involved in? His guests at the House Party were presumably not discussing European civilisation. She had

[228]

a shrewd idea that Mr Papadopoulou and Mr Skorbatov had some new enterprise in hand for a start. She suddenly thought about the swimming pool that no one was allowed to see. Or rather the hole in the ground that would one day be the new pool. A hole in the ground, while it lasted, might come in rather handy for other purposes. Burying radioactive material, for example. Or a body. More than one body, even. A regular supply of bodies. Mr Skorbatov no doubt had a capacious cold-store on his yacht. He might be giving Mr Papadopoulou a regular contract to do his undertaking for him. She felt a sudden coldly dismal lurch in her stomach. Marine diesel spares! She had noticed the crate on the waterfront that morning. No! Not possible! Was it?

But if it was, then perhaps he wanted to know a little more about his business partner. Something he could have to hand if Mr Papadopoulou ever took it into his head to increase his charges.

She watched Mr Skorbatov put one of the grapes in his mouth. His jaw snapped shut on it, and was still again. The grape had gone.

She looked at Mrs Toppler, sitting all unawares beside him. I could talk to her now, thought Nikki, while Dr Wilfred is talking to Mrs Skorbatova.

She was just about to move when she saw that Dr Wilfred had turned away from Mrs Skorbatova and was talking to Mrs Toppler again.

She stopped, and stood watching the catastrophe approach, unable to move, as in a dream.

42

Oliver Fox had now told Mrs Skorbatova all about the difficulties he had got himself into in the days when he had been
Oliver Fox, and she had gazed at him throughout without
saying a word. She was obviously interested, though; particularly, it seemed to him, in the parts that involved his smiling his smile, and brushing aside the lock of hair that from
time to time fell into his smiling brown eyes. And above
all in the parts where he recounted how negatively so many
people reacted to the very mention of the name Oliver Fox.
Each time it made her smile in her turn and raise her eyebrows, and sometimes lightly slap his hand.

Now Mrs Toppler's hand was on his other arm. 'You're a
genius, Dr Wilfred!' she said. 'No one else has been able to
get a toot out of her! How did you do it? You don't speak
Russian, do you?'

'No,' said Dr Wilfred. 'I just tell her . . .' He turned back
to Mrs Skorbatova and whispered in her ear. 'Mrs Toppler
wants to know what I tell you to make you laugh,' he said.
'But that's our little secret. The fact that I'm Oliver Fox.'
Mrs Skorbatova laughed again, and gave him a little punch
on his arm.

'This is what we need to replace Christian,' said Mrs Toppler. 'Someone like you, who can get on with people. Even
with an ice princess who can't speak English, but who just
happens to be married to one of the richest men in the world.
You seem to be able to do anything! And stay so calm about

it all! Look at me. I'm in such a state! Can't eat, can't think – and all I've got to say is these two pages! "Our guest of honour tonight needs no introduction . . ." Whereas you . . .'

She stopped and looked around.

'Your lecture!' she said. 'The script of your lecture! Where is it?'

'Oh, yes,' he said. 'My lecture.'

'You hadn't forgotten about it?'

'Of course not,' he said, though in fact just for the moment he had, under the pressure of events.

'So where is it?' she said in alarm. 'The script – the text – the words?'

He shrugged. 'Inside my head.'

'You've learned it by heart?'

'No, I thought I'd just make it up as I went along.'

She gazed at him.

'It'll be fresher that way,' he said. 'More spontaneous. I'll take myself by surprise.'

'I've sat next to a whole slew of guests of honour since this place opened,' she said. 'But I've never met one like you. Well, if you can make things up as you go along, so can I! And here's an idea I've just had, straight out of the oven and on to the table, still bubbling . . .'

She put her hand on his arm, and began to murmur something that he had to bend close to hear.

*

Nikki watched Oliver Fox leaning towards Mrs Toppler with his head lowered and then sitting back in surprise. And in one of those eureka moments for which the real Dr Norman

Wilfred, she knew, had worked so hard to give some ordered explanation, she understood why Oliver Fox was so astonished, and why Mrs Toppler was now waiting so attentively for his response.

Not possible, though! No, no, no! Not possible!

But it *was* possible. *Anything* was possible. In the last twenty-four hours that horrible trickster with the modestly surprised look on his face had proved it over and over again.

This was her flash of insight: that Mrs Toppler had just invited Mr Oliver Fox to become the next director of the Fred Toppler Foundation.

Her flash of insight was followed by a second flash. Of anger. At Oliver Fox, at Mrs Toppler, at herself. And at last she knew how to explain to Mrs Toppler.

The passport. She would simply show Mrs Toppler the passport. The passport would say it all, just as it had to her.

43

'Suitcase,' said Annuka Vos into her phone, very loudly and clearly. She was standing in the floodlit garden of the villa, to make sure her words got through with a minimum of interference. 'Stolen. Has been. Suitcase. Mine. Yes . . . ? Oh, for heaven's sake! There must be *someone* in the Greek police who can speak English better than this!

'Yes, but this is the fifth time I've phoned you . . . ! Fifth! Five! Phoned! Five times . . . ! Oh, never mind . . .

'Busy – yes – I know you are . . . An event – yes – I know . . . ! I know, I know . . . ! *Big* event! I *know*! You told me before! But I have been travelling all day and I have no clean clothes to change into . . . Clean clothes! None . . . ! No toothbrush! Brush for teeth – no, none! No nightdress . . . ! Dress for night! Not got it . . . !

'Stolen – yes! And for the fifth time, the name of the person who stole it is Evers, E-V-E-R-S. Georgina Francesca Evers . . . Yes, because it's in her passport . . . Her passport was in her handbag . . . Not *my* handbag – *her* handbag . . . ! Not stolen, no, not the *handbag*! Left behind when she fled . . . ! *Fled* . . . ! F-L-E-D! Ran! Left! Went . . . ! Oh, let it go, it doesn't matter . . .

'Yes, because I found it under the lounger . . . The *lounger* . . . Forget it . . . Also in the bag were her money and her credit cards, so she won't have gone far. It can't be very difficult to find her . . . And she'll be easy to spot because she's wearing a mosquito net . . . *Mosquito* . . . M-O-S-Q . . . Hello . . . ? You haven't hung up on me . . . ?'

Georgie was not, in fact, all that easy to spot, even dressed from head to foot in mosquito netting, because she was hiding behind a clump of broom. It was true, though, that she hadn't gone far. She had started picking her way down the track, but in bare feet it was like walking on broken glass, and it was plain that she would be permanently lamed long before she reached any possible destination. Also she was frightened of somehow missing Oliver when he at last arrived. Not that she had any great desire, now that she had discovered he was expecting her to share their week together with the cleaning woman, ever to see him again, except perhaps, once she had recovered some shoes, to kick him in the balls. But Oliver and whatever vehicle he eventually arrived in seemed to be her only hope of ever getting away from this horrible house and its horrible occupant. So she had picked her painful way back to the villa, and sat down to wait on the dry, stony ground behind the clump of broom opposite. She was so close to the villa, in fact, that she could see the woman standing in the garden, shouting into her phone again. She could even hear some of the words. 'Suitcase . . . stolen . . . five . . . passport . . . handbag . . .'

Her passport, yes, and her handbag. That was another reason for staying until Oliver got here.

The woman went back into the villa and slammed the door. The garden lighting went out, and the first faint dusting of stars appeared overhead. The ground that Georgie was sitting on became harder and harder. The emptiness of her stomach became more and more painfully noticeable. Ants spread through every part of her mosquito netting.

And then, at last, she heard the distant whine of an engine labouring uphill in low gear. At each turn in the road it grew louder. A spill of moving light appeared on the track below her, then two blinding beams, rocking and dipping over the potholes. She struggled to her feet, so stiff that she could scarcely manage it.

She hesitated for a moment as the taxi stopped in front of her, uncertain whether she was going to throw her arms around Oliver as she had once so longed to, or whether she was going to stick with her revised plan of inflicting some kind of painful injury on him as best she could in bare feet, or whether she was going to embrace him first and then kick him.

As Oliver got out of the taxi the garden of the villa lit up like fairyland once again, and it wasn't Oliver, it was Wilfred. Of course. Wilfred, back yet again. She might have guessed from the soapy look on his face when he went that she hadn't really managed to get rid of him.

So she didn't embrace him. She didn't kick him. She waited while he lifted something off the back seat, slammed the door, and opened the garden gate. He was holding whatever it was in front of him covered in a sheet, like a nurse carrying a bedpan. But already she was getting into the taxi. The driver turned round and gazed at her. She pulled the mosquito netting more closely around her, then realised that there was something reassuringly familiar about the man's face, or about the wart in the middle of his bald head.

'It's Spiros again, isn't it?' she said.

'Stavros,' said Stavros. 'Where you go?'

Yes, where she go? She had not the slightest idea. Nor, now she thought about it, how she was going to pay the fare without her handbag.

'Don't tell me,' said Stavros. 'I know.'

'Do you?'

'Of course!' He nodded at her mosquito netting as he started to turn the car round. 'Where else in Skios you going tonight in evening dress except only Fred Toppler?'

*

Still holding his covered platter of canapés, Dr Wilfred lifted the wrought-iron knocker on the front door of the villa, and then hesitated. He wasn't sure, now that he was here, that Georgie would be as pleased to see him as he had assumed. If she opened the door and found him standing on the step she might just possibly jump to the wrong conclusions, and close it again before he could explain.

She would surely be pleased to see the food, however. It might be sensible to make sure that she saw the food before she saw him. He went round to the side of the house, with the idea of showing her the platter through the glass panes of the garden door. This is why he had come, after all, to bring her something to eat. It was the canapés he was thinking about, not her moles or her vertebrae. He was simply going to give her the canapés and leave.

There was no sign of her on the other side of the glass door, though, so he gently pushed it open and listened . . . She was in the bathroom – he could hear the water running. All right – he would leave the platter on the kitchen table for her to find when she emerged. Though now he was here, he might as well lay the table for her. Only one place, of course. Well, two, just in case she insisted on his having a few of the canapés to keep her company.

He moved around the big kitchen, opening cupboards and drawers. Plates, yes. Crisp white damask napkins. He arranged the canapés as tastefully as he could, and put two more slices of bread in the toaster. He found two silver candlesticks, and two long red candles to go in them, to make her lonely supper seem a little more festive.

He thought of the other dinner that was being eaten even now at the foundation. Of all the idiocies that were being uttered by all the idiots packed in around the overdressed tables, and not heard for the roar of all the other idiocies being uttered by the idiots around them. Of the false Dr Norman Wilfred watching the courses come and go, feeling his mouth getting drier and drier as the time drew ever closer when he would have to rise and deliver his lecture. And what lecture was he going to deliver? The only lecture that any imaginable Dr Norman Wilfred might give was here on the table beside the canapés, in the safe keeping of himself, the real Dr Norman Wilfred, the lucky Dr Norman Wilfred, the happy Dr Norman Wilfred, the Dr Norman Wilfred who had known how to build the great house of his career – and then known the moment to walk out of the front door and abandon it.

He heard the bathroom door open, and then Georgie's approaching footsteps. His own mouth was a little dry, he realised, even though he didn't have to deliver a lecture.

She was standing in the doorway, wrapped in a dressing gown. There was a sharp rasp of suddenly indrawn breath.

'*Now* what's going on?' she cried.

But her voice had changed, had gone large and dark. He looked at her, suddenly fearful. Yes, her face, too, had changed, like a face in a dream. Everything about her had changed, and changed out of all recognition. It had all gone large and dark.

He drew out a chair from the table and sat down.

Something, in the last twenty-four hours, had gone radically wrong with the world. The Gulf Stream of good fortune that had bathed and warmed his shores from the age of twelve or so had without warning turned aside and left him in an unfamiliar and inhospitable new climate.

44

The passport was lying on the desk where Nikki had left it. She picked it up as if it were infectious. It was as alien as an old love-letter from someone who had proved false. She remembered how unsettled she had been by the sight of his unsmiling face in it even before. It had been revealing. When he stopped smiling there was something cold about him. Something cruel – something perhaps even verging on the psychopathic. She found herself turning the pages in spite of her distaste, and looking at the photograph again. Yes, there was a mean, watchful light in his eyes, and a hard set to the mouth.

He looked very different from the smiling impostor she had been so dangerously close to falling in love with. In fact he looked very different from the unsmiling version of himself that she had seen in the photograph before. All his blond hair had fallen out – he was half-bald. His cheeks were lined and pouched, his jowls baggy. He was fifteen or more years older. It was like the picture of Dorian Gray.

No, he was someone else entirely. The passport had changed its identity, like Dr Norman Wilfred himself. The entire world had begun to deliquesce around her.

She looked at this stranger's name.

Yes, of course. In all her anxiety about what to do, and her anger at the false Dr Norman Wilfred, she had failed to think about his other victim. Now here he was, looking out at her from the ordinariness of the past, from the quiet dullness of things before all this had started to happen: the real Dr Norman Wilfred.

*

'We'll wait till he stands up to speak,' said Annuka Vos to Dr Wilfred. 'Some idiot will introduce him. Everyone will clap, and then there'll be a moment of silence before he opens his mouth. That's our cue to stand up and make the biggest, most embarrassing public scene anyone has ever witnessed.'

Dr Wilfred was sitting beside her in the back of the taxi, holding on to his lecture with one hand and his safety-belt with the other, as they plunged down the mountainside, and the potholes and hairpin bends sprang towards them out of the darkness. They had eaten most of the canapés and drunk several glasses of Petrus's brandy while he had recounted to her the injustice he had suffered at Oliver Fox's hands. The indignation she felt on her own account had been inflamed even more by her generous outrage on Dr Wilfred's behalf than it had by the brandy. They had both been hideously abused. And now she knew where to find their abuser.

'The trouble is,' said Dr Wilfred, 'that no one will believe it's me. They didn't before.'

'If any doubts are expressed, leave them to me. I will deal with them. By force if necessary. I don't know what this lecture of yours is about, and I don't care. But *you're* going to give it, not him. Even if we both have to shout him down.'

Dr Wilfred was silent for a pothole or two. 'I don't really want to,' he said. 'I've rather gone off the whole idea.'

She gazed at him in amazement.

'What? You want to let that ridiculous little fraud give your lecture for you?'

Dr Wilfred held up his typescript. 'He can't give *my* lecture.'

'No, he's going to be doing what he always does – he's going to make it up himself as he goes along! Some complete rubbish of his own! You're someone well known, are you? You're going to be a lot better known still when people hear what you're supposed to have said! You're going to be a public laughing stock!'

Still this poor broken specimen was silent.

'Come on!' she said. 'Wake up! Make an effort! This little rat has stolen your life!'

God, the effort one always had to make with men! It should have been the other way round! It should have been *him* struggling to persuade *her*!

'You're not worrying about your starving lady friend, are you? I'll tell you where she is by this time. At the dinner! With him! Eating her head off!'

He seemed to have forgotten about her, though. She had blown into his life by some sequence of mistakes and coincidences. Now, by some further sequence of mistakes and coincidences, she had blown out of it again.

'I've had a rather difficult day, one way and another,' he said. 'I think what I should really like to do is go back to the villa, if that's all right with you. We could finish the canapés. Get an early night, perhaps.'

She looked at him. He wasn't beginning to nourish any illusions about *her*, was he? It would be typical, of course. A bird in the hand – just what Oliver could never resist.

Yes. Well. Nevertheless. She modified her approach a little.

'We're going to be doing this together,' she said softly, and kept her eyes fixed on him until he felt the pressure of her gaze, and glanced round at her. She smiled. He looked away, then looked at her again. She switched on the interior light, so that perhaps he could see, in her wide open dark Latin eyes, the tawny splash of Baltic amber in the pupils.

She had plainly unsettled him a little. She had unsettled herself a little, too, she realised, now that she was looking at him so hard. He wasn't quite as old and broken as she had supposed. In the dim light of the taxi, with the red baldness of his head and the scruffiness of his clothes hidden in the shadows, he was, well, not so insignificant, after all. Some lingering traces remained of the importance that he had described to her over the canapés. He wasn't remotely the man she knew in her heart that she really deserved, that quiet, laughing, considerate giant, who would be romping with the children when she came back from an exhausting day of negotiations with her fellow-bankers in Zurich and who would break off to throw his arms round her and whirl her around until he and she and all six children collapsed laughing on the hearthrug in front of the crackling log fire. He was obviously something of a figure in the world, though. In demand to speak at international conferences and festivals. She saw heads turning and cameras flashing as he and she arrived in Montreal or Montevideo for their joint presentation . . .

An absurd thought. All the same, she made sure that when he looked round at her again he found her still softly gazing at him. He smiled. A little ruefully, perhaps, a little awkwardly, but resignedly.

So – they were going to do it. They were going to finish Mr Oliver Fox once and for all. Slay the dragon at last that had wrought such havoc up and down the land.

She leaned towards the driver.

'Step on it, will you, Stavros? It is Stavros, isn't it?'

'Spiros,' said Spiros.

Instead of going faster, though, he was slowing down. The taxi was ploughing through some sort of obstruction. It appeared in the headlights to be a broken suitcase that someone had abandoned in the middle of the road, with a long trail of dusty shoes and clothes spilling out of it.

'Disgusting, what some people do with their rubbish,' said Annuka Vos.

Dr Wilfred said nothing.

*

Still Nikki stood in Parmenides, holding Dr Norman Wilfred's passport. So where was he? The real Dr Norman Wilfred?

In London, perhaps. Had missed the flight. No, he'd caught the flight – she'd spoken to his PA. And the flight had arrived. She'd been at the airport to meet it. So he had reached Skios. And yet somehow, on the spur of the same moment in which Oliver Fox had appointed himself to be Dr Norman Wilfred, he had come into possession of Dr Norman Wilfred's passport.

So he had somehow made the real Dr Norman Wilfred vanish. Had abducted him. Kidnapped him.

How, though? He could scarcely have done it on his own. Particularly since he had been with her all the time, enjoying himself by watching her become ever more hopelessly entangled in the web he had spun. He must have had people working with him. They would have had to do it, not on the spur of the moment at all, but according to a careful plan made long in advance. They would have had weapons and safe houses.

So perhaps this wasn't a joke, after all. It was something quite different. Into her mind came the picture of Mrs Toppler talking to Oliver Fox, her hand on his arm, telling him everything. And then of Oliver Fox turning to talk to Mrs Skorbatova. And of Mrs Skorbatova suddenly able to understand English.

And of Mr Skorbatov cutting the grapes with those tiny silver scissors. She thought about the way he had been holding them, the surgical ruthlessness with which he had used them, and then how each grape had vanished into his mouth, snap, like a fly into the mouth of a lizard . . .

45

Behind the bougainvillaea that screened the car park the fat limousines and four-by-fours purred as contentedly as well-fed cats, while the chauffeurs tipped their seats back and settled to an hour or two of air-conditioned sleep.

In the lodge Elli yawned and phoned her mother in Ioannina.

At the barrier in front of the lodge Giorgios had taken over while the rest of the security staff had their supper break. There was nothing for him to do. All the guests had arrived long since. He sat down in the darkness under an oleander and lit a cigarette. He had scarcely taken his first consoling drag, however, when the lights of an approaching car appeared. He got himself wearily to his feet and stubbed the cigarette out. This job had certain perks, it was true, but there was even less chance for the occasional relaxing smoke than he would have had looking for gas leaks.

The familiar ΣΚΙΟΣ ΤΑΞΙ. Spiros or Stavros? Stavros. Giorgios wandered over and shook hands while Stavros's passenger, a woman wearing an evening dress made of complex folds and swags of tulle, got out of the back. Giorgios and Stavros had quite a lot to talk about. Stavros's mother was a cousin of Giorgios's aunt, and they hadn't seen each other since Uncle Panagiotis had run off with the girl from the ice-cream bar.

'Hey!' interrupted Stavros suddenly. He jumped out of the taxi and looked round. His passenger was just disappearing under the barrier, into the darkness inside the foundation, her tulle hoisted up around her.

'Invitation!' shouted Giorgios, and ran after her.

'Thirty-two euros!' shouted Stavros, and ran after Giorgios.

*

There was another slight disturbance occurring in the harbour. An incoming yacht, *Happy Days*, registered in Izmir, had just collided with something large and solid in the darkness.

'Sorry about that,' said the man at the helm, in an expensively educated English voice. 'Only paintwork, though.'

'Patrick's arseholed again!' said a second matching voice. 'Someone else take the wheel!'

'Trouble is,' said a third voice likewise, 'all the rest of us are arseholeder than Patrick.'

'Look at it, though!' said a fourth voice. 'Is that what we hit? It's the size of an aircraft carrier!'

Heads had appeared over the rail above their heads, shouting in a foreign language.

'Oh my God!' said the third voice on *Happy Days*. 'Russians! And they're waving things at us!'

'Sub-machine guns,' said the second voice.

'Do beg your pardon!' the fourth voice shouted up to them. 'Helmsman arseholed!'

Happy Days motored gently on into the darkness and hit the dockside with reassuring firmness. All three men who weren't holding on to the wheel for support fell over and laughed.

'Anyway, he's got us there,' said the third voice. 'Good old Patrick!'

'Yes, but *where's* he got us?' said the second.

'Skabulos,' said the third.

'Skrofulos,' said the fourth, taking a line ashore.

'Who cares?' said the third. 'As long as it's dry and it's not rocking about.'

'And there's somewhere we can get a few beers,' said the fourth.

'I can see a taverna!' said the second. 'Look! Candle-lit tables! The works!'

'Women!' said the third. 'I can see women!'

'No women for Patrick,' said the fourth voice. 'He's in a serious relationship.'

'Well, I am,' said Patrick. 'So fuck off. Though since she's in Switzerland at the moment . . .'

*

In Empedocles Christian at last roused himself from his long meditation. He brushed the grey veil of hair away from his face and tucked Oliver Fox's passport carefully away beneath his prayer shawl. He sighed deeply. Eric Felt, dozing on the other side of the low table, started awake at the unaccustomed sound, and then gazed in astonishment.

Christian was getting to his feet.

Eric hastily scrambled up as well, and stood bulging excitedly. The moment had come.

*

In Parmenides Nikki looked in the bathroom mirror. Her hair had gone flat and brooding. She quickly brushed it up with her hand. She removed the sour and vengeful look from her face and restored its usual pleasant openness. She carefully clamped Dr Norman Wilfred's passport on to her clipboard. It wasn't Mrs Toppler she needed to show *this* passport to – it was Mr Papadopoulou. He was the one Mr Oliver Fox had in his sights.

And he was the one with people who could take care of things like this.

*

Giorgios had abandoned the chase after Stavros and his passenger, and returned to guard the barrier, still out of breath. He arrived just in time to find another taxi, Spiros's this time, delivering two more late arrivals – an oddly matched couple, she expensively dressed and groomed, he apparently some kind of down-and-out. The man began fumbling in his pockets to pay Spiros, but already the woman was propelling him impatiently towards the barrier.

'Invitation,' said Giorgios, whereupon the woman knocked him unceremoniously aside with her handbag. Giorgios, discouraged by the pain in his elbow, and still short of breath from his last attempt to preserve the foundation's security, watched her push her companion under the barrier. He turned back to discuss the news about Uncle Panagiotis with Spiros. But Spiros was already ducking under the barrier in his turn.

'Thirty-two euros!' he was shouting.

46

On the agora the last moments of pleasure were being savoured before the serious business of the evening closed in. Coffee cups and brandy glasses were being drained, the crinkled silver paper off chocolates flattened on tablecloths. Legs were being stretched, bladders emptied, tables hopped, empty chairs smilingly leaned across. On the way to and from the gents elbows were being amiably squeezed and distant acquaintanceships renewed. In the queues outside the ladies hair tints were being insincerely commended and husbands half-sincerely disparaged.

Mr Papadopoulou had sat down in the seat next to Mr Skorbatov, left temporarily vacant by Darling Erlunder, who had got Wellesley Luft mixed up with Ludleigh Wells, and was telling him how much she loved his best-seller about how prayer could improve one's orgasms. Mr Papadopoulou was talking earnestly and sincerely, with much touching of Mr Skorbatov's arm and putting of his mouth conspiratorially close to the Russian magnate's ear as he looked past the back of his head, while Mr Skorbatov said nothing, but half-closed his eyes and sketched the faint iconic suggestion of a smile.

In the shadows nearby Nikki was lurking, waiting for the conversation to end so that she could show Mr Papadopoulou the abducted Dr Wilfred's passport.

From the shadows, too, a pair of glittering eyes looked out from a face as motionless and austere as a skull beneath its veil of grey hair, with an orange-trousered stomach twitching in anticipation beside it.

'Also,' Mrs Fred Toppler was saying to the current Dr Wilfred, 'if you were the director here, you could exercise that other amazing skill of yours, and give me a little massage whenever I need it.'

Dr Wilfred leaned a little closer to her and discreetly slipped his left hand under her silken top, then down inside the waistband of her trousers. It was now completely dark. Only the candlelit frontsides of people still existed. 'Just *there*?' he said.

'Oh my God,' she said, 'that is so blissful! And so calming! If only you could keep your hand on my butt while I make my speech! You're like Dieter, Dr Wilfred – you give me confidence! We could do such great things together! We could make all the wonderful dreams he had for this place come true at last. He wanted to see the foundation reach out all over the world! South America – India – Russia! House Parties on every continent! Civilisation spreading out over all the hurts of the world like oil on troubled waters!'

Dr Wilfred looked up at the candle flames swaying in the warm darkness, and knew that everything was possible. He could do it. He could deliver the lecture. Then all the rest would follow. After the lecture Nikki would be waiting for him. Tomorrow Georgie would turn up. He would find a way to get rid of Annuka Vos. No, he would win over even Annuka Vos. Then he would become director of this delightful place. He would spend the long summer days and short summer nights rubbing Mrs Toppler's back, and making Mrs Skorbatova laugh.

With the fingers of his left hand still deep in the bulge of flesh around the base of Mrs Toppler's spine, he took another sip from his wine glass, then put his right hand on Mrs Skor-batova's wrist.

'This is what every man needs,' he said to her. 'To be Nor-man Wilfred to the lady on one side of him, and Oliver Fox to the lady on the other.'

Mrs Skorbatova let her wrist remain under his hand, and laughed again. At last she spoke.

'No!' she said. 'No, no, no, no, no, no!'

'No?' said Oliver Fox.

She gently detached her wrist, seized the end of his nose, and waggled it from side to side. 'No!' she said. She pointed to the heavy gold ring on the third finger of her left hand, then waved the index finger on her right warningly from side to side.

'No focks!' she said.

*

Right, thought Reg Bolt, the Director of Security, watching from the shadows opposite the top table, as everyone finally settled back into their rightful places. They were all assembled. The guests, the hosts. The speaker. Nikki and Eric. The waiters, bodyguards, and personal security advisers. He checked each of their dimly lit faces in turn. The director was shut away in his darkened villa, and everyone else was here on the agora, and settled for the lecture. The darkness around him deepened as a pool of bright light lit up the lectern on the top table. He eased himself carefully back, deeper into the shadow, and slipped quietly away into the night.

For the next hour at least he and the lads had the rest of the foundation to themselves. There would be just time to do the job. The big one. The one that was so big that even the least curious bystander might begin to ask questions. The one that could only be done in the darkness, when all eyes and ears were safely here, and bent upon Dr Norman Wilfred.

*

'OK?' said Mrs Toppler. Dr Wilfred nodded. She rose and hammered with the olive-wood gavel. Beyond the little pool of brightness in which they were bathed he was aware of the darkness being softened by the indistinct paleness of faces turning towards them. The reassuring static of conversation subsided into an unnatural calm.

Mrs Toppler looked down through a pair of folded spectacles at her script.

'Our guest of honour tonight,' she said, 'needs no introduction . . .'

47

Everywhere beyond the agora a soft nocturnal peace descended upon the grounds of the foundation, as upon a little town where everyone was indoors celebrating Christmas or watching the football. The warm darkness of the night was made more profound by the flecks of silver floodlight glimpsed through the branches of the trees, the quietness made more palpable by the scribbling of the cicadas and the faint amplified echoes of Mrs Toppler's voice off ancient stonework.

Outside the kitchens little collapsed white heaps began to become visible in the darkness, as Yannis and the kitchen crew emerged from their stainless-steel hell and sank down on to the ground, too tired even to eat the leftovers.

In the harbour the dark water slapped tenderly at the moored yachts. The landward-facing windsock by the helicopter pad sank as the light daytime breeze off the sea died away, then lifted again to face seaward.

Chris Binns, the writer in residence, gazed out of the window of Epictetus, murmuring to himself over and over again the first stanza of his poem – *The goddess, looking wise,/ Whisky sour in hand,/ Nibbling the excellent local cocktail olives/ And pushing the stones down the back of the sofa/ In the most civilised manner*. What he hoped was that, if he repeated it often enough, it would prove to be the run-up to an effortless leap into the still undecided-upon main verb and the still unwritten second stanza. No leap had so far occurred.

He was, however, becoming slowly conscious that the silence was not quite the usual silence, or the darkness the usual darkness. Some of the trees had a faint silvering of light among their branches. Someone somewhere was speaking. He couldn't distinguish the words, only an occasional North American vowel, and an electronic timbre. Yes, something was certainly going on out there. He had forgotten what it was, but at least he now remembered that he had forgotten.

'The goddess,' he murmured, 'looking wise ...'

*

Back on the agora Mrs Toppler's voice came and went, came and went, according to the varying closeness of her acquaintance with the microphone.

'... public bodies far too numerous to list here ...' she said, very audibly, and then somehow let the relationship lapse again. '. . . mention only the Board of Governors . . . the Joint Standing Committee . . . the Council for the Preservation . . . for the Abolition . . . the Expansion . . . the Limitation . . .'

It all came back to Dr Wilfred, sitting modestly beside her as she spoke. The boards, the committees, the councils. The books and papers. The prizes and fellowships. What an astonishing amount he had packed into his life.

'. . . and last but by no means least . . . his keen interest . . . his lifelong devotion . . . never spared himself . . . somehow found time for . . . an avid follower . . .'

The shadowy faces in front of Mrs Toppler gazed respectfully up at her out of the half-darkness. Here and there eyelids and heads sank in sympathy with her sinking voice, but often rose again as the voice returned. Behind the faces thoughts were thought: memories and regrets, plans and hopes, reasonings and computations.

V. J. D. Chaudhury, for example, was regretting that he had not taken the opportunity to relieve himself when it had been offered. Davina Smokey was worrying about her grandchildren's table manners. His Excellency Sheikh Abdul hilal bin-Taimour bin-Hamud bin-Ali al-Said was trying to calculate the proceeds from a rise of 0.073 % in the royalty on 4.833 billion barrels of light crude. K. D. Clopper was absorbed in the Yankees/Orioles game on his phone behind the tablecloth. The Bishop of the Hesperides Archipelago was re-examining the Orthodox Church's position on original sin in the light of recent advances in neurology. Wellesley Luft was fast asleep, deep in yet another dream about Jackie Kennedy. Mr Papadopoulou's personal bodyguard was checking the safety-catch on his gun. Norbert Ditmuss was waiting patiently for a chance to ask his question.

And at the back of the audience more shadowy new faces were still arriving.

*

The moon put its head cautiously above the hills to the east of the foundation, was evidently reassured by the peacefulness of the scene, and emerged completely from hiding.

On the hillside to the west, from behind the screens around the site where the new swimming pool was being built, something else no less cautiously began to emerge to face the moon. Something not gracefully round, but obstinately rectangular.

Evidently reassured, like the moon, it slowly, slowly rose into the whiteness of the moonlight beneath the sheltering arm of the contractors' crane. More and more of it, vaster and vaster. Not two feet high, like the moon. A crate. Not five feet high, though, like the crate of marine diesel spares. Seven feet, eight feet. And still, inch by inch, it came. More and more of it. Nine feet, ten feet. Now a stencil, just legible in the moonlight. Not marine diesel spares this time. Refrigeration plant.

'Come on, come on!' whispered Reg Bolt urgently into his walkie-talkie as he watched. 'They'll have finished the lecture before she's halfway down the hill!'

*

Dr Wilfred became aware that Mrs Toppler had turned towards him, and heard in retrospect the recently spoken words that were still hanging in the air around her: '. . . not come here to listen to me . . . without further ado . . .'

There was the sound of applause, and of people coming back to life. Someone was leaning over and moving the microphones to stand in front of him.

He rose. He smiled and brushed the hair away from his eyes. He nodded his acknowledgement to Mrs Toppler, then to the audience. He waited for the applause to die away and then raked the agora with his soft brown eyes, from left to right, from front to back. He suddenly felt not like Dr Wilfred at all, but like the old Oliver as he had been so many times before, with the familiar abyss opening in front of him, now deeper and darker than ever. The earth's gravitational field reached out to him from the depths, dragging him down, pulling on the nerves of his legs, of his stomach, of his whole body.

He took two good lungfuls of air and opened his mouth.

48

So all the many elements were now in place that would shape the culmination of this year's Great European House Party. The various storylines were obviously about to come together to produce a single event of great complexity and significance. A showdown. The grand dénouement.

Exactly what form this event would take no one at that point knew or could know. Most of the participants no doubt had expectations of some kind, but even these were confused and indefinite, and hopelessly mixed up with what they *intended* to happen, or *hoped* would, or *feared* might. In any case, none of them had more than the most partial knowledge of the factors involved – nor much time to think about it, since the present moment of stasis while Oliver was drawing breath and opening his mouth to speak was so brief.

If they had been living in a story, of course, they might have guessed that someone somewhere had the rest of the book in his hands, and that what was just about to happen was already there in the printed pages, fixed, unalterable, solidly existent. Not that it would have helped *them* very much, because no one in a story ever knows they are. And even Dr Wilfred, with his doggedly Newtonian faith in causality, wouldn't claim that future events in the real world have that kind of already-achieved actuality. Even if he had known the position and movements of everyone involved, and understood all their feelings and intentions – even if he hadn't been so involved in the proceedings himself – he would have conceded that, according to the present state of scientific thinking, what the previous state of the universe had determined for the future was a set of probabilities. The Bishop of the Hesperides Archipelago, for that matter, whose public pronouncements sometimes suggested that God possessed very clearly established plans and purposes with which he himself as bishop was well acquainted, would have had to agree that even these were probabilities rather than settled states of affairs, since God surely had the right and the power to change his mind at the last minute, just as a mere bishop like himself might.

Nevertheless, those probabilities, as both Dr Wilfred and the Bishop saw them in their different ways, must themselves have been real entities. They existed already in that brief moment between Oliver's standing up and beginning to speak, when the event would become simply part of the established furniture of the universe. They *must* have existed! Surely. What kind of a probability is it that doesn't actually exist?

If someone with a mind as synoptic, comprehensive, and swift as God's had attempted to catalogue them they would surely have been these:

Dr Wilfred will be forced to his feet by Annuka Vos to deliver the real Fred Toppler Lecture from the text that he has so carefully kept with him through all the vicissitudes of the trip. He will be disconcerted, however, to find that Oliver is not wearing orange skateboarding trousers, and will hesitate for a fatal fraction of a second himself, which will allow Georgie time to realise that the Dr Norman Wilfred at the lectern is her missing boyfriend, whereupon she will be unable to resist waving to him. This tiny anomaly in the proceedings, insignificant in itself, will be like the last crystal dropped into a supersaturated solution. Around it the whole invisibly overloaded mass will change its state, because

Stavros, spotting Georgie as she waves, will step forward to demand the thirty-two euros she owes him;

Georgie, looking round for someone to borrow the thirty-two euros from, will see the real Dr Wilfred, and beg him to help her out;

the real Dr Wilfred, now even more confused to find Georgie holding his hand and looking up into his eyes, will fumble for his wallet;

Spiros, seeing Dr Wilfred finding the thirty-two euros for Stavros, will demand the thirty-two euros that Dr Wilfred and Annuka owe *him*;

Annuka Vos, ready to shout down any opposition to Dr Wilfred, will take time out first to demand that Georgie returns the suitcase she has stolen;

Georgie, at the sight of Annuka, will give a cry of alarm, and warn Dr Wilfred that this is the cleaning woman from the villa, whose extreme religious convictions make her a danger to society;

Nikki will hurry discreetly forward to deal with the disturbance;

Georgie, believing Nikki to be in Switzerland, will be unable to prevent herself crying out in astonishment, 'Nikki!';

Nikki, no less astonished, her normally greater self-control briefly failing under the accumulated strain of events, will reply 'Georgie!' almost as loudly;

several members of the audience will indignantly try to hush them, and whisper for everyone to sit down;

Patrick, nevertheless, seeing Nikki with her clipboard and

air of authority, will slip twenty euros down the front of her bra and ask her to find him a table, even though the place is so busy, with four Carlsbergs while they're waiting;

Georgie, at the sight of Patrick, will give another clearly audible gasp of surprise, and say, 'You!';

Patrick, at the sight of Georgie, will gasp in his turn and say much the same;

Oliver, as he watches the developing chaos in front of him, will brush the tangle of blond hair out of his soft brown eyes and say nothing;

on the hillside above Epictetus the refrigeration plant will be quietly swung clear of the screens, carefully lowered on to the waiting truck, and loaded aboard *Rusalka* of Sevastopol;

somewhere about now Christian and Mr Papadopoulou will produce the two incriminating passports . . . the police will be called . . . Oliver Fox will be arrested . . . Dr Norman Wilfred will have a stroke . . . Annuka will deliver the Fred Toppler Lecture on his behalf . . . Christian will reclaim his kingdom . . . Eric Felt will enter into a civil partnership with him and become his formal heir apparent . . . Mr Skorba-tov will conclude whatever secret business it is that he is engaged upon with Mr Papadopoulou . . . Nikki will marry one of Patrick's drunken yachting companions . . . Georgie will take the veil . . . prices will rise . . . rain will fall . . . a cure for baldness will be found . . . and so on and so on . . .

Thus Oliver, standing there at the lectern with his mouth already open to bring into existence the wild series of inventions which would have sent the world off on a completely different causal trajectory, will have been pre-empted by the great gear-chain of cause and effect – as it turns out to be with hindsight, now that it is actually happening. He set it in motion at the airport the previous evening, he is forced to realise, and the overwhelming probability is that it will now operate just as Newton, Einstein, and the real Dr Norman Wilfred would wish. Each cause, he will almost certainly find it instructive to note, trails an effect at its heels like an obedient dog, each effect gratefully acknowledges a cause as its legitimate master. There is no room for any ridiculous impromptu interventions.

Clunk-click. Click-clunk. If only the initial conditions had been fully understood, and hindsight had been foresight, the whole sequence of events could have been predicted in time to be included in Newton's *Principia* or the Book of Revelation.

However . . .

*

However, in the instant before Georgie waves and finally sets this well-prepared scenario upon its unstoppable course, something else occurs that stops it even before it starts. This is a completely unconnected and irrelevant event. A triviality, a passing thought in someone's head, a velleity that comes out of nowhere and has no imaginable significance or place in any self-respecting causal chain.

One of the guests, Sheikh Abdul hilal bin-Taimour bin-Hamud bin-Ali al-Said – someone with no grievances, suspicions, or schemes of his own – happens to notice, in the dish of petit-fours on the table in front of him, a single remaining cube of Turkish delight. He doesn't much like Turkish delight, but (as he explains at the subsequent government inquiry into the disaster) there is something unsatisfactory about the sight of one single Turkish delight sitting on its own in the dish, something that jars slightly with the natural order of things. So he reaches out idly to take it. And within the next few seconds the world has veered off the course that had been so carefully and elaborately prepared for it.

In reaching for the Turkish delight the Sheikh has leaned across a candle. There is a smell of burning, and by the time he has popped the gelatinous cube into his mouth, and crushed it between tongue and palate, his robes are engulfed in flames. The people around him scramble to their feet in alarm. Chairs turn over. A voice, identified at the inquiry as belonging to either Suki Brox or Darling Erlunder, shouts 'Fire!'

Whereupon someone does.

It's only a short burst in the first place, out of the darkness somewhere behind the speaker, probably from one of Mr Papadopoulou's security advisers, and exactly what he thinks he's firing *at* it's difficult to guess; but it's followed by a second burst, which is most likely Mr Skorbatov's people firing back, after which the firing becomes general, and for a few moments the noise of shooting and screaming obliterates all possibility of rational reaction to events, and any semblance of ordered causality.

49

The screaming continues for some time after the shooting has ceased. By the time it has subsided, and people are beginning to emerge from where they have taken refuge behind pillars and under tables, the spotlights have been shot out to provide cover for the withdrawal of the more important business interests. The Sheikh has also been extinguished, in this case by the Bishop, who has wrapped him in his own robes, fire-proofed against the candles used during the Orthodox liturgy, and the only illumination comes from the first faint moonshine and the few candles which have not yet guttered out or been knocked over in the panic.

When Dr Norman Wilfred, or Oliver Fox as he has now in his state of shock reverted to being, gets up from the floor behind the table he finds the chairs in the darkness on either side of him empty; Mrs Toppler and Mrs Skorbatova have apparently been hurried away with their menfolk, together with the dead and wounded on both sides. Many of the other guests have fled as well. Some of those remaining are weeping or whimpering as they wander about in a state of post-traumatic shock, crunching broken glass underfoot, and falling into each other's arms as they find their loved ones, or even their unloved ones, still alive.

Oliver recognises one or two faces he had not expected to see looming up out of the darkness. Georgie . . . Annuka . . . As confused as everyone else, he wonders what they are doing here. Wasn't Georgie coming tomorrow? Wasn't Annuka remaining in London? Or had he heard a rumour that they were now living together somewhere?

Some of the people he knows seem to have been as unaware up to now of each other's presence as he was of theirs, and a number of the predestined encounters do take place in one form or another. Everyone is too confused to be as surprised as they should have been, though, and the events have little of their expected force.

'I thought *you* were supposed to be giving the lecture, Wilfred?' says Georgie to a balding man who is distractedly trying to collect up scattered pages of typescript. There is something that strikes Oliver as familiar about the name Wilfred, but he can't remember what it is.

'Was I?' says Wilfred.

'Georgie?' says Nikki doubtfully. 'So you're here, then?'

'Nikki?' says Georgie likewise. 'But you're in Switzerland.'

'Am I?'

'Yes, and so are you,' says someone else to Georgie – a man Oliver remembers seeing somewhere once, a month or two before, who for some reason has the words 'Happy Days' printed across his tee-shirt.

'If I'm in Switzerland,' says Georgie, 'why are you spying on me here?'

'Theta function,' says a little man in broken spectacles. 'Lambda . . . phi . . .'

'Sixty-four euros,' say two bald-headed fat men suffering from warts. 'Plus twenty-six euros waiting time.'

'Blood over my shirt!' says Annuka irritably. 'A napkin, someone! Water! Oh, it's from me. Someone fetch a dressing, please!'

[265]

There is a silence while Annuka dabs away at her shirt with her right hand, and bleeds on to it with her left.

Another man Oliver has never seen before is lying on the floor in tee-shirt and skateboarding trousers, bulging in a hopeless, bloodstained kind of way. A strange creature is bending over him, holding a candle, and either feeling the victim's pulse or robbing him. The creature's lank grey hair falls around his face like some kind of mourning veil, and when he straightens up, his gaunt and wizened face in the candlelight reminds Oliver of a troll he once saw in a computer game. The creature gets to his feet and holds a small book aloft towards Oliver in a way that suggests silent accusation. For a moment Oliver believes it might be *The Thoughts of Chairman Mao*. He can see a picture of Chairman Mao's face, but when the man brings book and candle threateningly closer, Oliver sees that the face is his own.

'Thank you,' he says. He takes his passport out of the troll-like creature's hand and departs.

50

Within seconds of the eruption on the agora a kind of shock wave was radiating outwards through the rest of the foundation, as the guests scattered in terror to the shelter of their villas, or scrambled into their waiting limousines. Events by this time had become so complex that it was impossible to give any remotely adequate contemporaneous account of what was going on. It could only be reconstructed and recounted retrospectively. The *Journal of Science Management* was the publication best placed to do this, since they had a correspondent on the spot, and they would have had an authoritative world exclusive on the disaster, if Wellesley Luft, still hopelessly jet-lagged, had not slept through the entire proceedings. The official inquiry, though, was eventually able to put some sort of narrative together from what could be seen in the silent recordings of the various security cameras, and most of this material is now available on the internet for anyone interested.

So here are two of the limousines silently colliding in the rush to get away, and blocking the exit from the car park. One of the security staff (Giorgios), tries to part the drivers, who have got out and started fighting, but they both turn on him, and he retires with his hand over his nose while some of the cars behind try to struggle past the blockage by forcing a way through the screen of bougainvillaea.

The scenes from the cameras along the waterfront are even more confused, as crewmen and security staff bundle their employers into dinghies and tenders, and scramble with such haste to cast off that a number of people are left attempting to jump ever more impossible gaps from the quayside. One important-looking woman in low-cut evening dress and high-piled hair can be seen standing on the dock waving her arms at the departing boats, apparently pushed aside in the rush and forgotten about. A speedboat registered with *Why Worry* of Dubrovnik is run down by *Happy Days* of Izmir. A helicopter scrambled from the helipad hovers over the scene, possibly with humane intentions, and shines its searchlight down upon colliding boats, people in the water fighting to grab lifelines, and empty lifebelts. One of the boats capsizes in the downdraught from the helicopter's rotors. Surprisingly, only thirteen bodies were recovered from the water by police later.

*

Events up on the hillside at the site of the new swimming pool above Epictetus were harder to reconstruct, because Reg Bolt had evidently turned all the security cameras off. The crane driver must presumably have fled at the sound of shooting, just as he was beginning to lower the enormous crate on to the truck waiting below, and so must the driver of the truck, because the crate had evidently come crashing down out of control, tumbled end over end down the hillside, and split open to reveal its contents.

Nikki, it turned out, had been wrong about them burying bodies behind the screen. They were digging them up. Long-buried bodies. Beautiful bodies, that belonged, now they had been found, not to Mr Papadopoulou or the Fred

[268]

Toppler Foundation but to the Hellenic Republic and mankind at large.

Or should have done.

*

It was the biggest and most beautiful of all the exhumed bodies that had burst free of the packing that imprisoned her. The first to see her was Chris Binns, watching at his window in Epictetus, struggling with his second stanza, and with no idea what all the noise and running around had been about. Suddenly, there she was, out of nowhere, a towering white figure in the darkness above him. She was wearing a helmet and carrying a shield, and there were serpents writhing at her feet. In the moonlight her face had an unearthly pallor. She stood gazing out over the lights on the agora, the classical ruins, the villas, the fishermen's cottages, and the lapping water in the harbour. Her right arm was upraised, as if she was surprised by what she saw and was giving it her blessing, or laying a curse upon it. It was impossible to guess from the look on her face, though, what her intentions were, or what she thought about the world before her. Her expression was impassive, unshakeably serene, a blank.

Chris recognised her immediately from her helmet and her long white robes – her *chiton*, just as Wikipedia said. She was Athena, the goddess of wisdom and civilisation, of craft and war and justice, the tutelary deity of the island.

For some moments he was so surprised that he couldn't breathe. He had conjured her back from the underworld where the old gods live, and he had done it by imagining her, through the sheer power of the words in the poem he was writing about her.

She wasn't a real physical object, he understood that clearly enough. She was some kind of hallucination, a projection of his own mind on to the external world. Of course. But his residency in Skios was justified. His choice of career. His whole life.

He felt in the darkness for pencil and paper. His long-awaited second stanza was already writing itself.

*

The confusion at the entrance by this time had grown worse because, just as the cars struggling to get out had begun to free themselves from the wreckage of the bougainvillaea and smash their way through the barrier, they came up against the flashing blue lights and howling sirens of the island's arriving emergency services.

Soon arms and clubs were being waved, first demonstratively and then in earnest, and soon after that the confrontation between police trying to reach the massacre and participants trying to escape from it was complicated by the violent intervention of a woman who loudly wanted the police to arrest someone for some other offence entirely. It was very difficult in the circumstances prevailing for police officers with only limited English to understand who was to be arrested for what – whether it was someone called Wilfred for impersonating someone called Fox, or the other way round; and whether the man whom the woman was propelling so urgently towards them, and from whom she was snatching some kind of typescript to wave in their faces as evidence, was Fox or Wilfred; and where Fox was if this was Wilfred, or Wilfred if this was Fox.

In the end, so as to get on with the job they had been sent to do, they arrested whichever man it was they had to hand, and later, in the calmer conditions of the police station, charged him with attempting to leave the scene of a crime, inciting public disorder, wasting police time, being an accessory in the deaths of a still undetermined number of people, and bringing the Hellenic Republic into disrepute. Annuka Vos, his accuser, or defender, who had attempted to prevent them throwing him into the van by battering the chief of police about the head with her handbag, and who had thereupon been thrown into the van after him, they charged only with attempted murder.

*

Among the last of the wounded to be collected was Cedric Chailey, the token Brit. 'I knew there was going to be trouble,' he said to Rosamund Chailey, as he lay on one of the tables in the now almost empty agora, with his wounded leg stretched out in front of him and bound up as best she could in a tablecloth. 'As soon as they said he was Norman Wilfred. I was in college with Norman Wilfred. That fellow wasn't Norman Wilfred. And if anything should happen to me you'll see that Control gets this.'

He handed her the mobile phone he had removed from Mr Skorbatov's shirt pocket, containing all the great oligarch's contacts, codes, and passwords.

*

By the time Oliver had packed his suitcase – or at any rate Dr Wilfred's suitcase – and arrived at the entrance, the counterpoint of sirens from the departing police and ambulances winding their way back through the mountains was becoming fainter. There was no one to be seen, and no limousines or taxis. He tapped on the window of the lodge. Tapped and tapped – banged with his fist – because Elli had her headphones on, oblivious to the world around her.

'Sorry!' she said, when she at last slid back the glass. 'I'm talking to my Auntie Soussana in Patras. What tricks those people in Patras do! You never imagine! So in what way my help you?'

'A taxi, if you would.'

'Oh, were you at the lecture? Is it all over? How did it go? No rain? I thought I heard thunder.'

51

On the agora the last few candles guttered out. The moon rode ever higher in the sky, and poured a soft classical peace ever deeper into the ruins. The warm air was sweet with the blossoms of the Mediterranean night. From the hillside where she had emerged from her abductors' crate the white goddess looked serenely down upon her little protectorate, and held her guiding hand over it once again as she had held it three thousand years before. She had restored peace and civilisation to her island.

Here and there in the moonlight some of the exhausted cooks and waiters, who had only stirred uneasily in their sleep at the noise of gunfire and screaming, opened their eyes and perhaps pecked at a little abandoned baklava or took a restorative swig from a forgotten bottle of brandy. Giorgios, who had settled down at last to smoke his so long awaited and so richly deserved cigarette, only to discover that the pack had fallen out of his pocket during his exertions, located a box of cigars and made do with one of them.

At a moonlit table in one secluded corner Georgie cut Nikki another handful of grapes, and Nikki poured Georgie another glass of wine.

'I really knew,' said Nikki. 'From the moment I set eyes on him. In my heart.'

'So did I,' said Georgie. 'I always know if they're duds. Quite easy, actually, because they always are.'

'What was that one at school called?'

'You mean Mr Wossop?'

'No, the boy you hid in the changing rooms . . . Mr *Wossop*? That awful little man who took us for Comparative Religion? You didn't!'

'Not really. Only once, on that retreat thing to the nunnery place.'

'Georgie!'

'You were too busy retreating to notice. You were so ghastly when you were head girl, Nikki!'

'Was I? What, a bit . . . scrungy?'

'Scrungissimo. I hated you.'

'No, you didn't. You had some kind of thing about me. Creeping up and peering at me all the time.'

'I didn't have my lenses then. Oh, Nikki, all that being ghastly of yours, and where's it got you in the end? She'll never make you director now!'

'No. Nothing much left to be director of, anyway.'

'Nikki, it's no good, is it? Suddenly trying not to be ghastly, if ghastly's what you are.'

They sipped their wine. Nikki refilled their glasses.

'Anyway,' said Georgie, 'he seems to have vanished.'

'Norman?'

'Oliver.'

'I still can't think of him as Oliver.'

'Not that it matters much which. If they shot him.'

'Maybe the cleaning woman got him.'

They laughed. They stopped laughing. They reflected silently for some moments on life and its vicissitudes.

'I like it here,' said Georgie. 'We could find somewhere to live. A Greek fisherman's cottage. With or without Greek fishermen.'

'You mean – together? You and me?'

'Why not? Then if Patrick rings, no problem. You wouldn't have to invent anything, because there I'd be.'

'So where would Patrick be?'

'Somewhere else. Wherever he is now. Back on the boat with his chums. Floating about.'

They poured another glass of wine.

'I'm so pleased you don't live in Switzerland,' said Georgie. 'I shouldn't have wanted to live in Switzerland.'

'Switzerland, Switzerland! Georgie, what *is* all this?'

'That time before when I phoned to say I was staying with you. You kept going on about skiers.'

'Skiers? In Skios?'

Georgie thought about this. 'Oh, I see,' she said.

'Georgie,' said Nikki, 'you're such a dumbo!'

'Dumbissimo,' said Georgie.

Nikki gazed into her glass of moonlit wine, Georgie at the moonlit goddess gazing down upon them.

'So peaceful here, though,' said Georgie. 'So kind of like eternal. All these statues and things.'

Nikki turned to see what Georgie was looking at.

'Never seen that one before,' she said.

*

'*Phoksoliva?*' said Spiros, as he and Oliver together struggled to lift the heavy suitcase into the boot of the taxi. 'Thirty-two euros. In advance.'

Oliver took out a handful of the spare banknotes he had found in a secret compartment of Dr Wilfred's suitcase. 'Airport,' he said. He was going to start his studies in neurology as soon as he was back in London. Or perhaps in some other branch of science. It would be interesting to know what a Wexler whatever-it-was was.

In the headlights, as Spiros let in the clutch and the taxi moved forward, appeared a familiar and improbable figure – a woman in low-cut evening dress, with strong bare shoulders and a construction of brass-coloured hair on her head like the dome of a Russian church. She stood in front of the taxi waving her arms.

'No!' she said. 'No! No! Please! Taxi! Yes! Thank you!'

'Oh, hello,' said Oliver. 'You want a lift?'

'No, no, no!' said Mrs Skorbatova, getting in beside him.

'I thought you'd gone. So what, you didn't leave with your husband?'

'Yes!' said Mrs Skorbatova.

'No, you didn't. You got left behind, because here you are.'

'No, no, no!'

'OK?' said Spiros. 'Airport?'

'Airport!' said Mrs Skorbatova. 'Yes, yes!'

'Wait!' said Oliver. He smiled his soft, melancholy smile at her, as if he had foreseen the whole thing, and all the beauty of it, and all the sadness that would inevitably follow.

Spiros waited, watching the performance in the rear-view mirror. 'Or *Phoksoliva*?' he said.

'Exactly,' said Oliver. '*Phoksoliva*.' If he started his studies a few days later than he had planned he could always catch up later. And he had surely earned a bit of a break.

'*Phoksoliva*?' said Mrs Skorbatova. She laughed, seized the end of his nose again, and waggled it from side to side.

'No, no, no!' she said. 'No *phoks*! No, no, no, no! No, no, no, no, no!'

'No problem,' said Spiros.

*

Millimetre by millimetre in the moonlight Athena began to lean a little closer to the settlement she was responsible for, as the ground subsided beneath her weight. Gradually she leaned a little less slowly, until she passed the point of no return, and measured her length on the ground. She managed it with reasonable dignity, like a duchess overcome by drink, though she broke her arm in three places and her head fell off.

'She's gone,' said Georgie.

'Everyone goes,' said Nikki, closing one eye to sight the last centimetre of wine left in her glass. 'Dr Wilfred. You. Me. The cleaning woman.'

'No, that white statue thing.'

'Things come, things go,' said Nikki. 'Statues, temples. European civilisation. Three thousand years. Constant flux.'

'Your boss is back, though,' said Georgie. 'I thought she was dead.'

Nikki turned to look. From somewhere in the shadows Mrs Fred Toppler had appeared. She seemed to be dazed, and was walking as if under water, or in a deep sleep. Slowly she found her way to the microphone. She was holding up a crumpled sheet of paper to read, though there was only moonlight to read it by, and the microphone was as dead as the old gods and goddesses. But Nikki knew what the words were.

'I just want to say a big thank you to our distinguished guest,' Mrs Fred Toppler was saying, 'for making this evening such a unique and special occasion, and one that I'm sure none of us here will ever forget . . .'

Also by Michael Frayn

ff

Headlong

Martin Clay, a would-be art historian, believes he has discovered a missing masterpiece. The owner of the painting is oblivious to its potential and asks Martin to help him sell it, leaving Martin with the chance of a lifetime: if he can only separate the painter from its owner, he would be able to perform a great public service, and make his professional reputation – perhaps make rather a lot of money as well. But is the painting really what Martin believes it to be? As Martin is drawn further into this moral and intellectual labyrinth, events start to spiral out of his control . . .

Shortlisted for the Booker Prize, Whitbread Novel Award and the James Tait Memorial Prize for Fiction

'A knife-edge thriller/farce about a missing Bruegel masterpiece and its rightful custodians.' *Independent*

'Frayn's plot – a high-precision feat of fictional engineering – accelerates exhilaratingly . . . a black and brilliant comedy of uncertainties.' *Sunday Times*

'Ingenious . . . As entertaining as it is intelligent, as stimulating as it is funny.' *New York Times*

ff

Spies

'A beautifully accomplished, richly nostalgic novel about supposed second-world-war espionage seen through the eyes of a young boy.' *Sunday Times*

In the quiet cul-de-sac where Keith and Stephen live the only immediate signs of the Second World War are the blackout at night and a single random bombsite. But the two boys start to suspect all is not as it seems when one day Keith announces a disconcerting discovery: the Germans have infiltrated his own family. And when the secret underground world they have dreamed up emerges from the shadows, they find themselves engulfed in mysteries far deeper and more painful than they have bargained for.

Winner of the Whitbread Novel of the Year Award

'A novel with a vivid sympathy for how lonely, scared and helpless being a child often feels, and how easily and eagerly we forget it . . . A pleasure to read.' *Guardian*

'This brilliant and serious novel is Frayn on absolutely top – if unashamedly smart – form.' *Daily Telegraph*

'Deeply satisfying . . . Frayn has written nothing better.' *Independent*

ff

Faber and Faber is one of the great independent publishing houses. We were established in 1929 by Geoffrey Faber with T. S. Eliot as one of our first editors. We are proud to publish award-winning fiction and non-fiction, as well as an unrivalled list of poets and playwrights. Among our list of writers we have five Booker Prize winners and twelve Nobel Laureates, and we continue to seek out the most exciting and innovative writers at work today.

Find out more about our authors and books
faber.co.uk

Read our blog for insight and opinion on books and the arts
thethoughtfox.co.uk

Follow news and conversation
twitter.com/faberbooks

Watch readings and interviews
youtube.com/faberandfaber

Connect with other readers
facebook.com/faberandfaber

Explore our archive
flickr.com/faberandfaber